KU-751-181

Marina Oliver has published almost fifty novels under various pseudonyms, plus half a dozen non-fiction books. She has written historical novels as well as twentieth century sagas, contemporary romances and crime.

Marina was the Chairman of the Romantic Novelists' Association and also lectured in America and on Cunard cruise ships. She has edited magazines and novels and runs many writing courses and workshops.

Marina now splits her time between rural Shropshire and Madeira and is married with four children and several grandchildren.

For more details on the author visit Marina's website: www.marina-oliver.net

SCANDAL AT THE DOWER HOUSE

When Catarina's elderly husband dies, she moves to the Dower House where things are about to change dramatically with the arrival of Catarina's young sister Joanna. Tricked by her cousin Matthew into a sham marriage, Joanna is now pregnant and alone. Catarina has a plan to hide her sister's disgrace, but then tragedy strikes suddenly at the Dower House. What will be the fate of Joanna's unwanted child?

MARINA OLIVER

SCANDAL AT THE DOWER HOUSE

Complete and Unabridged

ULVERSCROFT
Leicester

First published in Great Britain in 2010 by
Robert Hale Limited
London

First Large Print Edition
published 2010
by arrangement with
Robert Hale Limited
London

British Library CIP Data

Oliver, Marina, *1934* –
  Scandal at the Dower House.
  1. Illegitimate children- -England- -Fiction.
  2. Widows- -Fiction. 3. Sisters- -Fiction.
  4. Domestic fiction. 5. Large type books.
  I. Title
  823.9′14–dc22

  ISBN 978–1–44480–445–4

Published by
F. A. Thorpe (Publishing)
Anstey, Leicestershire

Set by Words & Graphics Ltd.
Anstey, Leicestershire
Printed and bound in Great Britain by
T. J. International Ltd., Padstow, Cornwall

This book is printed on acid-free paper

Dedication

To the Romantic Novelists' Association,
just completing fifty successful years, and
all the members, past and present, who
have helped to make this the best writers'
group of all.

1

'You have very pretty manners, my dear. No trace of the shop floor.'

Lady Keith's voice was penetrating, and the door to the dining room was still open. Catarina, Countess of Rasen, knew the men must have heard, and did not know whether to be offended, embarrassed, amused or furious. But recalling her pretty manners she refused to reply, instead leading the way into the formal drawing room. After just a few hours in the lady's company she had concluded Lady Keith was the type of arrogant dowager who prided herself on always saying what she thought, however hurtful or silly. Though in her sixties, she dressed in clothes more suitable to a young girl, with far too many flounces of black satin ribbon and lace, and was adorned with a profusion of jet beads and mourning brooches.

Catarina felt dowdy in comparison. The only black gowns she possessed dated from six years ago, when Lady Unwin, the wife of Walter's best friend, died. She had not had time or inclination to order more in the few days since Walter's death.

Her young sister Joanna had no intention of letting the slur pass.

'Papa never served in or owned a shop,' she protested. 'He was a very well-known wine importer; he sold wine to all the best people within a hundred miles of Bristol!'

'But a merchant, my dear, is not so very different, though I understand your father came from a good family. It seems so vulgar for a gentleman to go into trade, even if he did make a vast amount of money.'

'Joanna, would you be so kind as to fetch my shawl? I left it in the library earlier, when I was sorting out the papers for his lordship, and I find it grows chilly.'

Joanna, recalled to a sense of decorum by Catarina's firm tone, blushed and made her escape. Catarina asked her guest if she had visited this part of Somerset before and, by the time Joanna returned, the conversation was proceeding in the well-worn tracks of comparing opinions about places they had visited. It seemed that Lady Keith despised everywhere apart from London and Bath, her childhood home in Gloucestershire, and her late husband's castle in Scotland.

Catarina tried to include the fourth member of the party, Olivia, in the conversation, but she seemed an exceedingly shy child, intimidated by her aunt, and stammered that she had never been anywhere except home and school. She still looked like a schoolgirl, in her simple gown and with her hair tied back in a long braid. Lady Keith's injunction to sit up straight, speak up, and look at people when she was answering questions simply threw the poor girl into greater confusion.

Catarina hoped the men would not sit long over the port. All the arrangements with the Reverend Eade had been agreed that afternoon, and Sir Humphrey Unwin would wish to leave for Chase Manor, five miles away, before it grew dark. It was a moonless March night, and he was of a nervous disposition.

Her wishes were granted. Almost on the thought the door opened to admit the new Earl of Rasen, Nicholas Brooke, the most elegant man she had ever encountered in his tight-fitting pantaloons which showed not a crease, discreet waistcoat, intricately tied cravat and a coat which, like his pantaloons, showed every muscle of a trim, strong body. His brother Jeremy, equally elegantly attired, the rector, in a state of genteel shabbiness, and Sir Humphrey, in clothes which had been fashionable twenty years ago, followed him. The latter immediately made his apologies and farewells, tried to deter Lord Brooke from escorting him to the stables and, in a flurry of thanks and promises of any further help he could give dear Catarina, backed out of the room.

Joanna cast a speaking look at her sister, but to the latter's relief refrained from comment. Catarina could read her mind and felt a great deal of sympathy. Lord Brooke had arrived at Marshington Grange just a few hours ago for the first time, but was already assuming control. It was his right, she reminded herself, but she had been mistress of the house for so long it was hard to relinquish its management to another. It was, however, something she would have to accept when she moved to the Dower House.

★ ★ ★

Catarina tried to curb her impatience. Surely the funeral was over by now. She was seething with suppressed annoyance as she tried to reply politely to Lady Keith's inane, often insulting comments. The woman was, she thought, rather like an inquisitive bird with her sharp nose, receding chin and scrawny neck. She had, since her arrival the previous day, found nothing but fault in the house, which was too small and furnished in such an

4

old-fashioned way; the park surrounding it, which had too many trees and not enough deer for her liking; the church, which was undistinguished and at an inconvenient distance; the servants, whose mourning clothes were shabby and who treated Catarina with far too much friendliness and did not keep the proper distance from their mistress who, even if her origins were suspect, was an earl's widow. At dinner she had picked at her food, tasted each dish and then pushed it away. It was too cold, too tough, too sweet, or tasteless. No wonder she was so skinny.

Catarina moved restlessly to the window overlooking the long sweeping driveway, but none of the returning carriages she hoped to see had yet appeared. The elms, still starkly bare of leaves, were swaying in the March wind, and overhead a canopy of grey cloud made it a fitting day for a funeral. She was paying less than full attention to Lady Keith, until a few stray words made her swing round and stare at that lady.

'Jeremy?' she asked. 'But I understood he is in the army.'

'Of course, but now that monster is secured on Elba I expect he will sell out. Nicholas has several houses; he can have no need of another. Marshington Grange is rather small, but will do admirably for his brother. I expect the rents from the estate will be enough for its upkeep.'

'But Bonaparte has escaped from Elba! Sir Humphrey heard the news only yesterday. He told me before the men went to the church.'

Lady Keith went pale. 'Escaped? But where is he? And why was I not told immediately?'

'I believe he has landed in France, but Sir Humphrey considers there is no cause for alarm. He doubts the French will want to be involved in more fighting.'

'What does he, a mere country squire, know about it?'

'He is a Justice of the Peace, like Walter was. He may live in obscurity now, but he used to be sent on diplomatic missions before his health broke down and he could not tolerate long journeys,' Catarina said sharply, unable to hide her annoyance. Sir Humphrey had been a good friend ever since she had married Walter, and she would not allow this ridiculous old woman to belittle him.

'The coaches are coming,' Joanna interrupted, and Catarina gave a sigh of relief. It would soon be over, tomorrow Lord Brooke, his siblings and their appalling aunt who had accompanied them, she had been informed, as a chaperon, would be gone, and she could be left to mourn Walter and begin to order her new life without him.

She had been married to him eight years ago when she was barely sixteen. Her uncle, Sir Ivor Norton, who had become their guardian when their father had died a year earlier, had been only too glad to dispose of her so advantageously. It had not mattered to him that Walter, recently inheriting from his elderly father, was forty years her senior. He had an ancient title, was much respected; Marshington Grange was an old, prestigious house and the connection gave Sir Ivor and Aunt Hebe a good deal of satisfaction. They expected her to introduce her sister to similarly grand prospective husbands, but Walter despised London society, and very rarely visited the capital, so those hopes had been unfulfilled, and they blamed her for it. She had been naïve, straight from the schoolroom of the Bath seminary, and had been told so often she had believed it, that parents and guardians knew best, and girls accepted any matrimonial arrangements made for them.

It had not been an unhappy eight years. Walter had treated her more as a favourite daughter than a wife, and she had been truly shocked, feeling lost and rudderless, when he had been brought home on a hurdle, having broken his neck in a fall from his horse.

She swallowed hard. For just one more day

she had to be strong. Then Lord Brooke would be gone, Joanna returned to Sir Ivor's house near Bristol, and she could make her own plans.

The coaches were at the door, and she had to show a calm demeanour until the neighbours and friends departed. Bracing herself, smoothing down her skirts with hands which had suddenly become clammy, she moved away from the window and sat in her accustomed chair to one side of the fireplace. Staines, the butler, followed by a footman and two of the housemaids, processed into the room carrying large trays of refreshments.

'Bring the tea things to me, Staines; I will pour as your — Lady Brooke will be too upset,' Lady Keith ordered, and Staines, casting an agonized glance at Catarina, hesitated.

Catarina, feeling that she was behaving in a pusillanimous manner, but unwilling to cause embarrassment by insisting on her rights, nodded. She was no longer the mistress of Marshington Grange. The estate was entailed; soon she would not even live here.

The men who had attended the funeral came into the room and all was bustle. The local farmers and landowners, who had not seen Catarina since Walter had died, came over to express their condolences and then, as soon as they decently could, departed.

'Phew, at last!' Jeremy exclaimed. 'I thought they would never go and leave us in peace.'

Catarina considered the man who was likely to be her new neighbour. The same age as herself, he was tall, dark and looked every inch a soldier. He was in one of the top cavalry regiments, she knew, and no doubt turned many female heads when in his regimentals. Even in his mourning clothes he had a foppish air, with everything slightly exaggerated. But he seemed very young to her, used as she was to being with Walter and his friends.

He would be thought handsome in almost any company, but his brother was in every respect more striking, though without the excesses of Jeremy's costume. He was slightly taller, his hair a shade darker with a deeper wave. His eyes were a darker brown, almost black, his nose more aquiline and his lips more generous. Sometimes, though, he had a rather sardonic air which gave him a devilish look and made Jeremy's teasing of him as Nick the devil seem apt. She found it odd that he was, at thirty, unmarried. Rich, handsome and heir to an earldom, he would be a big prize on the marriage mart. Was he too aware of his own qualities to consider any girl a fitting mate? Though she had made herself content with Walter, in her girlhood dreams she had wished for a young, handsome suitor. She decided, however, she would not like one so apparently arrogant.

Jeremy was full of smiles, and Catarina suspected he was having difficulty in suppressing his naturally high spirits in a house of mourning. Lord Brooke, on the other hand, seemed to bear the weight of the world on his shoulders. Catarina had yet to see his face relax in a smile. Though perfectly correct in his manner towards her, he was cold, distant, and she wondered if he disliked her.

When all the guests had departed, Walter's solicitor, Mr Mowbray, who had come down from London the previous day, gave a discreet cough.

'Your lordship, perhaps it is convenient now to read my late client's will?'

★　★　★

Catarina barely listened as Mr Mowbray read out a long list of minor legacies, money to the servants and his tenant farmers, personal mementoes to his friends. He had discussed them with her several years ago when the will was drawn up. Then she heard her own name, and glanced up.

Her father had been wealthy; she and Joanna were his only children and she had brought a small fortune to the marriage. She knew she would have that as her jointure, and would have a perfectly adequate, indeed generous, income from the funds where it was invested. She also had her share of the profits in the wine business, which Mr Sinclair, her father's partner, still ran, and which Walter had always insisted she should have.

'I leave Marshington Grange, Oaktree Manor and all other entailed property to my cousin, Nicholas Brooke, who will inherit my title. All the non-entailed property is to go to my wife, Catarina, in gratitude for her love and patience during the years we have been together.'

Mr Mowbray pushed back his spectacles. 'Oaktree Manor, where the late Earl lived before his father died, is let, as you may know.'

'And just what does that unentailed property consist of?' Lady Keith interrupted. 'How much of the estate is entailed? I must say, these legacies to servants are unduly generous in my opinion. How will simple folk know what to do with a hundred pounds or

11

more? It's asking for trouble to treat them above their station in life.'

'It was Cousin Walter's wish,' Lord Brooke interrupted, and to Catarina's surprise, his aunt reacted to the sudden steely tone in his voice and sat back in her chair, lips pursed, but mercifully silent.

Mr Mowbray glanced from Lord Brooke to Catarina, in obvious embarrassment.

'I would like to know too,' Catarina managed. She'd known about the jointure, of course, and had expected some personal memento, perhaps, such as the portrait of her by Sir Joshua Reynolds that Walter had commissioned soon after their marriage, but had supposed the bulk of the estate would go to the new earl.

Mr Mowbray glanced down at his papers. 'I have a schedule here. There is the London house in Mount Street, which has been let for some years now. The house in Bath, the hunting lodge, and half-a-dozen farms adjacent to the original estate which his lordship purchased many years ago. Then there are his commercial interests. He was, you may recall, very interested in the developments in the textile industries and the mechanical innovations there and elsewhere. You will have, at a rough estimate, my lady, the same income from these sources as from your own jointure.'

It was a distressed Catarina who eventually escaped to the privacy of her room. Lady Keith, restrained while Mr Mowbray had been present, had vented her fury on Catarina the moment the solicitor had departed. None of Lord Brooke's protests, Olivia's startled tears, or Jeremy's embarrassed declarations that it was nothing to do with him, could stem the venom as she insisted that Walter's money should remain in his family, and help to support the cost of the estate. She accused Catarina of influencing a senile, besotted old fool, and hinted she would make it so unpleasant for her that Catarina would never again dare show her treacherous face to Bath or London society.

Finally Catarina lost her temper and told Lady Keith she was an interfering, jealous old bat who had not cared a jot for Walter when he was alive, had never visited him or paid him any attention, and was resentful that he had found happiness with her.

'He told me you tried to inveigle him into marriage when he was barely twenty,' she said, 'and how thankful he was to have escaped being married to a harridan. For the moment this is still my home and you are no longer welcome here. I expect you to have left before I have to see you again in the morning.'

* * *

Later that night, when all the guests had retired, Catarina crept downstairs. She could not sleep and had left the book she was reading in the small parlour. It was a book of sermons, not something she normally chose to read, but it had seemed appropriate after Walter's death. Perhaps that would send her to sleep.

As she passed the door of Olivia's room she heard sobbing, and paused. Was the child ill? She had looked pale and unhappy all the time she had been in the house. Catarina knocked gently on the door and the sobbing ceased. She went quietly into the room to find Olivia huddled on her pillows, looking with terrified eyes towards the door.

'Oh, it's only you!'

'Who did you expect?'

'Aunt!'

It was said with such heartfelt horror Catarina felt inclined to laugh. But the child was clearly afraid of Lady Keith. She closed the door softly behind her and went to sit on the side of the bed. Taking one of Olivia's cold hands in hers, she stroked it gently.

14

'Tell me. I won't give you away. What has she done?'

Olivia sniffed. 'She's taking me to London, for the Season. She says that because of our cousin's death I can't have my come out this year, I have to wear mourning, and I hate black, but she will make me go to call on her friends and things, and I know I'll hate it! Her friends are all odious; they spend all their time at the British Museum, looking at old stones and Roman things!'

Catarina tried not to laugh at her woeful tone. 'What does your brother say? Is he willing?'

'He says she knows best. But whenever I am with her I feel so stupid and I never know what to say. She scolds all the time and I seem to shrivel!'

'I know just what you mean!'

'I'd much rather go home to Brooke Court and stay with Shippy.'

'Shippy?'

'Miss Shipton, my governess. I was sent to school for a year, but I hated it, and Nicholas asked Shippy to come back. He says she's more of a companion, but she can still help me with my drawing and French. But Aunt Clara says she will be dismissed. She would have sent her away by now if we hadn't had to change our plans and come here.'

'Tell your brother how you feel; perhaps say you would like to delay going to London for another year. How old are you?'

'I was sixteen in December.'

'Much too soon to have to go to grown-up parties, and perhaps be betrothed next year,' Catarina said with feeling.

She had never been out in Society before she was married off to Walter, and afterwards, as his wife, she knew she had been awkward and not fully aware of all the proprieties when they went to stay for a few weeks in Bath, and once, on an occasion she looked back on with dismay at her naivety, to London, where she had known no one, and made so many gaffes she had pleaded with Walter to take her home. They had visited London only twice more, and Catarina thought she would be happy never again to set foot there.

'He won't listen to me,' Olivia said, her voice breaking on a sob.

'Tell him, and try not to weep as you do. Gentlemen hate to see females in tears. Explain you don't feel you are ready. Say that if you are too shy to talk to anyone there is no chance of your making a suitable match. You do want to be married, in time, I suppose?'

Olivia blushed, and her hand in Catarina's trembled.

'Well, yes, if he is kind to me.'

16

Cynically, Catarina thought that if Lady Keith had any say in selecting a husband for Olivia, kindness would be the least quality she would look for.

'Have you any friends who may be making their come outs next year? Friends from school, perhaps?'

'I think so. I still write to some of them. It wasn't the girls there I hated.'

'Then tell him you would be so much more confident if you were able to be with them.'

Olivia looked doubtful, but she smiled slightly, and slid down under the covers.

'Thank you, you've been kind.'

'Go to sleep now.'

Catarina left the room and continued in her quest for the book of sermons, trying to decide whether it would do more harm than good if she were herself to speak to Lord Brooke and explain how his sister felt.

★ ★ ★

The sermons were of no help and thoughts of Olivia's distress kept Catarina wakeful. After such a sleepless night Catarina wanted nothing better than to breakfast in bed and stay there until the guests departed, but she knew that would be cowardly, and when Rosa, her maid, came in bringing hot water

17

she forced herself to get up and dress. An apology for her outburst was due; she would think less of herself if she avoided making it.

Her hope that Lady Keith would have breakfasted in bed was dashed when she entered the breakfast room. The lady was seated to one side of the long table, with nothing but a cup of coffee in front of her. Joanna was the only other person present, but the used plates indicated that the others had eaten and left.

Catarina took a deep breath, 'My lady, I have to apologize for what I said last night. It was unpardonable of me and I ask your forgiveness.'

Lady Keith glared at her. 'You were abominably rude, but that is no more than I might have expected from a shop girl whose mother was a Portuguese peasant!'

Joanna gasped. 'Mama came from a wealthy, aristocratic family! She was not a peasant!'

Catarina clung to the shreds of her temper. 'Have you had breakfast, Lady Keith?'

'Since I am so unwelcome here I do not care to abuse your hospitality by eating at your board. I have been persuaded to drink coffee, but soon, madam, we will leave. Nicholas has gone to see to the carriage. Then you may begin preparing to move to the Dower House, and the sooner you do so the better, so that my nephews may take possession, even though they have been cheated of much of the inheritance.'

Catarina bit hard on her lip. She would not rise to these taunts. Turning away, she helped herself to coddled eggs, all she felt she could force down her throat. As she sat down Joanna began to chat with forced brightness about their uncle, Sir Ivor, and his wife and family.

'I need not return tomorrow if you would like me to stay and help you move, Catarina,' she offered.

'Let us decide later, when I have had an opportunity to inspect the Dower House and plan what needs doing there.'

'I suppose it is furnished?' Lady Keith asked. 'To whom does that belong? Or do you propose abstracting furniture from this house?'

'As it all belongs to Catarina, since as far as I know furniture cannot be entailed in the same way as houses, she could take what she wanted and sell the rest!' Joanna informed Lady Keith, accompanying her words with a triumphant smile.

Catarina was saved from having to rebuke Joanna by the door opening and Lord Brooke's entrance.

'The coach will be at the front door in five

19

minutes, Aunt Clara. I've informed your maid, and your luggage is being brought down. Lady Brooke, may I have a few words with you before we leave? Let us go into the library.'

'I wish to speak to you on another matter, my lord.'

He held open the door for her, and Catarina, abandoning her cold eggs and full cup of coffee, escaped. Only a few more minutes and the appalling old besom would be gone.

Lord Brooke closed the door of the library, ushered Catarina to a chair drawn up before the fire, and began to pace the room. He glanced across at her, one eyebrow raised, and she wondered if he was trying to intimidate her. She raised her chin in response and stared back unsmilingly.

'I must apologize for my aunt,' he said stiffly. 'She was the only older female available, and I did not feel I could stay in your house without a chaperon. She is still suffering from the loss of her own husband two years ago, and the deaths of both her sons. They were with the army in Spain. It has embittered her, but she should not have said what she did.'

'Neither should I and I have apologized,' Catarina told him, putting a slight emphasis on the second 'I'.

She glanced up at him and was surprised to see a gleam of something like amusement in his eyes. When he was relaxed he could be a very attractive man. But it was so fleeting she wondered later if she had imagined it.

'You will soon be left in peace. I intend to take some papers away with me that I have not had opportunity to study. I trust you have no objections?'

'They are yours now, my lord.'

'I also wanted to tell you there is no need for you to move yet. I understand the Dower House has been unoccupied for some years and will need work.'

'Thank you, but I will go as soon as possible.'

Catarina knew she would feel uncomfortable if she thought she was in any way reliant on this man's consideration. She was uneasy in his presence and would be so in his house.

'Please inform me when you do. There are a few matters I need to check, so I will come down for a few days when I can spare the time.'

'Of course. Will your brother come to live here?'

'It is one possibility, but he has his career in the army to consider, and would not be here most of the time, so I may prefer to find a tenant. Whatever is decided, I will keep you informed as to our plans. Now I must go; we are on our way to London, a long drive, and Aunt Clara does not like the coach to travel at much more than walking speed for fear it causes her discomfort.'

There was what looked like another gleam of amusement, but it was gone so swiftly Catarina could not be certain.

'What did you want to say?' he asked.

'I found your sister in tears last night. She is dreading being in London. My lord, she is not ready for Society! I should know, I was barely sixteen when I was wed to Walter, and I was utterly lost.'

He stiffened and she was expecting a rebuke. His tone was cold.

'My aunt can be trusted to know best.'

'You have just apologized for her rudeness to me. Think how much worse it can be for a young girl who feels that, as she is a member of the family, she has to be obeyed!'

'I hardly think that is your business, my lady.'

'I agree, but at least give Olivia an opportunity to explain. She will be stiff and feel stupid, and gain a reputation she can never throw off. If you want her to make a good match she needs to be presented in a better light than your aunt is likely to provide for her. That is all I have to say, but I hope you will be considerate of your sister's feelings!'

He did not reply, but pursed his lips, and she hoped she had not made things even worse for Olivia.

She went with him to the front door to discover Olivia waiting to get into the ponderous travelling coach, while Jeremy, looking dashing in his breeches and riding boots, his coat lapels just an inch too wide, and his shirt collars an inch too high, held the reins of two magnificent riding horses.

Olivia dropped Catarina a curtsy and muttered shy thanks for her hospitality, then gripped her hands convulsively and tried to say something else. She could not speak, and turned guiltily in obedience to her aunt's command to stop dawdling and get in the coach. The maid followed, the steps were raised, the doors shut, and the two sturdy horses set the coach moving in lumbering motion.

Catarina turned to the men to bid them farewell, just as Joanna came out of the house.

'Has that dreadful old woman finally gone? Oh, I'm sorry, I didn't see you there,' she said, giggling, and looking from under her eyelashes at Jeremy, who grinned back at her.

'And we must be gone too, though at the

speed that coach moves we could spend another few hours here and still catch them up long before they stop for the night,' Jeremy said. 'How about you showing me more of the gardens than I have seen so far, Miss Norton?'

To Catarina's relief his brother vetoed the idea. 'You will have plenty of time to see the gardens in the summer, when there will be more to see. Now we must escort the ladies. Goodbye, Lady Brooke, Miss Norton, and thank you for your hospitality.'

He took the reins of a black, strong-looking stallion from Jeremy and swung up into the saddle. Jeremy seized Catarina's hand and raised it to his lips, looking at her with laughing eyes as he did so.

'Farewell, Cousin. You too, Miss Norton,' he added, releasing Catarina and taking her sister's hand. 'I trust we will have many more meetings, on less sad occasions.'

Joanna dimpled. 'Oh, yes, so do I.'

Catarina wanted to chastise Joanna, tell her such flirtatious behaviour was indecorous, but she was feeling too stressed from the past dreadful few days to take the risk of another argument. They watched the brothers ride after the coach, and Joanna gave a little skip of excitement.

'Let's go and inspect the Dower House.

24

I've never been inside, but it looks a pretty house, square and compact, not rambling like the Grange. I love planning rooms and decorations. There is a big double drawing room, isn't there? What fun! You will let me help, won't you?'

2

Lord Brooke said little in reply to Jeremy's comments as they rode away from Marshington Grange. There was a great deal to think about. He was angry with his aunt for her unfortunate remarks, with Catarina for her interference over Olivia, even angrier with himself that he had not made more effort to find a different chaperon. He knew what Lady Keith was like and might have anticipated her abrasive behaviour. He had few female relatives, but if he had stopped to consider he could surely have found a suitable older woman from the ranks of his late mother's many friends. It had been an unfortunate introduction to his cousin's widow. Perhaps he should reconsider the plan for Olivia to stay in London. Then he felt angry again that he was permitting someone else's opinion to influence him.

He tried to think of other things, but the vision of Catarina telling his aunt some much deserved home truths made him want to laugh. She had looked just a slip of a girl, in her rather outdated mourning clothes. He could scarcely believe she had been married for eight years. And she had faced him at his most imperious, flinging up her chin in defiance when she had expected him to scold her. No other girl he'd met had done that to him. Most were too anxious to make a good impression. Perhaps that was why he had never wished to make any of them an offer. Once again he tried to force himself to think of other matters.

Marshington Grange would be an ideal small estate for Jeremy, and he could probably break the entail in order to gift it to him, but his brother had no intention of quitting the army. With Napoleon at large again, there was every prospect of more fighting, and too many of the crack troops from the victorious Peninsular army had been sent to far off corners of the globe. Others had been pensioned off. He himself had left the army when his father died a few years before, but he was seriously wondering whether he ought to re-enlist. Wellington might need all the experienced men he could find.

Ought he to ask Catarina — he couldn't think of someone so young and beautiful as a countess — to remain at the house, in charge of the estate, or could he find and install a suitable tenant? Despite his annoyance with her over her criticism of his plan to send

Olivia to London, he accepted that she had seemed to him a superbly capable young woman. The tenant farmers had spoken well of both his cousin Walter and Catarina. The house had run smoothly, the servants were well trained and from the brief tour he had made of the estate it was obviously in good heart, though there were a few matters he hadn't had time to investigate which worried him slightly, and he meant to deal with them as soon as possible.

Most of the villagers were still using the old three-field system, which was wasteful and inefficient. That would need to change. Yet if he did ask her to oversee everything she might resent it, consider he was imposing on her. She was much younger than he had expected. He'd known Walter had married a much younger wife, but he was surprised at how beautiful she was, despite the unflattering and outmoded black gown. The two branches of the family were so distantly connected, he himself had been in the army at the time and, as Walter rarely went to London, Nicholas had not known more than the barest facts. Had she wanted to marry a man so much older? Had the title persuaded her?

He had never expected to inherit the title. There was a shortage of men in the family so it had been a tenuous relationship: Walter's grandfather and his own great-grandfather had been brothers. And once Walter married a young wife he would have been expected to sire his own sons. An ancient dispute between his grandfather and Walter's father had ensured the families were not on more than terms of civility when they met accidentally. They never paid visits, even though their principal houses were but a day's ride apart.

Unlike Lady Keith, he had no quarrel with Walter's will. He was wealthy enough to be able to maintain the estate, even if the revenues from the entailed property proved insufficient. His father and grandfather had both married heiresses who had brought substantial fortunes into the family.

His thoughts swung to Catarina again. She was a difficult woman to dismiss from his mind. He knew little about her, but his aunt's strictures on her parentage were, he suspected, spiteful guesses. A younger son, her father had made his own fortune by importing wine. He knew that much, and that her uncle was well-regarded in Bristol where he was influential in the town. If Joanna's remarks were accurate, their mother was from a good family. Both girls seemed well educated, and ladylike, despite Joanna's tendency to flirt with his brother.

He glanced at Jeremy. The boy was handsome, popular amongst his fellow officers, a welcome guest in Society whenever he was on leave, and had an adequate income from what his mother and grandmother had left him. He was, however, too young at four and twenty to contemplate marriage. He himself, six years older, did not yet feel the need to marry and set up his own nursery. There were too many complaisant young matrons bored with their husbands and offering distractions for him to want to lose his freedom just yet.

When they reached the inn where they planned to spend the night he shrugged off his preoccupations. There he might hear more news about Bonaparte's escape.

★　★　★

It was a lovely morning in May and Catarina, having admired the spring flowers in the meadows as she walked to the Dower House, and picked some bluebells to brighten up the drawing room, had been talking to the estate carpenter about the final details to the changes she was making there. She had just turned to walk back to the Grange when Sir Humphrey Unwin appeared.

She sighed. He and Walter had been friends

since childhood, had done the Grand Tour together and, when they had both settled down on their estates, been fellow Justices. He rode over almost every day, offering all sorts of advice and help, and looking hurt and woebegone when she refused. He often brought news of what was happening in France, the progress of Bonaparte and the mobilizing of the Allies in Belgium, but he pooh-poohed the idea that it would come to a battle.

'You should not worry, my dear. The French will see sense.'

She could hardly tell him she was not worried. It all seemed rather far away from her present concerns.

As she was wondering whether she ought to invite him to take a nuncheon with her, the sound of an approaching carriage made her glance towards the lane.

A very smart curricle was turning into the driveway to the Grange, which ran past the Dower House. Seeing her, the driver, wearing a many-caped coat, halted his equipage and alighted. Catarina recognized Lord Brooke and her pulse began to beat rapidly. It was the shock of suddenly seeing him, she told herself. Before she could wonder what brought him here he had handed the reins to his tiger and was striding up the path towards her.

'Good morning,' he said. 'I'm pleased to have met you, as I have very little time, I have an appointment with my agent soon. Your servant, Sir Humphrey. Lady Brooke, may I have a few words?'

Sir Humphrey, looking disgruntled, acknowledged the greeting and turned to Catarina.

'I had better take myself off, my dear, if you have business with his lordship. You won't want me to interfere. Perhaps I will ride over again tomorrow, if there is further news. Goodbye.'

Before she could prevent him, he seized her hand and raised it to his lips. Over his shoulder Catarina could see Lord Brooke's sardonic gaze, and resisted the temptation to snatch her hand away.

Eventually he was gone and Catarina turned to Lord Brooke.

'Come inside, my lord, and take a glass of wine. What brings you back now? The Dower House is almost ready for me; I will be moving in next week.'

'It was about some other houses I came. One of my reasons. I have discovered your late husband was contemplating removing the villagers from their present cottages to a point a mile away. He intended, I understand, to provide himself with a better view by so doing. I came to stop it.'

'Stop it? But why?'

'I didn't know your husband, but from all I have heard he was a good landlord, so I find it desp — disappointing, to hear he is dispossessing the villagers of their homes.'

'Have you seen those homes?' Catarina asked.

'No, except for seeing their roofs from the house.'

'Those pretty thatched roofs are full of vermin, and the nearest water, apart from the river, is half a mile away. They are floored with earth, low lying, near the marsh, and very damp in winter. Occasionally they are flooded. A dozen houses share one privy.'

'Those things can be improved and I mean to see to it. I do not wish to criticize Walter, but I would have thought, as he was reputed a good landlord, that he would have done something about it.'

By now Catarina was fuming. 'He did do something about it! Those hovels are a disgrace. You will find the villagers are only too anxious to move to the new cottages Walter has caused to be built near the church. Good, stone cottages, with roofs of slate, each with its own privy, and a well within a few yards.'

'Such improvements could be achieved where they are at the moment. Don't the

33

people work on the farms, or in the house? Will they appreciate a long walk, at least a mile, to and from work?'

'They will be closer to their friends and families who already live in the cottages Walter has been building for the past eight years. They will be close to the church, and there are shops in the village. They are closer to the commons and their animals. And to their taps.'

'Taps?'

'The strips in the common fields. Ask them, my lord, and listen to what they want before you prevent them from acquiring better houses at the same rents as before!'

* * *

The estate room, when Nicholas went into it, was untidy, with papers scattered all over the desk and others lying on the floor. There seemed no kind of order. He sat behind the desk and was reading some of the papers when the agent, a young man of his own age, rushed into the room.

'My lord! You should have told me you meant to visit; I would have had it all tidy for you.'

'Should have told you?' Nicholas drawled, his tone icy.

The other man's eyes widened and he swallowed hard.

'I-I only meant, well, that I'd have been prepared for you!'

'It should be tidy at all times. You might then even find it possible to hide your depredations of the estate.'

'I-I don't know what you mean, my lord!'

'No? Then perhaps I had best explain. Your late master was building new houses in the village. You had the task of paying the builders, but I find from comparing the amounts you put in the accounts books and the receipts from the builders that you seem to have been stealing small but steady sums from the late earl and, I presume, from me. I have not been able to compare the books since the funeral, but I intend to.'

'I must have made an error in calculation, my lord,' the wretched man said. 'If you permit me to check them, I will soon discover the mistake.'

'A systematic cheating is no error. How did you become agent here at Marshington? You are young for such a responsible position.'

'I'm old enough,' the man replied, looking frightened. 'I came when my father died. A year ago, that was. He'd been agent here for many years and the late earl had promised him I would have the position after him.'

'What did you do before?'

'I worked for a merchant in Bristol, as a clerk in the counting house.'

'Then I suggest you apply to have the post back, for I will not permit you to remain in my employment, cheating and lying to me. I will not, of course, be able to give you a reference.'

★　★　★

Nicholas helped Catarina into the curricle and she directed him towards a side path which led towards the cottages. He stole a glance at her to confirm his memory. For some reason he had not been able to forget her. She was truly lovely, though the stark black mourning dress did not flatter her golden skin. Her face was oval, her eyes a golden brown, and her mouth wide and kissable. She seemed to have gained weight since March; her cheeks were fuller, as was her bosom, partially revealed by the lighter gown she wore and visible under the shawl casually draped round her shoulders. He felt a frisson of desire. Why on earth had such a girl married a man so much older? There must have been other suitors apart from Walter, for her money as well as her delicious person, even when she was only sixteen.

Recalling Sir Humphrey's unctuous leave-taking he had an unwelcome thought. Surely Catarina was not contemplating a connection with him? Not with another elderly man. She deserved something better. In any case it was far too soon for her to be contemplating another marriage.

Then he recalled a conversation with Olivia soon after they reached home, when he had agreed to her pleas that she might return to Brooke Court and Miss Shipton for another year. He had, besides, promised that he would find someone other than Lady Keith to sponsor her debut into Society. She had been in a confiding mood, such was her relief.

'Joanna was expelled,' she had told him,

'Expelled? From your seminary? I didn't know she had been a fellow pupil.'

'Yes, but she is two years older than I, and we had little in common. She had her own friends. She remembered me, of course, but I don't think she'd have recalled my name if I had not been with you.'

'Was she as outspoken there?'

'Yes; she never cared what she said, but that wasn't the reason she was expelled,' Olivia blushed. 'She was caught climbing out of a storeroom window to meet a young man!'

Somehow that had not surprised Nicholas. All the time they had been at Marshington Grange for Walter's funeral, Joanna had been flirting, discreetly but with intent, with Jeremy. Was Catarina similarly inclined, another flirt? She had not seemed like that. Had there been some scandal which had induced her guardians to marry her off? It was not unusual for girls to wed straight from the schoolroom, and Walter, though so much older, had been a good match, but from what he had seen of Catarina's spirit, he would have expected her to protest. Yet she seemed to be encouraging Sir Humphrey.

He pushed aside such distasteful speculations as they came to the first of the cottages. What had looked picturesque from the terrace at the Grange was, close to, rather more squalid. Several cottages had, it appeared, already been demolished, and piles of rubble showed where they had stood. The thatch was old and in dire need of renewing. The wattle and daub walls were pocked with gaps where the mud had fallen away. The window frames sagged, with spaces through which the wind would whistle.

'These things can be repaired,' he said to Catarina, as he halted the curricle and took stock of the scene in front of him.

'Of course, but I must show you the houses

in the village and you will see how much better they are.'

'I deplore the fashion of clearing away whole villages just to improve the prospect from a house.'

'So do I, if that is the sole reason, and especially if no other suitable provision is made for the villagers. But these people want to move. Ask them yourself.'

She scrambled from the curricle and vanished through a low doorway in the nearest cottage. Nicholas climbed down slowly, handed the reins to his tiger, and wondered whether he was meant to follow.

Before he could decide, Catarina reappeared tugging at the hand of a small, slight, bent old woman who glanced up at him shyly as she tried to curtsy. Several small children followed her out of the house and stood nearby, joined soon by two more women and an ancient man smoking a foul-smelling pipe which had in it, Nicholas thought, something far more obnoxious than tobacco.

'Moll, this is the new earl. Tell him why you want to move from this house.'

Moll took a deep breath. 'Well, surr, it be mortal damp in't winter. See t'river, it floods in't winter. An' we don't 'ave nowhere ter go, see, can't, we don't 'ave more'n the one room.'

Nicholas glanced at the cottages and belatedly realized the thatch came so low it was impossible for there to be an upper storey, even a loft. 'What do you do,' he asked, 'when the houses are flooded?'

'It don't often reach wall beds, so we can sleep in't dry. We just 'as ter wade through it. But it covers fireplace, so we can't cook. Surr, when will our new cotts be ready? Old Marge went just afore 'is lordship were killed, an' says it's 'eaven, so close ter new well an' all.'

'Will the new houses be ready soon?' Nicholas demanded.

'Before the winter, if you don't stop the building,' Catarina told him. 'And even if you preferred to rebuild here, you would need to find somewhere for these people to go while it's done. How many still live here, Moll?'

There were three cottages remaining, so when Moll told him there were ten adults and as many children he looked at them again, wondering how on earth so many people fitted into their single rooms.

'You'd prefer the new houses near the church? Rather than have these rebuilt, with upper floors and more room?'

Moll looked frightened. 'Oh, surr, you bain't goin' ter stop us 'aving our nice new 'ouses? The old earl promised, and we'm lookin' forward to being close ter them who've already gone.'

There was a murmur of agreement from the adults surrounding them.

Nicholas nodded slowly. 'Very well, I'll make sure the builders finish your new houses as soon as possible.'

'Bless you, surr!'

'Do you want to see the new houses?' Catarina asked as they drove away.

'I think not. I really must be getting on. I intended only to make a quick visit to see my agent. I am on my way to Brussels.'

'You are rejoining the army? Now that the threat from Napoleon seems greater? Is there really going to be more fighting? Sir Humphrey does not think so.'

'I fear there will be. Perhaps he is trying to reassure you, prevent you from worrying.'

'He is very considerate.'

Was he? Nicholas ground his teeth.

'The duke needs all the experienced officers he can find. Jeremy is already there, in Brussels, but so far all he appears to do is go to balls and parties.'

'Then I wish you good fortune, my lord. My mother's family in Portugal suffered during the French occupation. Several cousins were killed, either in the fighting, or when the French massacred all the people of Evora.'

41

'Do your family live there?'

'No longer in Evora. The Quinta das Fontes is near Oporto. That is the main estate, though various members of the family have their own houses along the Douro. They are mostly producers of wine.'

'Which I suppose is how your parents met?'

'Papa did a lot of business with the family, but her parents were not pleased when he wanted to marry Mama. They had hoped for an alliance with one of the wealthy, well-connected Portuguese families.'

'When did they die?'

'Mama was ill for a long time after Joanna's birth. There is six years between us and several babies were lost before Joanna was born. She was only four when Mama died. Papa died four years later, of a fever he contracted when visiting a vineyard in the Canaries.'

'And his brother became your guardian?'

Catarina merely nodded. He glanced at her and saw that her lips were pressed firmly together. Though she had talked freely about her parents, she was clearly unwilling to speak of her uncle. Was that because he had forced her into marriage with Walter? All he had heard about Sir Ivor Norton indicated the man was stern and unyielding. His own sons were reputed wild youngsters, though

Nicholas barely knew them.

They had reached the Dower House and he helped Catarina to alight.

'Will you take a glass of wine, my lord? I can offer you some of Papa's best Madeira.'

'I must decline; I have a long way to travel. But my thanks for your . . . guidance over the cottages. By the way, I have dismissed the agent and my own man, Mr Trubshaw, will be arriving to take over. Perhaps you will talk to him? I know he would appreciate it.'

'Dismissed? But why?'

'He had been defrauding your husband, falsifying the accounts over the cost of the building materials for the new cottages, and telling me lies. Of all things I most abominate being lied to.'

She clearly wanted to know more, but Nicholas shook his head.

'I'll explain another time. I really must leave now.'

He drove away. He did not know what to feel. He was so accustomed to managing his own estates, where no one queried his decisions, that he was a trifle piqued at having had to accept Catarina's advice. At least he would now have a reliable agent here.

He shrugged, and forced his attention back to the situation in France. Wellington and Napoleon had never met in battle. From all reports many of Napoleon's former soldiers were flocking to join him, and the allied army was a heterogeneous collection of untrained and inexperienced men. If anyone could mould them into a proper fighting force it was the duke. The sooner he got to Brussels the better.

★   ★   ★

Two weeks later, Catarina and Rosa, her maid, were in the Dower House putting away Catarina's gowns.

'Such a pity you can't wear colours,' the maid said. 'Black doesn't suit you.'

'There's no one to see me,' Catarina said. 'I can't go out in company yet, and I have no wish to.'

'Sir Humphrey calls almost every day.'

'He's been very kind. As one of his lordship's oldest friends he's made it his task to look after me.'

Rosa suppressed a smile and Catarina frowned. She knew what her maid, who had been with her since her marriage, thought. Sir Humphrey was a widower, his wife having died six years ago, and his children were all married and living at a distance. He made no secret of the fact he did not enjoy living a bachelor existence. And he had never hidden his admiration for Catarina. Fervently she prayed he would not make her an offer. She had been fond of Walter, but she had no desire to wed another man of his age. She had no desire to remarry at all, whatever romantic notions Rosa had. Perhaps it was her own imminent wedding to the son of one of the tenant farmers that directed her thoughts in such pathways.

They finished putting away the gowns, and Catarina picked up the older, less fashionable ones she had determined to give away. Walter had been a generous husband, and she had more gowns than she would need now. Besides, the Dower House had only four principal bedrooms, all far smaller than hers at the Grange, and there was insufficient room for them all. She would harness the gig and take them to the rectory. Mrs Eade would know who needed clothing, and her sewing circle, made up of the few gentlewomen in the parish, a couple of farmers' wives, and two favoured shopkeepers, would enjoy using the material and making over the gowns into apparel more suitable for needy villagers.

Rosa packed up the bundle, while Catarina sent Staines to order the gig. Walter's butler, who had been with the earl for more than thirty years, had insisted he wanted to remain in her service.

'I'm getting on, my lady, and I can't be doing with the sort of changes a new owner will want to make. I'd be better suited, much more content, looking after you at the Dower House.'

Touched, she had agreed. With him, Rosa, a cook, kitchen maid, two housemaids and two gardeners, who also looked after her two horses and did odd jobs about the house, she was well served.

She was entering the village just as a mail coach pulled away from the Bear inn. Then she frowned. Surely that female standing before the inn, a carpet bag at her feet, couldn't be Joanna? But it was. As soon as her sister saw her she abandoned her bag and ran to meet Catarina.

'Oh, Cat!' she cried and burst into tears.

'Joanna, what on earth's the matter? Why are you here?'

'I-I can't tell you here.'

'Get in. Let's collect your luggage. I must take these gowns to Mrs Eade, then we can go home and you can tell me what brings you here, and in such a state. Now dry your eyes.'

Joanna sniffed, employed the handkerchief Catarina offered and tried to calm herself. Fortunately Mrs Eade was out, so Catarina did not have to refuse any offer of refreshment, and half an hour later she was guiding Joanna into the Dower House.

Staines, without being asked, brought a pot of tea and some of Cook's almond biscuits. Ellen, her cook, was no older than Catarina herself, and she had hesitated before employing her. She had been accustomed to have much older women, plump and comfortable, as cooks, but once Ellen, on a week's trial, had produced some of her delicious dishes, Catarina had had no more reservations. Ellen seemed to spend all her time reading old recipe books, and told Catarina she had inherited them from her grandmother, who had been cook to gentry.

Joanna tossed her travelling cloak over the back of a chair and curled up in a small ball in one corner of a big sofa. She seemed disinclined to speak and Catarina did not press her. She poured tea for them both. Joanna took the cup with a bleak smile, then she attacked the plate of biscuits and ate voraciously.

'I had no breakfast,' she explained. 'I had to leave in the middle of the night to catch the mail in Bristol.'

'Does Uncle Ivor know you have come? Has he been unkind to you?' she added, thinking back to the few months she had herself spent with her uncle's family between leaving school and marrying Walter.

Joanna paled, 'No, and you must not tell him I'm here! Promise, Catarina! He'll make me go back!'

'They will guess you have come to me.'

'No, they won't. I left a note saying I was going to a friend's in London.'

Catarina frowned. She appreciated Joanna's fear of their uncle's anger, but she did not approve of telling lies.

'He and Aunt Hebe will be worried.'

'They've never cared for either of us except in the way of duty. They disapproved of Papa and never accepted Mama. But they'll want to drag me back and, Cat, I can't!'

'Why not? Have they been unkind to you?' Catarina repeated.

'No. Not them,' and Joanna burst into tears.

It took time and patience to calm her, but eventually she sat up, pushed herself away from Catarina's comforting arms and wiped her eyes. Then she took a deep breath.

'Cat, I'm — oh, I can't tell you!'

'You must if I'm to help you. And you must want my help, or you would not have come to me.'

Joanna nodded, and turned away her face so that she did not have to look at Catarina. Her words were muffled and low, but Catarina heard them.

'I'm increasing; I'm having a baby.'

3

Nicholas put his lack of interest in accepting any of the many invitations waiting for him in London to his concerns about the coming struggle with Napoleon. Many of the people who normally spent the Season in London had flocked to Paris and Brussels, taking advantage of the opportunity to visit Europe, the first for many years, though it appeared that a few, apprehensive at the approach of the Corsican monster, had fled back to London.

One of the young matrons with whom he enjoyed a discreet liaison sent a brief note saying her husband was away for a week, and she hoped to see him before he, too, left for Brussels, but he tossed it into the fire. He had no appetite for her frivolity. Lady Keith, furious that he had countermanded her decision to have Olivia in London for the Season, sent an imperious command ordering him to dinner the following day, and to this he sent polite apologies, mentioning a previous engagement. He was in no mood to listen to her complaints.

He could not dismiss thoughts of Catarina

from his mind. Used as he was to ordering his own affairs, it rankled that she had been better informed than he about the old cottages. However much he told himself that as she lived there it was only natural she would know the situation, he disliked the experience of having to admit he was wrong. She had not, however, known about the agent's dishonesty, but that had no doubt been Walter's province.

She was an enigma, and to his annoyance he could not rid his mind of thoughts of her. Going through Walter's papers he had discovered several letters from an elderly Colonel Carsley, a member of White's, and it seemed they were old friends. Almost without being aware of it he found himself entering the club later that day.

The colonel was reposing in a deep armchair, his eyes closed and a glass held loosely in his hand in imminent danger of tipping the port it contained on to his lap.

Nicholas drew up another chair and coughed loudly. The colonel started, opened his eyes and drained his glass.

'What? Who? Oh, it's you, young Brooke. Thought you were down in Somerset. How did poor Walter's funeral go?'

'That was over two months ago; I have been busy elsewhere since. But I was at

Marshington Grange last week and met his widow again. A pleasant girl, but rather younger than I expected.'

The colonel uttered a salacious chortle. 'Walter was an old dog. Didn't know he had it in him. I wouldn't have minded bedding that filly meself!'

Nicholas found his hands clenched into fists. He forced himself to relax.

'We were such distant connections I hadn't met Walter since I was a child. My father always said he would never marry, but when he did we assumed he wanted to secure the succession.'

'Wants aren't always granted to us. You should be grateful. You get the title and the estate. He was a warm man, Walter, never spent above his income and managed to increase his fortune.'

'Why did he choose a girl just out of the schoolroom? I'd have thought he might have preferred someone older.'

'He didn't confide in me, but I understand he was visiting her uncle in Bristol for some reason and saw the chit. He was smitten and the uncle — Sir Ivor Norton, wasn't he? — caught his fish. An odd man, Norton, not the sort to take kindly to having to take on two schoolgirls. Got a sister, I believe? Did you see her? Is she another beauty?'

'She's pretty, yes, but Lady Brooke is the more handsome. But enough of her. What's the latest news from Brussels?'

★ ★ ★

Catarina closed her eyes and shuddered. 'Who was it? Were you forced?' she asked, thankful that her voice sounded normal.

'It was only once or twice. Well, a few times,' Joanna muttered. 'Just after I went home after Walter's funeral. Matthew and I were married, but secretly, and he was leaving to join the army in Belgium. Oh, Cat, what shall I do?'

'Our cousin Matthew?'

Catarina tried to suppress her anger. Matthew was Uncle Ivor's eldest son, just a couple of years older than she was, and she had always detested him. As a child he had delighted in playing cruel pranks on other children, lying to escape any punishment and quite willing to blame anyone else for his own misdemeanours.

'Joanna, how could you! He was the most dreadful little sneak and he was expelled from Harrow for stealing. It's a wonder he hasn't been kicked out of the army too!'

Joanna sniffed. 'I thought he had changed. He was different from when we were little, friendly and fun. Cat, you can't imagine how awful it is living with our uncle! He promised to take me away from it all, and anyway we were married! Or at the time I thought we were.'

'Thought you were?' Catarina didn't know whether to shake her sister or weep for her. 'How can you be uncertain? Tell me all about it. When did this marriage take place, where, and who else was present? Didn't you know that you needed Uncle Ivor's permission as you are only eighteen? If the marriage was secret how could you have had it?'

'Matthew said it would be all right,' Joanna said, her voice sulky. 'It was late at night, I couldn't get away at any other time, but I managed to climb out of my window and down the wistaria outside.'

Catarina groaned. 'Like you did in the seminary. Oh, Joanna! Won't you ever learn?'

'It's no good being cross with me now. I need your help, Catarina. I thought you'd be willing to help me.'

'I will. Go on.'

'It was at that nice little church just a few miles away — St John's. You know it, the village has moved, it's now further up the hill and the church stands all on its own.'

Just right for a clandestine wedding ceremony, Catarina thought, but did not voice it.

'Who else was there?'

'Two of Matthew's army friends, he said they were. I hadn't met them before. And the curate, of course.'

'They were witnesses, I suppose. Did you sign the register? I remember I had to when I married Walter.'

'I signed in a big book. I suppose that's what you mean.'

'I don't understand why it had to be a secret. Why did Matthew not wish his father to know?'

'He had got plans for Matthew to marry someone else, a girl Aunt Hebe met the last time she was in Bath taking the waters.'

'Does he know about the baby? Have you written to tell him?'

Joanna nodded and gulped. 'I wrote as soon as I suspected. I had a reply yesterday. That was why I had to come to you. Cat, darling sister, you will help me, won't you?'

Catarina's foreboding increased. 'What did he say?'

'He said I had been a fool to believe him; he'd never married me, the ceremony was a joke and the curate was just another of his friends. And he said he was now betrothed to a girl he'd met in Brussels. He gave me the address of a woman in Bristol who — who helped girls in my situation. He meant she

54

would get rid of the baby for me. But, Cat, one of the girls at the seminary went to one of these women and she died!'

'Do you still have the letter?'

'Yes, I brought it to show you just how — how horrid he's being.'

'Give it to me. I'll keep it somewhere safe and if I get the opportunity one day I will do something drastic to Cousin Matthew. Perhaps it would serve him right if we sent a copy to this girl he says he's betrothed to. Did he tell you her name?'

'Here's the letter.' Joanna took it from her reticule and handed it to Catarina. 'Read it. He didn't tell me who it is.'

'Then perhaps it's no one. He may be saying it just as an excuse.'

Catarina's emotions were too complex for her to distinguish them. There was utter fury and disgust at Matthew's calculating cynicism; anger at Joanna for being taken in by him and permitting such intimacies; dismay at the scandal that would arise when their friends learned of the situation; and, under it all, a shameful jealousy that her sister knew more about this aspect of life than she did herself.

She and Walter had led celibate lives. On their wedding night he had confessed to her that, due to an accident some years before, he was incapable of fathering a child. They had never lived as man and wife, though no one but themselves knew this state of affairs. She suddenly had a vision of Nicholas Brooke and wondered guiltily what it would be like to have such a handsome man make love to her. Before her wedding she had often wished for a young, handsome knight to come and carry her away from her uncle's house, but when told she was to marry Walter had striven to banish such unmaidenly thoughts.

She pulled herself together. Kindness in a husband was more important than good looks. But Brooke had invaded her dreams too frequently for her comfort.

'Don't worry, Joanna. We'll think of a way round it without resorting to any dirty old woman in Bristol! Now I'll show you to your room, the pretty one with the rose-patterned wallpaper you chose, and in the morning I'll have thought of a plan. And think yourself lucky you are not really married to Matthew!'

★ ★ ★

In the aftermath of the battle, when the Emperor's army had been routed, Nicholas, filthy from the mud and so weary he wanted nothing better than to lie down in his soaking wet clothes and sleep where he was, knew he had to make sure Jeremy was safe. He'd seen his brother a couple of hours previously and, at that time, he had been alive and exalted with the success they sensed was coming. He set off, asking everyone he met if they knew where Jeremy's regiment was located, and was eventually directed to an inn on the road back to Brussels.

His horse, as weary as he was, stumbled along the *chaussée* and dropped his head the moment Nicholas dismounted. The road was filled with carts carrying the dead and wounded, soldiers straggling back to Brussels, people trying to go the other way, either to look for loved ones or, Nicholas suspected, to scavenge amongst the debris and rob the dead still lying where they had fallen. There was grass at the roadside, but his poor horse seemed too weary to bother eating. Nicholas knew how he felt. Though all he'd had in the past four and twenty hours was a small loaf of coarse bread, he had no desire for food, just for sleep.

There were several cavalrymen sitting on the ground outside the inn, but not Jeremy. Someone inside was screaming in agony and Nicholas winced at the sound.

'What goes on? I'm looking for my brother, Jeremy Brooke.'

One of the men gave him a sorrowing look.

A second gestured towards the inn.

'Don't ask, mate. It's butchery in there. He's no surgeon.'

'What?'

Nicholas pushed past them and found his way into the coffee room. The long trestle tables had been commandeered as beds, and several men lay on them, groaning, while others surrounded the furthest table. He glanced round swiftly but could not see Jeremy. Then he thought he heard his brother's voice, demanding to be let go.

'Pour some more brandy down his throat,' Nicholas heard and, fearing the worst, he pushed through towards this group of men.

Jeremy lay on the trestle, struggling to get free, but his arms and legs were being held down by four brawny fellows while a fifth was sharpening a large, wicked-looking saw. Jeremy's breeches had been cut away and blood was pouring from a wound in his left thigh.

Nicholas grabbed the man with the saw and demanded to know what was going on.

'Bullet lodged. Now get off, there's plenty more to be done. Have you got the pitch ready?' he asked yet another man standing beside him.

'Aye, nice and hot.'

'No! There must be another way. Bullets

can be dug out, there's no need to amputate.'

'Look, mate, I'm the surgeon, I know what needs to be done. If I don't take the leg it'll be gangrenous and he'll die a lingering death, much worse than a few minutes of pain here.'

'Nick?'

Jeremy, his gaze unfocused, began to laugh and mutter about old Nick and the devil. Nicholas, seeing what appeared to be the landlord hovering in the background, beckoned to him.

'Do you have a bed upstairs for my brother, away from these butchers? I'll pay well.'

'It's no more than a garret, but you're welcome.'

Nicholas gestured to two of the men assisting the surgeon and told them to carry Jeremy upstairs. They shrugged and, lured by the thought of his largesse, picked up Jeremy and carried him, still muttering alternate prayers and curses, up the narrow stairs into a small room under the eaves. Nicholas could hear the surgeon shouting at his other assistants, ordering them to move the next one over. Poor devils, in his murderous hands. But he had to do what he could for Jeremy.

Nicholas handed the men some coins and turned to the landlord.

'Have you some woman who could help me? And plenty of hot water and bandages please.'

'I'll send up my wife.'

Within a few minutes a buxom woman came in, carrying a knife and a linen sheet which she intimated could be cut into bandages. Another, younger woman carried in a jug of water. Nicholas took the first strip of bandage and began to swab Jeremy's wound. He could not see the bullet, which was buried deep, but the wound looked clean and, if he could stem the bleeding, he might be able to keep Jeremy alive until he could reach a proper doctor.

★　★　★

Catarina's prediction that Uncle Ivor would suspect Joanna had come to her was proved correct on the following day. Halfway through the morning his carriage drew up outside the Dower House.

Joanna, nervous, looked out of the window and gasped.

'Cat, it's Uncle Ivor! I won't go back with him! Oh, please don't tell him I'm here! I'm going to hide in the woods.'

Before Catarina could reply she had disappeared through the double doors dividing the front drawing room from the back half. Catarina had a craven desire to follow. She would have to lie to her uncle and convince him she knew nothing of the matter. She seized some embroidery, a seat cover she was making for the dining-room chairs, and tried to appear calm.

Staines let him in. Catarina trusted her uncle, who was high in the instep, would not stoop to asking questions of the servants. She gave him a look of surprise when he was shown into the drawing room, though her hands holding the embroidery were shaking so much she feared she would stab herself with the needle.

'Uncle Ivor! What a surprise. I was so sorry you and Aunt Hebe could not come to Walter's funeral.'

She had decided to attack and try to put him in the wrong at the start.

'We sent apologies. I really have too much to do to traipse all the way out here. You had your sister for comfort. She's the reason for my visit today. Is she here?'

'She isn't in my house,' Catarina replied truthfully. 'Why do you ask? Where is she?'

'The ungrateful wretch has run away, said she was going to a friend in London.'

'Then I expect that is where she has gone. You have wasted your time coming here. Do you wish me to accompany you to London in search of her?'

'You take this very calmly!'

'I know my sister. She is quite capable of making her own way to London if that was what she said she would do. Why has she left you? Have there been disagreements? Have you been angry with her? She does not take kindly to unfair chastisement.'

As he spluttered in annoyance, Catarina heard a horse neighing outside. A few moments later, Sir Humphrey entered the room. She greeted him more cordially than usual and introduced her uncle. Sir Humphrey looked gratified. Staines brought in some Madeira and, when his back was to the men, he winked at Catarina. She suppressed a smile. Her servants would not give Joanna away.

It was a tense half-hour, but eventually both visitors left, Sir Ivor saying he supposed he would have to ask at the mail offices. Fortunately Sir Humphrey had not known of Joanna's arrival, so he was able to sympathize with the other man as they bade Catarina farewell and departed.

★　★　★

By the following morning Catarina had her plan worked out. When Joanna, looking rather pale, appeared at breakfast she dismissed the servants and began to explain.

'It's possible to travel abroad more easily now, so I think it's time we visited Mama's family. We could travel on one of the ships Papa's partner, Mr Sinclair, sends to Oporto.'

'But we don't want them to know,' Joanna protested.

'They won't. It's the middle of June now, and you can't be more than two months' pregnant. No one will notice for at least another two months. We'll stay with them for a few weeks, then go further south, where we can rent a house and tell people you are the widow of a soldier killed recently.'

'Rosa will know I'm not.'

'Rosa is planning to get married, so I won't take her with us. We'll hire a Portuguese maid who doesn't know us.'

'What of the baby? I don't want it, Cat! It would remind me of Matthew all the time, and how he deceived me.'

'That we will have to decide later. You could give him, or her, away, or leave the child to be brought up in Portugal, It has been done before when ladies have found themselves in such a predicament. We can afford to pay for its keep.'

Joanna sighed. 'I suppose that's best. Oh,

Cat, I knew you'd find a way to help me. How soon can we go?'

★ ★ ★

Jeremy's bullet was dug out by a Brussels doctor, and he was told that with care he might survive.

'Though you will probably always walk with a limp. Some of the muscle has been torn. You should remain here for a while, not put undue strain on your constitution,' he was warned.

For a few days he was delirious. Nicholas almost despaired of him, but eventually the fever subsided and he was once more rational. Then he drove his brother to distraction by demanding to be taken home.

At last Nicholas decided that Jeremy would be less likely to fret himself back into a fever if they did go home, so he organized a large travelling coach and hired Bates, a soldier who had been a valet before he joined the army, who assured him he had been used to nursing injured men. They set off at the beginning of July, travelling as slowly as possible. It was agony for Jeremy, for the roads were poor and, despite all the coachman's care, he was inevitably jolted. He bore it stoically, but Nicholas was thankful when they boarded ship and Jeremy had not suffered a relapse.

When they reached Brooke Court late one afternoon, Jeremy was put straight to bed, but on the following morning he insisted on being helped to sit in a large chair by his bedroom window, his leg supported by a footstool.

'Nick, I'm a crock, useless for the army,' he stated, when Nicholas looked in to see how he did.

'It's too early to say.'

'I know it. I'll never be as active again, and I cannot bear the thought of anything less than proper fighting.'

'With your experience you could still be useful.'

'No, I'd go mad tied to some desk in London. Did you mean it about letting me live at Marshington Grange?'

'Yes. As you are my heir we might be able to break the entail, and I'll give it to you.'

'I'm truly grateful. I doubt the rents from the entailed farms will cover the upkeep, but I have the money Grandmother Talbot left me. I would like to try my hand at some of the new farming methods I've read about. I think I could make it profitable.'

Nicholas was amused. 'I didn't know you had an ambition to become a farmer.'

'Well, I didn't, before. I've always been

interested, though. One of the fellows in the regiment lives near Thomas Coke at Holkham, and he was telling me about the gatherings they have each year. Coke's Clippings they call them, because they hold them at shearing time. He invited me to visit him next year.'

'Would you have mainly sheep?'

'No. I think cattle would also do well, and I'd like to breed horses of some kind. I don't yet know what sort, riding or carriage types. I've been reading about what some of the other farmers do. There's a deal of marshy land which could be drained and made into good sheep pasture. I couldn't sleep last night,' he admitted, 'so I compiled a list of books I want. Could you have them sent down for me? While I'm laid up I can be studying and making plans.'

'Give me the list and I'll send someone to London to fetch the books,' Nicholas said, thankful to see Jeremy involved in new plans rather than repining over the end to his army career.

'But I ought to be down at Marshington as soon as possible, before the harvest, so that I can plan for next year. I saw there was a lot of common land still, so I will need to make some enclosures. And if I can persuade the villagers to agree to amalgamate their strips they can all benefit. Oh, I assure you I intend to be a model landlord!'

'You can't go down until you are fit enough to ride.'

'I'll be able to drive a gig in a few days.'

'I can't permit it. But,' he added, holding up his hand to stem Jeremy's protests, 'I'll go down myself and see what needs doing. Then if there is a need to introduce an Enclosure Act I can do it in the Lords.'

★　★　★

Catarina waited impatiently for answers to her letters. The one from Mr Sinclair came first and said there would not be another boat going to Oporto until the end of July, but she and Joanna would be very welcome to sail on her. He hoped they would spend at least one night with him and his wife before the departure. Some time later, her Aunt Madalene, her mother's older sister, sent to say how delighted she would be to see her nieces, and bemoaning the fact they did not intend to stay more than two weeks.

Joanna fretted at the delay, but Catarina had so much to do she was glad of the respite. The new agent, Mr Trubshaw, left to oversee matters on the estate, found his situation difficult, and he was for ever consulting her as to what her husband would have wanted him to do. No matter how often she told him that he should apply to the new earl, she had to admit that while Lord Brooke was in Belgium with Wellington's army she was the best person to make necessary decisions.

The news of Napoleon's defeat was greeted with great joy and thanksgiving. Catarina heard of the many deaths and wondered rather sadly what would happen to the estate if both Lord Brooke and his brother had perished. The thought of perhaps never again seeing Nicholas Brooke was unexpectedly painful. Who would be the next heir? Then she told herself sternly she ought not to care. Though she would be sorry, for they were pleasant men, it did not concern her. She felt a considerable lightening of her spirits, however, when a letter from Lord Brooke came to tell her Jeremy had been wounded and would be unable to travel to Somerset for a while, but he himself would visit Marshington Grange in the near future to make any necessary arrangements.

'Let's hope we'll be gone before then! I look such a sight!' Joanna complained.

Joanna was complaining rather a lot and sometimes Catarina wanted to slap her young sister. She had got herself into this predicament by being too gullible and ought to be thankful there was a possible way of hiding her shame.

'I hate black! It makes me look sallow,' she stormed, when Catarina told her that if she meant to go into the village she had to wear one of Catarina's mourning gowns, while her own were being made by the village seamstress.

'You must, out of respect for Walter, or you'll scandalize the village. And remember, when we are in Lisbon, and you are pretending to be a widow, you will have to wear it all the time. The Portuguese are very strict about that. If you were to remain there you would be expected to wear black for the rest of your life.'

'Then I shall return home as soon as I am rid of this incubus!' she stormed, rubbing her still slender waist.

'I can't endure this food,' she said the following day, pushing aside the plate of pork cutlets with Robert sauce. 'It turns my stomach.'

'If you make such a fuss at Aunt Madalene's she may suspect your condition,' Catarina warned. 'After all, she has had a dozen children herself, and has several grandchildren.'

'If I am forced to eat such messes I shall be sick!'

'You will control yourself. And unless you stop complaining and making yourself unpleasant to my servants, I'll call off the entire plan. I'll leave you there on your own once we have been to Aunt Madalene's.'

4

Nicholas arrived a few days later, and found Catarina in the Dower House garden, wearing an old white sunhat and picking peas. He'd forgotten just how lovely she was.

'Good morning,' he called over the hedge which separated the garden from the drive to the Grange.

She glanced up, then straightened her back and walked across to the hedge. She looked pale and somewhat harassed, he thought. There were shadows under her eyes which had not been there before, even at the time of the funeral, and there was a wary look in her eyes. Did she suspect him of planning things for the estate of which she did not approve? He felt a sudden desire to take care of her, to remove the worry from her eyes.

'Good morning, my lord. We received your letter. How is your brother? Was he seriously wounded?'

'A bullet in his leg. He'll probably always have a limp, but at least I was just in time to stop some butcher of a surgeon amputating the leg. I swear they killed almost as many men as the French did!'

Then as Catarina paled he cursed his unruly tongue. He hurried on.

'He is fretting to be down here. He will take up residence and has many plans for farming. He wants to emulate Thomas Coke and breed fine sheep.'

'Walter met Mr Coke once and much admired him. If he had been younger I think he would have liked to experiment, but he maintained he had too much else to do. His father had left the estate in a shocking state; it was all Walter could do to make it profitable by the time we married.'

'Jeremy plans to drain some of the marshland and turn it into pasture. I trust you have no objections to such a scheme?'

For the first time since they'd met, Catarina smiled, and Nicholas was taken aback at the transformation of her face. She had been beautiful before, but rather in the manner of the expressionless Madonnas the Italians were so fond of painting. This smile gave a hint of mischief, and Nicholas wondered what it would be like to make love to her and release those emotions.

'Walter was planning to do just that,' she told him.

'Then would you ride out with me and show me the best places? Had Walter made detailed plans?'

'I imagine there are maps in the estate office which will show what Walter was planning, Mr Trubshaw will know. He has been assiduous in trying to master all the details of the estate. I feel so ashamed we did not discover the problems with Mr Carter. As he was the son of our dear former agent we trusted him. It was fortunate you found out so soon.'

'I am accustomed to checking such matters. I will spend the rest of today consulting the plans. May I call for you at ten tomorrow? You have a riding horse, I hope?'

'Yes, my two horses were my own property,' she replied, and the smile vanished.

Nicholas cursed his thoughtless words. She clearly recalled Lady Keith's fury that she had been left anything beyond the minimum. He nodded and turned away.

'Tomorrow, then. I am grateful.'

* * *

As she went back into the house Catarina chastised herself for being so curt. Joanna's tantrums were affecting her own temper. The sooner they could be on their way to Portugal the better. She must make amends by being helpful and friendly towards Lord Brooke tomorrow.

She had two riding habits, one of dark green, the other cherry red. As she had not anticipated riding anywhere other than on the estate, and by herself, and would soon be going to Portugal, she had not bothered to have a black one made. Which should she wear? The green was closer to mourning, but the cherry red one suited her better, and was much newer, more fashionable. Nicholas, the earl, she kept reminding herself to call and think of him, had only ever seen her in dreary black, which did nothing to flatter her. She wanted to show him she could look more attractive, but shied away from considering why she wanted him in particular to see her as attractive. Would many people be scandalized if she wore the brightly coloured one? They would be on Grange land, or in the village, all the time, so perhaps it would not matter.

It wasn't difficult to be friendly, she found. He put himself out to be a charming, interesting companion as they rode towards the village. He was so attractive she wondered yet again why he had so far escaped matrimony. Perhaps there was a woman he loved, she thought, to whom he was betrothed, or whom he wished to marry. The thought gave her an unwelcome jolt of dismay. She was horrified as she realized she was considering what it would be like to be married to him herself. Hastily she cast about for something else to concentrate on. The army, the recent conflict with Napoleon, she decided.

When she asked, he told her about the battle, which was already being called after Waterloo, the village where the duke had made his headquarters.

'It was one of the worst battles I've been involved in, and I spent several years fighting in Portugal and Spain. If Blücher and the Prussians had not arrived in time, we could well have lost.'

'And your brother? Is he recovering?'

'Slowly. He will not be fit to come and live at Marshington Grange for quite a time, so I will be coming for a few days occasionally. In the meantime, may I hope you will keep a friendly eye on the estate and let me know if anything needs to be done that the agent cannot deal with?'

Catarina shook her head. 'I'm afraid that will not be possible, my lord.'

'You won't?'

'I can't. My sister and I are going to be away for some time. We have decided this is an opportune moment to visit Mama's family in Portugal.'

'Then I will have to depend on Mr

Trubshaw. Your family live near Oporto, I believe you said?'

'My Aunt Madalene and her family do, but there are many other cousins elsewhere. It is a large family.'

'A friend, another officer, married a Portuguese girl and lives near Oporto. He spoke the language and acted as liaison with the Portuguese soldiers, but he was injured, and this girl's family took him in and nursed him. I believe he is becoming an expert on growing olives. Thomas Winterton. Perhaps your family know him?'

'It could be so.'

'I'll give you his direction.'

Catarina tried to change the subject. Once they had visited Aunt Madalene she and Joanna planned to vanish, not contact any of Nicholas's friends. She pointed out the new cottages.

'All the people are now housed here, delighted to have the room and be near their friends and the common.'

'I saw the old ones had been pulled down. These look handsome.'

They were built in pairs, of stone and with slate roofs. Each had a plot of ground in which vegetables were growing. Most of the cottages had a run with fowls scratching at the dirt. Beyond them the ground rose slightly until it became a low range of hills. It looked like the common, and already the hay was harvested and the animals turned out to graze.

'The big fields are that way,' Catarina explained, pointing, 'and the marsh starts beyond them and curves round following the river we saw by the old cottages. Walter was planning to drain the nearest part first, but' — she swallowed — 'he never began. He was coming back from looking at them when something happened and he was thrown from his horse. We don't know what caused it, whether something startled the horse, or it stepped into a coney hole. It was a little lame when it returned to the stables. Then we began to search. It was some time before Walter was found, and by that time he was dead.'

'I am truly sorry. You were fond of him, clearly.'

'He was a good man. Now I think we should start back and go through the woods. The pigs won't have been turned out there yet. But they grow fat on the acorns and make a good meal for Christmas!'

★ ★ ★

To Catarina's relief Joanna behaved with all due decorum while they stayed with Mr and

Mrs Sinclair in Bristol. The sea voyage was calm and Joanna's spirits revived.

'I can see an end to this,' she said on their first evening at sea. 'I'm sorry I've been so obnoxious, but I felt nauseous and I was worried. Catarina, I'm so sorry to have caused you so much trouble.'

Catarina hugged her. 'You were foolish, but we'll manage it together. And what would I have done alone at the Dower House? At least we can see something of Mama's home. Papa always meant to bring us, but he said the war made it too dangerous.'

One of their cousins, Antonio de Freitas, was waiting to greet them when the ship docked at Oporto, and drove them the few miles to the Quinta das Fontes. It was far larger than Catarina had expected, a long, low house painted white, with green shutters at every window, and wings extending back to enclose a delightful courtyard. This was ablaze with flowers, many of which were new to Catarina, set in stone urns. All the rooms, on the ground and upper storeys, opened out on to shaded terraces and balconies. Colourful tubs of flowers adorned the balconies and all the steps, and bougainvillaea clambered up the walls. A fountain played in the centre of the courtyard, making a gentle tinkling sound as the water fell into an ornamental pool. The sun shone on the drops of water creating rainbow colours which flashed for a moment and then died. Aunt Madalene, having greeted them enthusiastically and remarked how like they were to their dear mother, took them out to where a table was laid in the shade.

'The fountain is from a natural spring,' she explained, as they drank tea and sampled delicious honey cakes, 'and gave the name to the quinta. There are other fountains in the garden, but we will show you those tomorrow. And the vineyards. Your Uncle Mario will explain how we make the wine. Oh, how delightful it is to have you here. I want to hear all about your lives in England. But I do wish you could make a longer visit.'

'Now the wars are over, we will come back often,' Catarina promised. 'This time, I'm afraid, we have promised to pay visits in Lisbon and Faro.'

'Do we know your friends? There are still many English officers in Lisbon looking after things while the court is in Brazil. Perhaps you will know some of them.'

For a moment Catarina wondered whether they should avoid Lisbon; she had not known about the English still being there. Then she decided that, as they would of necessity remain secluded, there was little chance of being seen or recognized. It was unlikely she would know any of them. She and Walter had not been much into Society, and since both she and Joanna were dark-haired and did not have the pale complexions of English girls, they would be taken as Portuguese.

Catarina was realizing how difficult it was going to be to keep Joanna's secret, their aunt being so hospitable and interested in their lives in England. Already she was telling lies, inventing excuses, and hating herself for the deception. Joanna had no qualms, though.

'We are visiting a couple of my friends from school,' she said cheerfully. 'One is married now and living in the south, which is why we want to travel there later, after we have seen the one in Lisbon.'

The two weeks they spent at the Quinta das Fontes were enjoyable, but both girls were glad when they could leave. One day Aunt Madalene had remarked that the good Portuguese food must suit them, as Joanna seemed to be putting on weight, and for a horrid moment Catarina thought she knew.

They left, promising to return the following year, driven by their uncle's coachman. Catarina insisted they take the public coach from Oporto, but she could not evade Antonio's escort. It simply was not possible for two young girls to travel on their own, they were told. She could not risk anyone discovering their destination in Lisbon, but Joanna's inventive mind provided the answer. They were, she said airily, to stay at a hotel for a night or so, as their hosts were away, and they would be collected as soon as the da Sousa family returned to the city. She had only a vague idea of the address where they would be staying, as the family had a couple of town houses and also a country estate.

Antonio was horrified at the notion of two ladies being alone in a hotel. They were afraid he would insist on remaining with them, but Catarina assured him it was considered acceptable in England and, to their relief, he said he had to go back home as there were people he had promised to meet there on business connected with the grape harvest.

Listening to Joanna, Catarina was thankful there were so few surnames in Portugal. There would be dozens, if not hundreds, of families called da Sousa and tracing an individual one would be difficult.

★　★　★

By mid-August Jeremy was fit enough to go to Marshington Grange. He was so restless Nicholas was thankful to take him there. At his own house he would have more to do, and

Nicholas meant to stay with him for several weeks and help him settle and get to know the people on the estate. Even to himself he did not admit that he hoped to meet Catarina again. She had not said when they would return from the visit to their Portuguese family, but surely they would be back before the winter.

Jeremy insisted he could ride around the estate, not have to travel in a ladies' gig, but he agreed to rest for a day or so after the tedious coach journey. Then he rebelled, telling Nicholas he was living up to his devilish name, so Nicholas went to the stables to make sure his saddle was put on a placid mare. Jeremy frowned when he saw her, but said nothing more. Nicholas trusted he was beginning to realize his limitations.

It was clear within the first few minutes that Jeremy was finding riding difficult and, after they had ridden as far as the village and seen the new houses, Nicholas insisted on turning back.

As they passed the Dower House Nicholas saw Staines in the garden and hailed him.

'When do the ladies plan to return?'

'Not for some months, my lord. I understand they are visiting several relatives.'

Nicholas thanked him, and was silent all the way back to the house. Jeremy, clearly in pain, did not wish to talk. He winced as he dismounted, and instead of following his normal practice of making sure his horse was properly looked after, he handed the mare to a groom, grimaced at Nicholas and said he would go into the house.

Before he went inside himself, Nicholas made sure there was a suitable gig and a pony to pull it. Jeremy might object and say he felt like a child or a female driving such a conveyance, but if he wanted to be able to tour his land he would have to endure the embarrassment.

After the first few outings Jeremy was reconciled. He met the tenant farmers, listened to their praises of the late earl, and tentatively began to discuss his own plans for improvements. One or two of the farmers approved, but he met considerable resistance from others.

'I'll have to go slowly,' he told Nicholas, as they sat over their port one evening. 'Do you think, if the dowager were here, she might persuade them? Several of them talked about her, and they seemed to respect her views. She has been good to many of them, sending help when they were in trouble. If she approved of my plans they would accept them more readily.'

For a few moments Nicholas wondered

who Jeremy meant by the dowager, then with a shock realized he was talking of Catarina.

'She's still a girl!' he exclaimed. 'How can you call her a dowager?'

Jeremy grinned at him. 'I know, it sounds ridiculous, she's the same age as I am, but as soon as you marry she'll have to get used to it. We can't have two countesses.'

'I'm not planning to marry,' Nicholas protested.

'Oh, come. You wouldn't want me to inherit the title, would you? Besides, you'll live to a ripe old age and I would be too ancient to make the most of it. I'll be content with the connection, the reflected glory. Seriously, Nick, you need to set up your own nursery soon. There will be even more debutantes on the catch for you now you have the title. Why don't you go up to London for the Little Season and survey the field?'

Nicholas grimaced. 'The whole business is like a horse fair. Dance with some chit at two consecutive balls, or drive her in the Park, and the dowagers are taking bets. Dowagers!' he added.

Jeremy chuckled. 'I'll hazard you don't meet many like our own dowager at Almack's!'

★ ★ ★

Catarina rented an apartment a week after they arrived in Lisbon. She hired a cook and a Portuguese maid, and they announced that Joanna, a grieving widow, would not be entering Society or receiving calls.

'That will explain how we don't know anyone here.'

'If we'd gone to a smaller town we could at least have driven out,' Joanna complained.

'And been more conspicuous. Here we are anonymous, and no one will notice us, or begin to speculate about us.'

Joanna nodded reluctant agreement. 'I am so bored!' she complained. 'I've read this book of poems so many times I could recite every one.'

'There are clothes to make for the child,' Catarina reminded her.

'I hate sewing. I have enough reminders of Matthew; I don't want to spend my time sewing for his wretched brat!'

Catarina sighed. Joanna insisted she did not wish to keep the child. In any event it would have been impossible, unless they moved from Somerset and all their acquaintances and settled in another part of the country where they could have maintained the fiction of Joanna's widowhood.

'I've been making enquiries. There is a convent nearby which takes in orphan babies.

They either find someone to adopt the children, or they keep them until they are old enough to be apprenticed to a trade. If I give them a large sum of money they will ensure the child goes to a good home.'

'I don't care.'

Catarina lost her temper. 'This baby is yours too! You are as responsible for creating it as Matthew. You can't be so heartless as not to care what becomes of the poor mite!'

'It was Matthew's fault!' Joanna muttered. 'I thought we were married, and he might have been going to his death at Waterloo.'

'You should have had the sense to know it was not all correct when it was done in a clandestine manner.'

'He said he didn't want Uncle Ivor to know, as he wanted Matthew to marry some girl with a title, not just a small fortune like mine.'

'He survived,' Catarina was horrified at her wickedness when she caught herself thinking it might have been better if he had not. 'His mother wrote to tell me, and also to announce his betrothal to a girl from Leicestershire. Will you tell him when the baby is born?'

Joanna shook her head. 'He doesn't care, He wanted me to get rid of it and, as soon as I can, I want to forget I ever had it. I mean it, Cat. This baby is not going to ruin my life.'

* ★ ★ ★

Nicholas and Jeremy were still at breakfast when their new butler came to say that Staines was in the kitchen, rather upset, and wanted to speak to them.

'We'll see him in the estate office in five minutes,' Nicholas said.

'I suspect some problem has arisen at the Dower House which he cannot deal with,' Jeremy said.

'There may be a message from Lady Brooke,' Nicholas said, but knew it was unlikely Staines would be coming to them so early in the day just to relay a message that the ladies were coming home. He wondered at his preoccupation with Catarina, Why did she occupy his thoughts so much? He admitted frankly that he desired her, wanted to make love to her, but he had desired many women, and then banished all thoughts of them either until the desire faded, which it often did, or an appropriate moment came to satisfy it. Perhaps, perversely, it was because he knew Catarina was not like his other conquests, bored married women who could love and leave their lovers as readily as he did himself.

Staines was standing by the window of the estate office when the brothers entered. He

87

swung round and took a few steps towards them, holding out his hands in supplication.

He had dressed hurriedly and not shaved. His hair looked as though he had spent the time of waiting thrusting his hands through it.

'What is it, man?' Nicholas demanded. 'Here, sit down, you're as pale as a ghost.'

'My lord, I don't know what to do,' Staines muttered, almost collapsing into the chair Nicholas thrust towards him. 'It's Cook. Ellen. She's dead.'

'Your cook at the Dower House? But she isn't an old woman. Has she been ailing?'

Staines shook his head and wrung his hands together. 'Wicked, it is!' He took a deep breath. 'It was her custom to go out into the garden last thing at night; she said a breath of fresh air helped her to sleep.'

Nicholas nodded. He knew many people who said the same.

'Who normally locked up after her? Did you see her? Was she looking ill then?'

Staines shook his head and groaned. 'She did herself. I saw to all the other doors and windows, but she'd lock the back door and go up to her room. I'd usually hear her, but not always. I was tired yesterday. I'd been helping Mr Lewis repair the roof of his barn, and must have gone to sleep the moment I put my head on the pillow Oh, why didn't I wait for her!'

'Are you saying she didn't come back into the house?'

He nodded. 'This morning she wasn't in the kitchen when I went for my breakfast, so I thought she'd overslept. I sent up young Liza, and she said the bed hadn't been slept in. Then — '

He stopped and dragged his sleeve across his eyes.

'Well?'

'The kitchen door wasn't locked. We went out, thinking she might have had a fall. But' — he gulped — 'she was down by the raspberry canes at the end of the garden and — and she was stone cold.'

'Dead? Had she fallen, could you tell?'

'She was covered in blood. Bludgeoned to death, poor lass.'

'Have you called a doctor? Or the constable?'

Staines shook his head. 'Dr Holt could do no good. I didn't know what to do, with my lady not here, so I came to tell you.'

Nicholas turned to Jeremy who had been standing by the door, listening. He looked horrified.

'Send a groom for Dr Holt and the constable. And saddle my horse, I'll go straight down. You bring Staines in the gig. Did you move her?' he asked, turning back to Staines as Jeremy, looking pale himself, nodded and left the room.

'I thought it best not to. There was nothing we could do for her, poor wench.'

'Good man.'

'I have to tell my lady, but I don't have her direction! She said she didn't know where they'd be after they'd visited her aunt. What shall I do?'

5

Joanna, having suddenly grown large and ungainly, so that even wearing a loose cloak did not hide her condition, refused to go out of the house apart from taking some gentle exercise in the small garden attached to it. Catarina, thankful to be away from her constant complaints, spent as long as she could over the daily marketing. She explored Lisbon on foot, admiring the many new buildings. Since convention demanded she take a maid with her she was thankful that Luisa had lived in Lisbon all her life and was proud of her city, so that she knew all the best places to see. At the same time Catarina was improving her grasp of the language, which she had rarely spoken since her mother died.

Sixty years earlier, on All Saint's Day, just as people were going to church, the city had been destroyed by a large earthquake, followed by a huge wave which had capsized many boats, and a fire that had raged for three days and destroyed most of what was left. Lisbon had then been one of the largest and most prosperous cities in Europe. Catarina had been old enough to remember her mother telling her how one of her uncles had been in Lisbon, one of the few survivors, and he had described how the house he was in had shaken. There had been a tremendous underground rumbling noise, and three terrific shocks, followed by the terrifying wall of water. Being on the outskirts, her uncle had been able to ride away.

'There was great destruction all over Portugal, Spain and Morocco too, and the high waves reached the coast of England,' Mama had said.

One day early in November she had escaped for a couple of hours, and was standing outside the Basilica de Estrela, admiring the white dome, when she heard her name.

'Surely it's Catarina Brooke? Catarina, how astounding to see you here! Are you visiting your mother's family?'

Catarina turned, slowly. 'Delphine. What are you doing here?'

Of all the people she might have met, her old schoolfriend Delphine was the worst. She had been a noted gossip in the seminary, seemed to spend all her time writing letters, and had never been able to keep any secret. She was fashionably dressed in an olive-green walking dress and slightly darker green pelisse; a chip straw hat was perched on her bright golden curls. An elderly woman, presumably her maid, stood slightly behind her, carrying a couple of parcels.

'Oh, my husband, Captain Pearce, is here, doing something about the roads. He is in the army. There is so little organization here since the French occupation, we are helping. But you must come to dine with us. We have a sweet little apartment near the castle. Are you staying with relatives? And don't you have a sister? Is she with you?'

Catarina thought rapidly. She dared not admit Joanna's presence, or Delphine would insist on calling to see her, and that would be fatal.

'I am staying with — with an elderly great aunt,' she said slowly, praying that Luisa, who was standing just behind her, could not understand. 'She has been very ill and I am keeping her company. Jo — Joanna is with friends in London.'

'Then I expect your aunt is not receiving — '

'No, not at all. She was rather reclusive before she became ill.'

Really, Joanna would be proud of her powers of invention, she thought wryly. She must be sure not to give Delphine their direction for, despite the mythical invalid, she suspected Delphine would contrive to visit.

93

'Can you come to dine tomorrow? We keep country hours here, unlike the Portuguese, so I will expect you at four. I heard about your husband's death, and I wrote my condolences, but I want to hear all about what you have been doing since. You are not a very good correspondent, Catarina!'

'Tomorrow?'

'It must be tomorrow, we are going back to England two days later. Oh, how wonderful to have run into you!'

What appalling timing, Catarina thought. Only three more days and this need not have happened. She considered her options. If she refused, Delphine would try to make a different arrangement, and would certainly insist on having her direction in order to contact her about it. She gave in to the inevitable and hoped she could maintain the fiction.

'I would love to dine. Thank you.'

'I will send a carriage.'

'No, no, that won't be necessary. I've no doubt my aunt will have some commissions for me that I will need to do beforehand. She usually does, so I will use her carriage. Where is your apartment?'

She escaped soon afterwards, when Delphine recalled all the various tasks she had to perform before they left for home and, after watching her friend and the maid walk away, Catarina turned back towards their own apartment, walking slowly so that she could think what to do.

★　★　★

Nicholas was relieved to see that the Dower House cook had not been so viciously attacked as Staines had suggested. There was a deal of blood, but it appeared to come from just one wound, a heavy blow to the side of her head. Doctor Holt arrived and pronounced her dead, which they all knew. Then the constable came and shook his head gloomily.

'Poor woman, but she was asking for it.'

'What do you mean?'

'Well, sir, Ellen was always a flighty piece. The despair of her parents, though they tried to keep it quiet. Lady Brooke couldn't have known what her reputation was when she took her on. After all, she came from ten miles away. But I've heard rumours lately she was meeting one of Farmer Lewis's men on the sly. Married, Dan is.'

'Mr Lewis's man? Mr Lewis who rents the home farm?' Nicholas asked. 'So that could account for her breaths of fresh air late at night. You think this might be a lover's quarrel?'

'Aye, that, or a jealous wife. Dan's missus Annie has a vicious temper and has given him a black eye or two since they've been wed.'

Jeremy was horrified. 'This isn't a woman's crime!'

'This was done with a heavy club, or more likely something like a heavy branch, not a fist,' the doctor said. He was still examining the body. 'Look, there are scraps of leaves and bark in her hair, which I swear didn't get there except from the weapon. The blood has stuck to them!'

'I'd best go and talk to Dan and his missus,' the constable said. 'And send a lad with a note for Ellen's parents. Poor souls, they'll be wretched. She was their only daughter. They may want her buried over their way.'

'Doctor, if you have finished, can we put her in an empty stable?' Nicholas asked, and the cook's body was soon neatly stowed.

Staines had remained at a distance, but now he came forward.

'My lord, how can I let her ladyship know? I don't have her direction, I don't know where her foreign relatives live.'

'It's near Oporto. I've no doubt her father's partner will know. I'll ride to Bristol and ask him. Jeremy, if I go immediately I may be able to return tonight. Can you deal with matters here?'

'Of course. Staines, should we employ another cook for now?'

'I couldn't say, my lord. One of the girls can do all we need while the mistress is away. I wouldn't like to take the responsibility of engaging someone else until she comes back.'

'If you need help, ask at the Grange. I have more servants than I need,' Jeremy offered.

Nicholas reached Bristol several hours later. The roads had been dusty and busy, and he decided he would have to remain the night as his horse was too tired for the return journey. He stabled the beast and booked a room at one of the main inns, then set out on foot for the wine importer's premises.

To his frustration, Mr Sinclair was not there and was not expected back until the following day. Nor was he at his home. His wife could not help, as she did not know precisely where Catarina's family lived.

'I once heard her mention the Quinta das Fontes,' he tried prompting her. 'Could that be it?'

'That sounds like it, but my husband will know.'

The next morning Nicholas was able to obtain the full direction and, as there was a ship leaving for Oporto the following day, he left his letter to be taken by it. It would probably be faster than by the ordinary mails. Then he rode back to Marshington Grange to hear from Jeremy that the jealous wife, loudly protesting her innocence, had been placed in the village lock-up.

'One of Catarina's maids had hysterics, said she would not under any circumstances stay here, so she has gone home,' Jeremy reported. 'I sent one of the grooms down to the Dower House to provide protection for the rest of them. Even Staines is badly shaken.'

'But if this woman Annie has been apprehended, they are in no danger.'

Jeremy grinned. 'Tell them that! They expect the husband to come wreaking vengeance on them. I must say village life is almost as exciting as Belgium!'

* * *

Catarina had spent a sleepless night concocting fiction in readiness for the dinner party, but she had little need for it. There were several other English people there. It was, she realized, a farewell party for Delphine and her husband, and most of the conversation was to do with the political situation in Portugal and speculation about whether the royal family would return soon from Brazil. The other guests were polite to Catarina, sympathized with her recent widowhood, and did not press her with questions.

'You must write to me when you return to England and tell me how you get on at the Dower House,' Delphine told her as she was leaving, but just then another guest captured Delphine's attention and Catarina made her escape without having to give away her own address.

On the way back to her apartment she wondered whether Lisbon was too full of English people, and whether they ought to move to some other town once the baby was born. Joanna was too far into her pregnancy for them to travel now, and all the arrangements had been made for her lying-in, but once she was able to go out Catarina knew her sister would be determined to make up for the months she had spent hidden away.

She did not want to return to England in the depths of winter. The sea journey would be rough, and while she was here she would like to see more of her mother's country. Perhaps they could go to the south, or even visit some of their cousins. Without the child they would be free. Joanna was adamant she did not under any circumstances wish to keep it, or even see it once it was born.

Catarina felt as though she had never really known her sister. She'd always been aware Joanna was light-minded and reckless in her behaviour, caring little for the opinions of others, but she had not previously realized how callous she could be. She began to worry about what would happen once they returned to England. Joanna would not be able to go back to live with their uncle, nor would she want to. When Catarina had written to tell him she and Joanna were planning to go to Portugal, his response had been curt and uncompromising. He never wished to set eyes on the ungrateful wretch again. The sooner she was one and twenty and he could hand over her fortune and all responsibility for her the better. Meanwhile, he would arrange for Joanna's allowance, which she did not deserve but which, as an honest guardian and trustee, he felt bound to continue giving her, to be sent each quarter into Catarina's charge.

With a sigh she supposed Joanna would have to come and live with her at the Dower House. It was not that she didn't love her sister, but rather dreaded the task of controlling her. What the girl needed was a stern husband, and perhaps in a year or so they could go to London for the Season where she might find one. Meanwhile they could spend some time in Bath so that Joanna might learn how to conduct herself properly in Society. Then she recalled Joanna's disgrace at the seminary. Maybe they ought to go to some other spa town such as Cheltenham, or even Tunbridge Wells. It would be better to be where there was less chance of meeting people who might know of Joanna's previous exploits.

★ ★ ★

Joanna was uninterested in anything but the discomforts of the last months of pregnancy. Their best estimate for the birth was the middle of December. Catarina had engaged a midwife who promised she could find a suitable wet nurse for the baby when the time came. Joanna had reacted in horror at the mere thought she might have to suckle the child herself. She insisted to Catarina she would be happy not even to see the child. Then, in the middle of November, she went into labour late one evening.

Luisa was sent for the midwife, while Catarina tried to recall all she knew about childbirth. She'd thought they would have more time for preparation, but at least she knew enough to set water to boil and collect as many clean rags and sheets as she could.

For several hours Joanna wept and railed against fate, then swore she would soon die of agony. The midwife came and looked at her, told her she would be several hours yet, and she had to attend first to another lady who was much closer to giving birth. She would return in the morning.

Joanna screamed abuse at her, demanded that Catarina find another midwife, or send for a doctor.

'There are doctors who act as midwives,' she wept.

By morning Catarina was exhausted. Joanna had wept or screamed the whole night, had clung to her hand with such force when the spasms gripped her that she felt they would never again be capable of holding anything firmly.

The midwife returned, examined Joanna, and told her, with considerable relish, that her previous patient had given birth to stillborn twins.

'And she did not make nearly so much noise about it as you do, my girl!'

'How dare you speak to me — *ow, ow, ow!* I'm splitting apart!'

'Should have thought of that nine months ago. Here, bite on this leather strap, it'll help.'

Joanna glared at her, panting. 'It's filthy! How many other women have bitten on it?

Ow, give it to me!'

An hour later a tiny girl was born and Joanna subsided on to the pillows with a sigh of relief.

'A good size, even though she came a few weeks early. She'll do,' the midwife said, wrapping the child in a sheet and placing her beside Joanna.

'No! Take it away! I won't have her!'

'Let me hold her,' Catarina said, and took the baby into her arms. She looked at the tiny face, red and puckered, the pale-blue eyes, the dark curly hair, the tiny fingers curling round her own and fell instantly in love. At that moment she determined that her niece would not be given away, to finish up heaven knew where, with some unknown family, or given, when she was old enough, into some kind of service. The baby was of her blood: Catarina had never expected to have a child, married to Walter. Joanna might reject her, but the child could depend on her aunt.

★   ★   ★

Nicholas wrote to the Quinta das Fontes and received a reply saying Catarina and Joanna had left months ago to visit friends in Lisbon. He was tempted to forget it, assuming they would be home soon, but Staines kept appearing whenever he rode past the Dower House, asking if he had any news.

'Dan's wife says she had nothing to do with the attack on Ellen,' he reported one day. 'She was at home and there are neighbours who support her story. But if Annie's convicted she'll be hanged, or sent to that Botany Bay the other side of the world, and she'll not see her family again.'

'Do you believe her?'

Staines rubbed his forehead. 'I believe the neighbours,' he said at last. 'And they can't have got the day wrong, as he was helping us with that barn roof. I wish her ladyship was at home; she'd help.'

So Nicholas thought of Thomas Winterton, the fellow officer who, wounded when Oporto had been recaptured six years earlier, and unfit for more fighting, had married the daughter of the family who had looked after him, and settled to grow olive trees in the Douro valley. Perhaps he could ask more questions and find a trace of Catarina and her sister.

He admitted to himself he was concerned, and would have gone to Portugal in search of the girls if he had spoken the language, but he accepted he would be of little use without it.

All he had from the quinta was the family name of the friends they had been meeting in

Lisbon and the hotel where they had stayed when their cousin Antonio escorted them there. They had said something about travelling further south, but Antonio had no notion where. Nicholas wrote to Thomas begging for his help, either in searching himself, or employing someone to do so. Thomas promised to do his best, but said he held out little hope without more clues.

Nicholas told himself that Catarina's return could make little difference to the accused woman. She had not been there; she could only give her a character testimonial, and there were others who could do that. But he was by now seriously worried for Catarina. She had, as far as he could discover, corresponded with no one in England since she had left. What had happened to her? He was missing her, thinking of her every day. He knew he loved her, wanted to see her, to hold her safe in his arms, to care for her for the rest of her life.

Jeremy, he knew, guessed something of this, but with rare tact his brother made no reference to it, pretending that the real reason for contacting Catarina was to help the suspected murderer.

'If she did not do it, who did?' Jeremy would ask, but no one in the village could supply a name. Ellen had, they discovered, been walking out with a young man from her own village before she came to work at the Dower House, but his friends vouched for him, saying he had been with them on the fateful night. They could discover no other liaisons, no one else with a motive.

Christmas came. Jeremy was by now able to ride around the estate, and Nicholas frequently rode over from Brooke Court. He visited London and his other houses occasionally, but remained away for no more than a few nights, Rationally he knew he would hear any news just as quickly in Gloucestershire, but in Somerset he felt closer to Catarina. He would wait there until they had news.

★ ★ ★

When Catarina told Joanna she intended to keep the baby herself, Joanna merely shrugged.

'As long as I don't have to have anything to do with her,' she said.

She even refused to select a name, so Catarina called her Maria, after their mother. She wanted to name her Brooke, but reluctantly accepted that if she did people would assume the child was her own, so she called her de Freitas, for her family.

'We will tell people she is a cousin's child who has been orphaned, and I have adopted her.'

'I really don't care what name you give the brat.'

Joanna had swiftly recovered her health, though she was plumper than before, with a voluptuous bosom. By the new year she was fretting to become involved in Lisbon society.

'It's a great shame your friend Delphine had to go home,' she said, more than once.

Catarina silently disagreed. She had been involved in so many uncomfortable lies since Joanna had been pregnant that she dreaded to have more to contend with. How could she account to Delphine for Joanna's presence in Lisbon when she had not been visible before? If people came to know about the baby they would soon realize the truth.

Joanna wanted to explore Lisbon, so Catarina sent her out with Luisa. She remained in the apartment, partly because the baby was ailing and she was concerned, partly because she did not wish to be seen with Joanna by any of Delphine's acquaintances.

Her precautions were, however, of no avail. The doctor had prescribed medicine for the baby and, when Catarina went out to fetch it from his dispensary, she met Joanna at the end of the street talking to an elderly Portuguese lady. The woman turned to Catarina and smiled.

'Oh, you too! You are both so like your mother,' she exclaimed. 'She was one of my best friends when we were children. That's why I spoke to your sister, to ask if you were related. I am giving a reception next week for some Brazilians who are about to go back home. I have also invited some of the English officers who have been administering the country. There will be some Portuguese friends there too, quite an international gathering. You must both come.'

There was no way to refuse without giving offence.

'But if we meet any English we know, how do we explain your presence?' Catarina demanded, when they were back in the apartment.

Joanna was unconcerned. 'We'll tell them I have just arrived in Lisbon after visiting friends.'

Catarina, who had considered herself honest before this imbroglio, thought she was turning into the most mendacious creature imaginable, she had told so many untruths in the past few months. The sooner they could leave Lisbon the better, but baby Maria was still frail, and they had been advised not to travel until the weather improved.

Joanna was thinking more of her first party. 'How do you like this blue silk? I am going to have a gown made of it.'

'I don't think you should wear colours yet. It isn't a year since Walter died.'

'Don't be so odiously correct, Cat! It's been almost a year; it's February now. I'm no longer pretending to be a widow. As it happens we didn't have to tell people that, so if I want to wear colours, I will! I simply refuse to wear this unflattering black any more!'

Catarina gave way and was herself tempted into half mourning, a silver-grey shimmering silk, and privately admitted she was glad to be wearing something which suited her after so long. Little Maria could be safely left with Clarice, her wet nurse, who adored her and regarded her as her own. She had lost her own baby, and her husband, a sailor, had been lost at sea some months before. She said she wanted to go to England with them when they ventured to make the sea journey. That solved a big problem, and Catarina longed for the day when she would once more be in her own home.

The reception was a large one, with many Brazilian and Portuguese guests as well as English. Joanna, enjoying her first party for months, sparkled, and whenever Catarina saw her seemed to be surrounded by admiring men. Surely, thought Catarina with an inward shudder, she had learned her lesson and would be careful not to make the same mistake again.

'It's quite a large delegation going to Brazil,' one of the men Catarina talked to informed her. 'There are many celebrations now the Prince Regent has given it the status of a Kingdom. It is only just, since so much of our wealth derives from there. Brazil, Portugal and the two Algarves will from now on be a United Kingdom of Portugal.'

It seemed rather remote to Catarina. She was on edge wondering what Joanna was doing. Joanna was fizzing with excitement as they drove back to their apartment afterwards.

'Eduardo Gonçalves has invited me to drive with him tomorrow. He's a Brazilian, incredibly handsome, and has a huge estate there. They found gold on it, and he is fabulously wealthy.'

'Is that all you care about?'

'Of course not; though he is so handsome and charming, having a great deal of wealth does add to a man's attractiveness. But he is sailing for Brazil in a week's time. There will be few opportunities for us to meet.'

Catarina was thankful. She wanted no further complications in their lives. Eduardo, when she met him, was suave but charming, and she looked forward to the day when he would be gone from Lisbon.

* * *

Nicholas went regularly to Marshington Grange, even though Jeremy was now fit enough to ride about the estate. His friend in Oporto could discover nothing of Catarina, and the anxiety made him short-tempered. What had become of her? Staines had no news of her return.

'Annie has been convicted,' the butler said, when Nicholas stopped to ask how they went on.

'I thought she had an alibi.'

'That was only for the first part of the evening. Apparently they went to bed early, tired like I was, and Dan slipped out, thinking Annie asleep. But she followed him. She was seen by old Simeon, who was out poaching. He let it out when he was drunk.'

'So she'll be executed?'

Staines shook his head. 'No. The sentence has been commuted to transportation. Dan's beside himself. Mr Lewis has threatened to turn him out of his cottage, since he does little work. He's incapable most of the time. I don't know where he finds the money for so much ale.'

Nicholas rode on, having asked Staines to inform him the moment he heard when his mistress was coming home. He had other problems more urgent to think about.

Jeremy was encountering considerable opposition to his proposals. The villagers welcomed the drainage scheme, for it would give them work, and some of them expected to benefit when he had more sheep. But life was harder for them than it had been for several years, and some of them blamed him.

'As if I could do anything about the high duties on malt and barley which leads to more smuggling of brandy and other spirits!' he complained to Nicholas, as they sat over dinner. 'Or the size of the tithe and the poor rate!'

'There will be proposals before Parliament soon,' Nicholas said. 'I hear some of them relate to imposing more duties to protect our own agriculture, and alleviating the poor rate.'

'Then I hope you will go and tell them how badly the people are suffering. Yet they won't see that the changes I am suggesting will help!'

Joanna went riding or driving several times with Eduardo. There was always a groom accompanying them and sometimes other friends of the Brazilian. Catarina relaxed, more concerned over the health of the baby. She scarcely listened to Joanna's chatter, merely thankful that her sister had recovered her high spirits and was no longer querulous and dissatisfied.

She did listen when Joanna told her Eduardo's ship was to sail that Saturday, relieved he would be out of her reach. Joanna was rather quieter than usual, and Catarina assumed she was dreading the parting. On Friday night, when they went to bed, Joanna hugged her tightly.

'I do realize how good you have been to me, Cat! Thank you.'

Catarina hugged her back. Perhaps Joanna was growing up.

On Saturday morning Joanna was gone, and the note she had pinned to her pillow announced she was leaving with Eduardo and would be married to him aboard his ship.

6

Without waiting for Luisa, Catarina ran from the house and hurried down to the quay, her emotions overwhelming her. She had little hopes of finding the ship, it would have sailed early, but she had to try.

As, ignoring the shocked glances of the inhabitants, she picked up her skirts and ran, the memory of her mother's frequent stories of the earthquake flitted through her mind.

Many people, Mama had been told, had gone down to the river Tagus in the hope of escaping the horrors of the falling city. Some had boarded boats, but these had been overturned and swept away by the enormous wave which then flooded much of the lower town. Those on the Quay de Pedra, newly built of marble, had drowned when the quay itself had collapsed and fallen into the raging river.

Catarina looked round anxiously, searching for one ship amongst the many moored in the broad river. It was impossible. Then she saw a man who, in his smart uniform, looked like some official.

'The ship, for Brazil, has it gone?' she panted.

He looked disapprovingly at her. 'What do you want with it?'

'My sister, she's on it. Has it sailed?'

'Sister? Or sweetheart who's left you?' he sneered. 'It's gone, hours since. Why don't you try to swim after it? Might catch it this side of the Atlantic.'

Chortling at his wit he turned away.

Catarina, accepting the truth, turned and walked slowly back to the apartment. Would Joanna never learn? She somehow doubted that Eduardo would marry her. Men did not fall in love with such rapidity and, since he came from an important family, it was likely there were plans for his marriage which did not include a foolish girl from England.

She breathed deeply. There was nothing she could do about it. She could scarcely chase after Joanna even if another ship were available. Her first emotion had been distress, then anger at Joanna's folly. Then a feeling of desolation had swept over her. She felt abandoned. Joanna was the only one of her family left. She did not think of her Uncle Ivor as family, since he had scarcely behaved like it. She had nothing in common with him, or his wife, and certainly not with Matthew. She doubted she would ever see Joanna again. Now she was truly on her own.

Then the anger returned. She had rescued

her sister from her folly once before. This time Joanna was out of reach of her help and would have to make the best of it. She would be fortunate not to end up in one of Rio's bordellos. But being Joanna, Catarina thought wryly, she would almost certainly find someone foolish enough to help.

She considered her own plans. As soon as the baby was well enough, and Maria seemed to be recovering, they would go home to England. Clarice had been sworn to secrecy over Maria's parentage and vowed she would not reveal it. She knew the situation, and that for it to be known Joanna had borne a child out of wedlock would be ruinous for her reputation. Catarina hoped she could trust her, but she was paying the girl well. As yet she spoke no English, and she had said it would reflect on her own reputation if it were known she was nursemaid to a bastard. Catarina had winced, but she knew the girl spoke the truth.

She would write to Mr Sinclair and ask when a suitable ship would be calling at Lisbon or Oporto. It would be better to embark from Lisbon if at all possible, to avoid the land journey to Oporto, which would be difficult with the baby. Also, there she ran the risk of meeting some of her family. While one part of her said she owed Joanna nothing more, another shrank from revealing her sister's disgrace. If Joanna ever returned from this mad Brazilian escapade Catarina could not be responsible for preventing her readmittance to Society.

★ ★ ★

Nicholas, on his way to the Grange, was driving past the Bear inn when he saw Mr Lewis going inside. He wanted a word with the man, so he stopped the curricle and walked into the taproom. Mr Lewis had seated himself at one of the small tables and spread some papers and a box in front of him. A line of men formed, and Nicholas realized the farmer must be paying wages to his labourers. He would have to wait, so he ordered some ale and sat down at the far side of the room beside a window overlooking the road.

A few minutes later, a short stocky man came in, blinking as he became accustomed to the dim light. Several more young men crowded in after him. He looked round cautiously and then pointed his finger at one of the men in Mr Lewis's line.

'You'm the one I want! It were your doin's my Ellen got killed! A good girl, she were, till you bedazzled her!'

Nicholas deduced that this was the murdered woman's former lover, come to exact vengeance.

The newcomer strode across to the line of men and yanked one of them, Dan, towards him. Before any of the others could grasp what was happening, the stocky man was dragging his victim outside, while his friends, blocking the doorway, made sure none of the locals could easily follow.

Dan's protests could be heard, but were soon drowned out by the tumult erupting inside the taproom. However much Dan's activities had been condemned by the village, these farm hands were not going to see one of their own attacked by foreigners from ten miles away.

The fight was vicious, but when the locals resorted to banging pewter tankards on the heads of the intruders, the latter were thrust outside and the villagers poured out after them. The fight continued, but outside the invaders had the advantage, as there were more of them. Dan was suffering, and Nicholas, observing what was happening through the window where he sat, concluded that Ellen's lover had considerable science. He must have had experience in the boxing ring.

Soon a thoroughly defeated Dan was being

tossed almost contemptuously into the duckpond and, with a cheer, the invaders disengaged and marched away.

Mr Lewis went and stood in the doorway, glowering.

'I'll finish paying you ruffians tomorrow. As for you, Dan,' he went on, surveying the bedraggled, weed-draped figure who had been pulled from the pond by his friends, 'this is the end. I've warned you several times of late. You've not worked well these past months. I've tried to make allowances, but I'll do so no more, if you bring such a rabble here. You can get out of the cottage by tomorrow.'

There were protests from Dan's friends when they realized they would be unable to buy ale until the following day, but they clearly held Mr Lewis in awe and, though they grumbled, they gradually drifted away.

Mr Lewis turned back into the taproom and began to collect his papers. He glanced at Nicholas and shrugged.

'You may think me hard,' he said, almost apologetically, 'but I haven't had a decent day's work out of him since it happened. And it was his own fault. If he hadn't been chasing that Ellen from the Dower House, poor Annie wouldn't have done what she did.'

'What will he do? Has he family?'

'No, he's a foreigner, from Devon. If I was him I'd want to go back there. The men might have fought for him today, but that was local pride. They blame him, and he doesn't have a pleasant time of it here. Annie was born here, see. Some of them think what she did was justified.'

'We spoke for her, but it didn't influence the judge. Mr Lewis, I wanted to have a word with you about the drainage scheme. I'll order some ale and we can talk about it here.'

★ ★ ★

It was March before Catarina arrived back at the Dower House. She had hired a post chaise in Bristol, refusing to accept Mr Sinclair's invitation to spend a few days with his family to recover from the voyage, which had been rougher than usual at that time of year.

'I need to get home to the Dower House as soon as possible; I've been away far too long,' she said.

They had been fortunate in being able to start at daybreak. Having docked late at night, Catarina had decided it was easier for them all to remain on board until morning, rather than move to an inn for just one night.

Clarice, to her relief, had proved to be a

good sailor, and when Catarina herself had to retire to her bunk, she had been thankful the girl could take charge of Maria. The child had thrown off her illness and was growing fast. Making up for being born early, Clarice said with a laugh.

The coach journey was, Catarina thought, almost as wet as the sea voyage. It rained incessantly, and from the drenched look of the countryside and the pools of water in low-lying fields, it seemed to have been raining for weeks.

It was dark before they arrived, but the house was ablaze with lights. She had written to tell Staines of her return, but had not been able to predict which day. He had clearly been prepared for her whenever she came and, when they clambered stiffly from the chaise and went into the house, Catarina blessed his efficiency as she almost collapsed, Maria in her arms, into a chair before a roaring fire of sweet-scented apple logs.

'Welcome home, my lady. I've sent the post boys round to the stables, and to get some food.'

He studiously avoided looking at the baby, who was smiling up at him. She was not, like some babies, shy of strangers, and occasionally Catarina felt a twinge of apprehension in case she turned out to be like her mother.

'This little one is Maria de Freitas,' Catarina said, 'and this is Clarice, her nurse. She is the child of a cousin, who died when she was born and, as her father had been killed in a hunting accident, the poor thing was orphaned. Her father's mother was English,' she added, thinking that this was the only partly truthful thing she was saying, 'so I have taken her in. We can turn the main guest room and dressing room into a nursery, since the Dower House is not supplied with one.'

'No, my lady. I will see to it at once.'

'Is there a fire there?'

'Yes. We expected Miss Joanna to be with you.'

Catarina had decided it was too difficult to explain in a letter. Besides, she had in some way felt that if she were present when people were told of Joanna's marriage, there would be less speculation. She took a deep breath.

'While we were staying in Lisbon Joanna met a Brazilian gentleman; she has married him and gone with him to Brazil. It will probably be some years before we see her again.'

If ever, she added to herself. Unless this romance is also a disaster and Joanna runs back to me.

Staines was imperturbable. 'Would Miss Clarice care to bring the little one upstairs? I will see that she has all she needs. Perhaps you, my lady, would prefer to have supper on a tray here in the library, in front of the fire? It is warmer here than in the dining parlour.'

'That would be perfect. But not a big meal. I'm sure Cook will know exactly what I need.'

'Yes, my lady,' Staines said, and turned away. He seemed about to say something else, but shook his head slightly, then indicated to Clarice to follow him.

Catarina relaxed. She was home, Staines was in charge and she could trust him to do all that was necessary. She wanted to know what was happening at the Grange, but that could wait until tomorrow, until she had slept in her own bed once more and recovered from the journey.

* * *

Perhaps it was being back at Marshington, Catarina thought, that induced dreams of Lord Brooke. She blushed as she recalled some of the images which had invaded her sleep. She could still remember everything about him; he had seemed so real, as though he had been in the room with her.

This was strange. She had thought little about him while she had been away, but she had been preoccupied with so much else during the past few months. She had not dreamed of Walter once.

Before descending the stairs for breakfast, she went to see how Clarice was settling in and whether Maria was content. She found her housemaid Liza, who had just brought up a tray for Clarice's breakfast, cooing over the baby.

'Oh, my lady, she's beautiful! She's got such lovely big eyes, a sort of hazel colour. Were they blue when she was born? They say they turn darker. Rosa will be so envious of this lovely hair. It's so dark and thick and curly. Her own little one has only a few strands of fair hair.'

'Rosa has a baby already?'

Her maid had been married just before they left for Portugal.

Liza giggled. 'A honeymoon baby! I told Rosa it was as well it didn't come a couple of months early. My lady, your breakfast will be ready in a few minutes. Would you like a tray, or will you come down?'

'I'll come down, thank you.'

She must find a new maid to take Rosa's place as soon as possible, so that Liza did not have that work to do as well as her own, She'd write to the Bristol Registry offices today.

Clarice said she was being well looked

after, had all she needed, but although she was learning some English from Catarina, she found it impossible to understand what Liza said.

Catarina laughed. 'She has a local accent. I'm afraid you'll find most of the people round here speak in the same way. But you will soon begin to understand. You have a quick ear, and have already learned much.'

She went downstairs into the dining room, where Staines brought her coffee, and helped her to ham and boiled eggs and sausages.

'I have missed these sausages,' Catarina told him. 'Now, while I eat, tell me all that has been happening. Is Mr Jeremy settling in at the Grange? Have they finished the drainage? What other news is there?' And, she added to herself, has Nicholas been here often? Would she be likely to see him soon?

When the butler did not reply she glanced up at him, eyebrows raised. He took a deep breath and turned away from her. When he spoke his voice was muffled and she had difficulty in hearing him.

'We tried to send to you, but no one knew where you were. His lordship wrote to your aunt, he even set one of his friends who lives in Portugal on to try and find you.'

Catarina slowly put down her knife and fork.

'What is it?' she asked. 'What on earth has happened to cause such trouble to be taken?'

'It's Ellen, my lady.'

'Ellen? My cook? Has she left? Is that all? Are you telling me you had to hire a new cook?'

'No, we didn't like to. Liza's been doing the cooking for us while you've been away.'

'Then what is the problem? We can soon hire someone else. I'll write when I ask about a new maid to replace Rosa.'

'It's not just that, my lady. It was a terrible thing to happen. Ellen — she was killed, struck down.'

Catarina stared at him, 'Killed? Ellen? Oh, how terrible. What happened? Was it a carriage accident?'

He shook his head. 'It was Annie; you know her, Dan's wife, him that worked for Mr Lewis. Dan, well, he was playing about with Ellen. Annie knew and came after Ellen with some sort of club. She killed her. Late one night, it was, and we didn't find the poor lass till morning.'

Sinking her head into her hands Catarina tried to take in the full, unexpected horror of it.

'Poor Ellen! But what has happened to Annie?'

'Transported, to New South Wales. Dan's

beside himself. He's lost his job and his cottage since he couldn't, or wouldn't, work properly. Mr Lewis turned him off in the end, though he'd been sympathetic to begin with.'

'Then what is he doing? Has he gone back to wherever he came from? He hasn't family here, has he?'

'He's seen occasionally in the village, but no one knows where he's living. He's not gone back to Devon, It's my belief he's living rough in the woods. When I've seen him he looks worse than he ever did, unshaved, hair grown long, and his clothes not fit for a Christian to wear.'

Catarina pushed away her plate. 'I'm sorry, Staines, but I've no appetite. I can't eat this.'

'I shouldn't have told you right away. It was stupid of me,' the man said. 'I should have waited.'

'No, things like this can't wait. But are there any other disasters I need to know of?'

★ ★ ★

Two days later a letter came from Joanna.

Catarina opened it in some trepidation. She felt as though any more bad news would be too much. But Joanna was clearly happy. She apologized for having run off without telling Catarina, 'But I know you'd have

127

stopped me, and I could not let such an opportunity go,' She had married Eduardo a few days into the voyage and he was a most considerate husband. 'He doesn't know about the baby, and he was so drunk on our wedding night he did not realize I was not a virgin.'

Catarina felt embarrassed at the knowledge her sister displayed. Where had she obtained it? And had Joanna deliberately encouraged Eduardo to drink too much? Was she so calculating?

She read on. Eduardo, it seemed, had known there was a baby in the apartment, for he had seen Clarice taking it for an airing. 'But I told him it belonged to you, that your husband had died before it was born. It can't do you any harm, Cat, for no one we knew there knows you in England.'

Were there any lies Joanna would not tell if it suited her? Catarina felt a spurt of anger against her unprincipled sister, but unless this entire letter was lies, she was at least happy and someone else had the responsibility for her. She hoped Eduardo was a strong but tolerant man, though in some ways it might do Joanna good to be beaten occasionally.

'I've written to Uncle Ivor, and so has Eduardo,' Joanna went on. Catarina knew this was inevitable. She could soon expect a visit from her uncle and she dreaded the forthcoming confrontation. He would blame her. It would make no difference to him that Joanna had secured a wealthy husband. He disliked all foreigners, and the further away from England they were the more he disliked and despised them. In his eyes, a Brazilian would be as bad as a Hottentot.

Catarina finished the letter. Eduardo had several houses, all of them delightfully spacious and sumptuously furnished, and simply miles of land, many huge plantations on which he grew sugar cane and coffee. Rio de Janeiro was a beautiful city and she had her own carriage and driver. The other Portuguese residents had made her welcome and she had been presented to the royal family. It would be such a shame when they decided it was safe for them to return to Lisbon, since many of the delightful courtiers would no doubt return with them. But that might be good for Eduardo, as he was much in the confidence of the prince, and might secure diplomatic missions, which would enable her to visit Europe, even London, and see her dear Catarina again.

There was no mention of Maria apart from that transfer of her parentage. Joanna, true to her resolve, wanted nothing to do with her daughter, did not ask how she fared, or even if she were still alive. When so many babies died in their first year it could have happened. Catarina felt a renewed anger against her sister and, in order to calm down, walked out into the garden.

It had rained almost continuously since they arrived back in England, but today, though the sky was full of scudding black clouds, it was dry, though not as warm as Catarina expected at the end of March. Perhaps, in the warmer climate of Portugal, she had simply become unaccustomed to a cold, wet and windy English spring.

She was looking across the hedge into the park, wondering whether she wanted to visit her old home, or whether it would bring back too many memories, when she heard the sound of horses and carriage wheels. She turned, saw a familiar curricle, and began to tremble. She was not ready for this, she told herself. She needed more time to prepare herself for meeting Lord Brooke.

He leapt down and strode through the gate a few yards away from where she stood, talking as he came towards her along the gravel path.

'Catarina! I didn't know you were home! Where have you been all this time? Oh, my darling girl, I've been so very worried about you,' he said, and before she knew what was happening, she was in his arms and he was smothering her face with kisses, pushing her hat away from her face so that he could look down into her eyes.

★　★　★

Nicholas held her away from him.

'You are more beautiful than ever,' he said, and trailed a finger down her cheek and across her lips. He felt her tremble and saw in her eyes the welcome she could not hide before she dropped her gaze.

'My lord,' she managed, but her voice was hoarse and he felt a stirring of joyous anticipation. She was far from indifferent to him. She was wearing a lilac muslin dress, half mourning, he realized, as it was trimmed with black ribbons around the hem. She had a green and grey Paisley shawl around her shoulders. Apart from her red riding habit, it was the first time he had seen her in colours instead of the unrelieved black she had worn after Walter's death.

'I've been away, in London, on Parliamentary business,' he said, his own voice a little husky. 'How long have you been home?'

'Just three days — I think,' Catarina began, attempting to straighten her hat. At that moment the rain began. 'Oh, do come inside, my lord. Send your man round to the stables. Come, you'll be wet through in moments!'

Laughing, they ran for the nearest door which happened to be into the kitchen. They were very wet, for the rain had been swift and heavy. Nicholas shook his head and droplets of rain spattered from his hair. Catarina threw off her hat, which had protected her own head, but the fabric of her gown clung to her legs. They were, he noted, as shapely as he had expected. He felt a surge of desire and had great difficulty in remembering the interested servants who were working in the kitchen.

'Come into the drawing room,' Catarina said. 'Liza, can you bring some wine? And I think his lordship might appreciate a towel to rub his hair.'

Nicholas could have done without the wine and the attentions of the servants, but he had to endure them. As he sat with a glass in his hand he was thinking that his somewhat ambiguous feelings for Catarina had solidified into a real resolve. He had desired her almost from the beginning, when she had been so controlled and in command at the time of Walter's death. She was beautiful, and he readily admitted he would like to take her to his bed. Now he knew his feelings were deeper than mere lust. The sudden surge of joy he had felt on seeing her was more than relief at her safe return, it was a primitive desire to possess her for the rest of his life. This, he told himself, was true love.

Should he tell her now, or give her time to understand? He had sensed, during that swift embrace, her own willing response, but to ask her to be his wife, so suddenly, might be premature. Didn't females prefer to be courted, to come to a gradual realization of a suitor's intentions? As he had never courted a girl with a view to marriage before he was astonishingly uncertain. He was still debating when there was a thunderous knock on the front door. Staines could be heard crossing the hall to open it.

'Come on, man, why do you take so long? I'm soaked! This weather is appalling, they haven't managed the spring planting yet, and unless the ground dries soon they will be far too late.'

'Allow me to take your hat, Sir Humphrey, and your driving coat. Have you sent your man to the stables?'

'Of course I have!'

Nicholas, suppressing his irritation at the interruption, muttered that the Dower House stables would be getting rather crowded.

Catarina chuckled, but Sir Humphrey was still in full flow.

'I've only just been told Lady Brooke is at home. I do think a message might have been sent to an old friend, not leaving me to hear by accident from one of my tenants.'

'I suspect her ladyship wished for a few days to settle back at home after her journey, Sir Humphrey. She is in the drawing room.'

And there, thought Nicholas, goes all hope of any private conversation with Catarina.

⋆ ⋆ ⋆

On the following day Catarina was in the small library writing a reply to Joanna when Staines came into the room.

'My lady, there are two of the village men come, asking if you would see them.'

Catarina sighed. 'It seems the entire village wants to call now it is known I am back.'

Mrs Eade had arrived soon after Sir Humphrey and, as soon as the rain had ceased, all three visitors had decided they ought to try to reach their homes before another downpour came. They were all wet and uncomfortable and wanted to change out of their damp clothes. There had been time for no more than basic civilities, no time for Catarina to tell them about Joanna's marriage. She knew that if she had mentioned it they would have wanted all the details, and at that moment, she did not feel capable of providing a rational explanation.

'Shall I send them away?'

'No, I suppose I had better see them now in case it is important. Bring them in, Staines.'

The men, two of the older villagers, came in rather sheepishly, wiping their hands over their hair.

'Tom, Billy, what can I do for you? Do sit down.'

'Well, my lady,' Tom began, 'we don' like ter bother you, but it's like this. No one else'll listen, and we thought perhaps, well, you might be able ter put a word in for us wi' Mr Jeremy.'

'Why can't you speak to him?'

'It don't do no good, 'e won't listen!' Billy said. 'But if 'e does it, what'll us do fer feed?'

'Feed?' Catarina was bewildered.

'Let me explain, our Billy. You'm too excited ter make sense.'

Billy scowled. 'Get on wi' it then.'

Tom took a deep breath. 'Mr Jeremy, see, 'e wants ter put fences round common. Ter keep 'is own cattle separate. Says they'm special, an' mustn't breed wi' ours. Can't see what difference it meks. A bull's a bull, ain't it, beggin' yer pardon, my lady.'

Catarina immediately saw the problem.

'Then where will you graze your own cattle and sheep?'

'We won't 'ave nowhere.'

'Us can't afford ter pay rent fer fields. An' the common's bin free fer generations back, since that there Magna Carta they talk about so much, an' such like. Mr Jeremy's got no right ter tek it from us.'

'And 'e wants ter change the taps. If we do as 'e says, an' change over so's all my taps are in one field, I'll 'ave all the poor land and none o' the good,' Billy said. 'It ain't fair.'

'So, my lady, we came ter see if you'd put in a word fer us, talk ter Mr Jeremy. If yer 'usband were still alive there's be none o' this silly changin' the way things be done. They've bin good enough fer us, an' our fathers an' grandfathers before us, fer generations.'

He stopped, and the two men looked at one another, then nodded slowly.

'Well, thanks fer listenin', my lady,' Tom said. 'We'd best go now we've 'ad our say.'

'I'll see Mr Jeremy for you,' Catarina said slowly. 'I can't promise it will do any good, but at least I will tell him he must find other grazing for your animals. Now go to the kitchen and Staines will give you some ale.'

7

Nicholas watched as Jeremy strode nervously about the room. He limped, but it was not too noticeable, and by now it discommoded him hardly at all.

'Nick, what can I do? They are so hidebound! They don't see how such improvements could benefit them in higher production and better prices.'

'They clearly have not understood.'

'But I've explained until I'm blue in the face, and most of them refuse to listen. They even turn away from me when I drive or ride through the village. When I first came they were friendly and tipped their caps whenever they saw me. Now I feel I'm hated!'

'Country folk dislike change.'

'Not all of them. Some, well, two, of the farmers understand me. But they've had enclosures for many years and have seen the benefits.'

'Can you not get them to explain to the others?'

'They say they've tried, but it does no good. Besides, one of the fellows said to me that if they grew richer they'd have to pay more to the poor tax.'

'Perhaps Lady Brooke might be able to explain. Have you been to see her since she came home?'

'No. I thought I'd let her settle in before calling. Do you think she might have any influence with them?'

'They liked her husband and they appreciated the changes he made. They haven't objected to the drainage schemes, have they?'

'No, and they have worked on them. It has given them extra wages.'

'Because it was of benefit to them and they could see it immediately. Jeremy, I think you must take this slowly, show them the benefits.'

'How? Unless they all agree to amalgamate their strips of land and create consolidated fields I can't demonstrate the benefits. And I'm not permitting my own animals to mate indiscriminately with their scrawny cattle and sheep, so I have to enclose the common and cut part of it off for my beasts. If they won't agree to do it I'll have to have an Act to make them.'

'Do you need all of it? Why not use the marsh pastures and just enclose a small portion of the common?'

'It seems ridiculous that I can't do what I choose with my own land and, even though it will be better for them, they oppose me!'

'Perhaps if Parliament reduces some of the taxes as is proposed they will consider it.'

'But that won't be in time to do anything this year.'

'You must not be impatient,' Nicholas said, and thought ruefully of his own impatience to go back to Catarina.

'I'm not impatient when I consider how many years it could take to improve the strain of cattle or sheep,' Jeremy said. 'But the sooner I can start the better. I feel I'll be waiting, doing nothing for a year or more.'

'Well, you can spend some of the time in London this Season. It will be a busy one, now the wars are over.'

'Unless half the people go off to Paris. And many of my friends died at Waterloo.'

Nicholas nodded. 'That does not mean you have to give up your own pleasures.'

'Are you going up soon?'

'I'm opening the town house for Olivia, if I can find a suitable matron to introduce her.'

'Not Aunt Clara?'

Nicholas laughed. 'She feels it necessary to visit Paris this year. Perhaps my offer to pay her expenses influenced her decision. No, I want someone more sympathetic. Olivia is shy; she needs to be encouraged rather than chastised all the time.'

'It's a great pity you haven't yet got into parson's mousetrap. Then your wife could present Olivia.'

Catarina had never had a Season herself, and she had spent little time in London, so would not know the right people. That would not do. Nicholas shook his head.

'I have a couple of dowagers in mind who will do it for a fee. Of course I must be in town for her ball, but otherwise my plans are uncertain.'

Until, he said to himself, he knew whether Catarina would accept his offer, If she did he would urge a speedy marriage.

★　★　★

Catarina pondered for a long time over what she could do to help the villagers. She understood Jeremy's desire to change things. Walter had been intending to do much the same, but Walter would have done it slowly, talked to the villagers, and persuaded them to his views before making the changes. He would not have allowed anyone to suffer. He had done this with regard to the cottages and the draining of the marsh. And he had been a much older man, with less time to achieve what he desired, she thought with a regretful sigh. He'd had less time than he'd anticipated. Jeremy was so much younger, but in so great a hurry.

Ought she to visit him, or ask him to come to her? She had not seen him since she arrived home. She was reluctant to go up to the Grange in case she met Nicholas. She had ceased thinking of him as Lord Brooke. His greeting, his words, his calling her his 'darling', had at first startled her, and then, when she had been unable to sleep for thinking of their significance, delighted her. She had not expected another opportunity for marriage to come to her, unless it was an offer from Sir Humphrey, and that she would certainly refuse.

Until now she had thought she would refuse any offer, and when she had seen a tentative admiration in her cousin Antonio's eyes she had rejected the very idea that he might wish to marry her. Now she was not so certain. She was still only five and twenty, no debutante, but young enough to marry again. Had Nicholas's words indicated he meant to make an offer, or had they just been the friendly greeting of a cousin?

It was a cold, wet day again and, as she sat before the fire in the front half of the big drawing room, she dismissed her thoughts during the night as ridiculous dreams, foolish imaginings. Nicholas had his pick of eager young debutantes, and since he had reached the age of thirty without succumbing to any of their blandishments, or feeling the need to marry and produce an heir, why should he choose an older woman? But he would want an heir eventually, and he would think her barren when there had been no child during her eight years of marriage with Walter. He would not know, and how could she tell him, that they had never lived as man and wife?

She was trimming one of Maria's dresses with coloured ribbon when Staines announced a visitor. It was Sir Humphrey. She tucked the dress into her sewing basket and rose to greet him.

'I did not expect any visitors while this rain lasted,' she said, giving him her hand.

'That's why I came today. Thought I had a chance of finding you alone. And I drove over in the carriage, so I'm not wet, even if my horses are. I sent them round to the stables, knew you would not object.'

'Of course not. I trust your coachman will go to the kitchen for something to warm him. Would you prefer wine, or coffee, Sir Humphrey.'

'Nothing, thank you, my dear. I don't want any distractions from what I have to say. Catarina, it's over a year since poor Walter died and I wouldn't have spoken before now, even if you hadn't been away, and despite my eagerness. But you're a young woman still, you ought to have the protection of a husband, be able to go out in Society and enjoy yourself, not hide yourself away in a small village miles from London.'

'I have no intention of hiding myself away,' Catarina interrupted, suspecting what was coming and wanting, if she could, to deflect it.

'A widow cannot entertain or go out in Society in the same way a married woman can. You must know that. And you are still young, and beautiful. My dear, you are wealthy with what your father and Walter left you. You'll be prey to all sorts of unscrupulous fortune-hunters, and you're not up to snuff. You need a man's protection.'

For a wild moment Catarina wondered just what sort of protection Sir Humphrey was offering.

'I may not be familiar with London Society, but I think I can tell whether men want me for my fortune or not,' she said, and then almost giggled.

Sir Humphrey was no more than comfortably off. Chase Manor was just a small manor house and he owned no other. Nor was his estate large. If he went to London, which was seldom, he stayed in an hotel, not possessing a town house, and in Bath he hired apartments in one of the best hotels. Could he possibly be thinking as much of her money as of herself?

'My dear, take it from me, you need a man's protection, that of a husband, and I am begging you to permit me to become that husband.'

'I — I do not wish to marry again, Sir Humphrey,' Catarina managed. And especially not another elderly man, she added to herself. 'I am flattered by your offer, but I must refuse. I esteem you, of course, and you have been a good friend to both me and Walter, but friendship is all I can accept from you.'

He did not appear at all put out.

'I am too soon. It is just as I expected. I respect your honesty, your reverence for Walter's memory, but he would not wish you to languish, a widow for the rest of your days. I will not speak of it again, just yet, but I know you will come to agree that becoming my wife will be the best for you. Now I must go, I have other calls to make.'

She avoided the kiss he attempted to drop on her forehead and moved quickly to ring the bell for Staines. As soon as Sir Humphrey was out of the room she collapsed into her chair and tried to stifle her giggles. She had been daydreaming about another proposal, one that would, she admitted, have been far more welcome. How could she avoid Sir Humphrey's threat to repeat his? It was a threat, she acknowledged. She'd known him for so long and recognized he was a stubborn man, prepared to hammer away at whatever he desired until the sheer weight of his persistence wore down the opposition.

Needing to calm herself she went up to the bedroom which had been turned into a nursery for Maria. Playing with her little niece, watching the baby smile as she clutched at the coloured ribbons and balls hung above her crib, always delighted her. She thought sadly of what Joanna was missing, and wondered yet again at her sister's unfeeling attitude towards her own daughter. Many women, she knew, sent their little ones to a wet nurse, often a villager near their country houses, and did not have them in their own homes for years. They might see them only occasionally until the children were a few years old. It was something she had never been able to understand. Watching Maria, and the almost daily changes in her, was a constant source of wonder.

How could she deter Sir Humphrey? He would come back, she knew. Marry someone else, said an insidious little inner voice. If

Nicholas proposed, would she accept? Did she feel fondly enough towards him? Was it love she felt for him, or just a sort of satisfaction that an attractive, eligible man appeared to want her? Did she love him in the consuming way Joanna appeared to love her Eduardo? She had not decided by the time she went to bed, and told herself she was worrying about nothing, since Lord Brooke would, when he married, want a well-connected young girl as his bride.

★   ★   ★

Before Nicholas could go to the Dower House again he received a message from Brooke Court that Olivia had suffered a fall from her horse. It was not serious, Miss Shipton said, just some bruising, but the message sent both of her brothers hastening to her side.

Olivia was shaken, badly bruised, but no bones were broken and the doctor said she would soon recover.

'It will not prevent our going to London, will it?' she asked, anxious. Her debut had been delayed once because she had suffered from an attack of measles soon after Christmas. 'The bruises don't show, and I will not be so stiff in a few days. Have you found someone to chaperon me yet? I was hoping to be in London by the beginning of May when Princess Charlotte marries Prince Leopold. I think that's so romantic, that she refused the man her father wanted and chose him.'

'I've written to Lady Mortimer, Mama's cousin. Do you remember her? I am expecting a reply any day now. But I will send the servants to open up the house so it will be ready for us whenever we wish to go.'

Olivia gave a sigh of relief. 'I was so hoping it would not have to be Aunt Clara after all.'

Nicholas grinned. 'Don't worry, I will find someone even if Lady Mortimer cannot oblige.'

The next day he received that lady's reply, which was favourable. She wrote she could start for London in a week's time and go straight to Grosvenor Square. Olivia insisted she would be able to travel in a few days, so he left her in the care of Jeremy and Miss Shipton while he made a quick visit to London to ensure everything was in readiness, and to learn what was happening in Parliament. Seeing Catarina would have to be postponed for a while, but as soon as Olivia was installed in London he could return to see her.

He had been somewhat shocked by his

instinctive reaction on meeting her and relief that she was well and safely back home. Despite his numerous liaisons, he had never before been in love, which was what he supposed his feelings for Catarina were. Those liaisons he had always treated lightly, diversions similar to a game of cards, or a day at the races. But he knew deep within himself that Catarina would be far more than that and the thought of possibly losing her, if she married someone else, was unbearable.

He had been made aware of Sir Humphrey's proprietorial attitude towards her when they had both been at the Dower House. Whether it was fatherly or something warmer he had not been able to judge. But surely Catarina would never again marry an old man? She had, at sixteen, little choice, but she seemed to have been content with Walter and sorry when he died. If she had freedom to choose, would she not prefer a man nearer her own age?

She had not repulsed his kiss; perhaps she had been too startled. The rain had started so soon afterwards there had not been time for anything but running into the house. Then Sir Humphrey had appeared, and any chance he might have had of talking to her had vanished.

He fretted all the way to London, had to

ask his Grosvenor Square housekeeper to repeat some of her questions, and paid little heed to the debates in the House. When Lady Mortimer arrived he was distracted; more than once she asked him if he had heard what she said.

'You seem like a man in love,' she commented, after dinner the first evening she was there. 'Who's the gal? Yet I gather you have been down in the country. Don't tell me some country miss has achieved what none of the debutantes of the past dozen years has managed.'

'Very well, then, Cousin, I won't.'

She laughed. 'I shall be watching you with more than normal interest. You will be coming back to Town soon, I hope.'

'Once Olivia is settled with you, I must go home for a while. Jeremy may stay, but he is having difficulties at Marshington. The people do not want to accept the reforms he is proposing.'

'Marshington? The Grange? Of course, you inherited the estate last year, did you not?'

'And I have given it to Jeremy. Or I will do as soon as the formalities of breaking the entail are completed.'

'I believe Sir Walter left a young and, if reports can be believed, beautiful widow,' she said slowly, and suddenly laughed. 'I shall

149

look forward to meeting her. No doubt she will be coming to London now her year of mourning is over. I shall insist you present her to me.'

'If she does come,' he replied, trying to sound as though it mattered nothing to him one way or the other. 'I believe her house in Mount Street is let. Now, have we settled all the details about Olivia? You will choose a day for her ball when you have had time to see what else has been planned by other debutantes' mothers. Have her bills sent to me, but no doubt there will be occasional expenses, so if the amount I have given you is insufficient let me know. I have no idea how much a come out will cost, but I don't want Olivia to economize.'

'I shall have great pleasure in spending your money, Nicholas. You have far too much!'

★ ★ ★

The day after Sir Humphrey's proposal, Sir Ivor Norton arrived at the Dower House. For once it was not raining and Catarina was in the garden, talking to her head gardener about the vegetables she wanted him to plant.

'Though it's been so wet the ground's not fit,' he said.

'Well, do what you can, when you can, and if you really think it would help to extend the glasshouses along this wall, arrange to have it done. I confess I would miss my early peas and potatoes, and would be happy if you can make them grow under glass.'

'The little 'un will be ready to enjoy some by then, well mashed up,' he said. 'My missus says it don't do to keep them just on milk, like some do, and she's reared six.'

'I'm sure she will enjoy them,' Catarina began, when she was interrupted by a harsh voice haranguing someone.

She heard him before, with a sinking heart, she turned to face Sir Ivor who was striding down the path towards her, followed by Staines.

'Catarina, I wish to speak to you. Tell this fool to stop bleating and go and order some refreshment. It's a long drive from Bristol.'

'Come into the house, Uncle. A nuncheon should be ready by now; no doubt you are hungry after your journey. Will ham and fruit be enough for you, or should I order some mutton chops to be cooked?'

'How do you get fruit at this time of year? Spending your money forcing it, or buying it at outrageous prices from Bristol, no doubt.'

'We still have apples — they store well — and yes, I do buy oranges. Papa's partner brings some on the wine ships.'

He snorted. 'I'll have a couple of chops.'

'See to it, please, Staines. This way, Uncle.'

He glared at the house.

'Far too big for you now you're widowed.'

'Not yet ready to have guests as the bedrooms need decorating,' Catarina said hurriedly. It would be disastrous if he expected to remain the night.

He waved aside her remarks.

'Bad organization. But I have to be back in Bristol tonight, however late it is. That wasn't what I came about. How dare you take your sister to Portugal without my leave? I'm her guardian and she's under age. Now I have this impertinent letter from some knave of a foreigner saying he's married her and wants her fortune. Well, he can whistle for it. She married without my consent, so not a penny will she have until she's of age!'

Catarina reined in her temper. She led him into the drawing room where Staines was ready with the decanter of Madeira, and excused herself, saying she needed to wash her hands and tidy herself after being in the garden. Hastening up to the nursery she warned Clarice not to bring Maria downstairs until the visitor had gone.

'But the weather is good, and fresh air good.'

'I know, but I don't want this particular gentleman to know about Maria, not yet.'

Clarice smiled and nodded. 'He not like children?'

That was the easiest explanation, so Catarina nodded and, on her way back to the drawing room, slipped into the kitchen to warn Liza and Staines also not to mention the baby.

'He . . . will not approve of my adopting her,' she said, and surprised a sceptical look in Liza's eyes. Did Liza not believe the story?

Dismissing the idea, she went back to Sir Ivor and managed to keep her temper during the meal. She explained to him that Eduardo was very rich, had large estates in Brazil, and a connection with the Portuguese Royal family, but none of it placated her uncle.

'How long had she known the wretch?' he demanded. 'Was that why you stayed there for so long, when you told me you were going to visit your mother's family? No such visit ought to last for months.'

'We have many cousins there,' Catarina explained. She did not need to tell him that they had in fact visited only her mother's sister. Also she did not want to admit how short a time Joanna had known Eduardo, or that she had gone with him on the ship without telling Catarina. She would, she decided, let people believe Joanna had known him for a long time, or even that she had left Portugal much earlier. It would also be better if they thought she had gone before Maria was born.

To her relief, having vented his fury on her, eaten some very good mutton chops and drunk a considerable amount of wine, he soon afterwards took his leave, saying he must be back in Bristol before it was too late. Feeling weak, she waved him off and almost staggered back into the drawing room. When Staines appeared at her elbow with a glass of wine she laughed.

'This is the good wine, my lady, not what I served at table.'

'You had better have one yourself, Staines. I am so sorry he was so rude.'

'I have had occasion to meet Sir Ivor before, my lady, so I knew what to expect.'

'I'm ashamed to be related to him!' she burst out.

'Most of us have relations we might prefer not to know. Cook is preparing your favourite syllabub for dinner and I have fetched up another bottle of the best wine.'

How fortunate she was with her servants. They took good care of her, were enchanted with the baby, and clearly capable of keeping their mouths closed when necessary.

So far very few people knew of Maria's existence. But she could not keep the baby hidden and had no desire to do so. The next time Mrs Eade called she must tell her the story she had told the servants, that Maria was a dead cousin's child. Then the entire neighbourhood would know within days.

★　★　★

It was two weeks before Nicholas returned to Marshington Grange. Catarina saw a carriage sporting the earl's crest sweep past the Dower House late one afternoon, but it did not stop. She knew it was Nicholas, and the following morning dressed in one of her best gowns and her most fetching cap, trimmed with more lace than the ones she normally wore about the house.

If he meant to make her an offer it would not do for her to be wearing mourning black, or even half mourning, so she pulled out a silk morning dress in deep cream which she had bought just before Walter's death, and never had an opportunity to wear. The sleeves were close-fitting; they and the bodice were trimmed with coquelicot embroidery, and a coquelicot rouleau edged the skirt. It suited her colouring and, with a shawl of the same colour round her shoulders, a pearl necklace and pearl drops in her ears, she told herself she was looking her best.

It was the middle of the morning before Nicholas came. It was another fine day, after several when it had rained almost continuously. Clarice had taken Maria outside to sit on a bench under one of the apple trees, where the baby could watch the changing patterns of the branches against the sky.

Staines, beaming, showed Nicholas in.

'His lordship, my lady,' he said, and Catarina, nervous, thought his tone was almost paternal. Did her servants suspect the same as she did?

'How are Jeremy and Olivia, my lord?'

'They are both in Town. Olivia makes her come out this Season, under the auspices of a cousin of our mama. Jeremy is there too, and I believe has for the moment given up trying to convince the villagers of the advantages of his proposed changes.'

'Olivia is looking forward to the Season?'

'With some trepidation, but Lady Mortimer is the sort of woman who can give her confidence.'

'Will you have some Madeira, my lord?' Catarina asked, suddenly aware of the decanters she had asked Staines to bring in earlier, so that she would have something ready to offer Nicholas if he came.

'No, thank you. Catarina. For once it's a fine day; can we not walk in the garden for a short while? I did not have an opportunity to see it the last time I was here.'

Catarina led the way through the doors at the back of the drawing room which opened on to the terrace, and they trod down the steps at the end on to one of the gravelled paths. Nicholas took her arm and they made stilted conversation as they walked through the flower garden and into the small walled garden where the new glasshouses were being built.

'You plan to grow more grapes?' Nicholas asked.

'Amongst other things. The weather has been so bad this year we are going to try some of the early vegetables under glass, but I'm not sure the new glass houses will be ready in time.'

They went on towards the small orchard at one side of the garden. As they reached the gate leading into it, Nicholas stopped, put his hand on it to stop her opening it, and turned towards Catarina.

'My dear Catarina, I think you must know how I feel about you. I was so worried when you were away for so long, without anyone here having any news of you.'

He reached out towards her, but just at

that moment Maria began to wail. Nicholas gave a start and turned round to see Clarice coming towards them, Maria cradled in her arms.

'I take her in, she hungry,' Clarice said, and, as she walked towards the gate, Nicholas hurriedly stepped back. He watched, silent, as Clarice came through the gate and held Maria out for him to see. 'See baby, pretty, no?'

'Whose baby is that?' Nicholas asked, his voice hoarse. 'Is it yours?'

'Yes. No. That is, yes, she is in a way. I have adopted her. She is a cousin's baby, the cousin died,' Catarina stammered.

He was looking at her so accusingly she was almost incapable of speaking. He watched Clarice go towards the house, then took a deep breath.

'I will speak to you another time. Goodbye, my lady.'

8

Catarina looked down at the letter in her hands. It was the round, unformed calligraphy of a schoolgirl, and Olivia had crossed the lines so much she had difficulty reading it. Besides, she was finding it hard to concentrate after Nicholas's abrupt departure the previous day. He had suddenly become cold when he had seen the baby. Did the notion of her having adopted a child make him change his mind? She had been so certain he was about to make her an offer. Was the thought of having to accept a baby as well as herself such a frightening one he had decided he did not after all want her as his wife?

She forced herself to concentrate on the letter. Olivia sounded happy. The dreaded Lady Keith had gone to Paris, so she was making her come out under the auspices of a cousin of her mama's. Already she had met a few other girls, and it wasn't nearly so terrifying as she'd expected. Lady Mortimer, her cousin, would be arranging a ball for her soon, and she did so hope dear Catarina would come up to Town for it.

Catarina shook her head slightly. The town house was let and she would not stay in an hotel. She had no friends she could visit, and if Nicholas remained cold she had no desire to meet him again, as she would be bound to do at Olivia's ball. Her thoughts swung back to the previous day and the unanswered question. Why had the sight of Maria changed him?

This dwelling on the matter was pointless. She stood up decisively. She would go for a ride. So far she had not been able to ride around the entire estate since she had returned to England, it had either been raining, or she had too much else to do. Even though she was no longer the owner, she would like to see some of the tenants. They had been her friends, many of them nearer to her in age than Walter and his cronies.

She sent to have her mare saddled, then rang for her new maid, Blodwen. She was a Welsh girl from Swansea who, when her former mistress died, had come to live with an aunt in Bristol to find another position. The registry had sent her and another cook, and so far Catarina had been satisfied with both of them. Blodwen spoke with a strong Welsh lilt, which confused poor Clarice even more than the local accent. Catarina herself, and Staines, were the only people in the house Clarice could understand properly.

Soon Catarina was cantering along the edge of the common. What ought to be hay in a few weeks did not look promising, the constant rain had flattened the grass. If there was not a good crop the villagers would have little with which to feed their animals during the winter. She turned towards the marsh, wanting to see what Jeremy had done with the drainage. The way lay alongside the woods, and she dropped to a walk, since the storms had blown dead and fallen branches across the path, and brought down a few trees. Ought she to suggest they be cleared, or would that be presumption? Then she recalled that although Jeremy was not here Nicholas was. But she would not inform him of the problem. She did not wish to have to meet him again. She had to stop thinking about him.

One particularly large oak had fallen right across the path. She was trying to find a way round it when someone rose up in front of her and caught the mare's reins. Catarina's heart gave a leap of fright. Perhaps she ought to have brought the groom, she thought in sudden panic, but she had always ridden alone, expecting to be safe on Walter's land.

It was a man, dressed in what looked like rags, his hair wild and tangled, his face and hands streaked with dirt. The mare, startled, tried to rear, but he held her firmly, and began stroking her neck, crooning softly so that she soon quietened.

'What do you want?' she demanded, thankful to find her voice calm and steady. Then she looked closer at him. 'It's Dan, isn't it? You used to work for Mr Lewis.'

'Aye, used to, missus. My lady, that is. I didn't mean ter frighten the mare. I'm sorry. But I 'as ter speak wi' someone. An' Mr Jeremy ain't 'ere.'

'I'm so sorry about your wife, Dan, and that you've lost your cottage. Where are you living? Have you another job?'

Looking as he did, he would have problems finding anything, she thought. She had heard that some of the people from villages nearby had left and gone to Bristol to find work, since there was not enough on the farms for everybody. Was that because of the enclosures everyone was talking about?

Dan was shaking his head. 'It were me own doin's; I were daft, an' my poor Annie 'ad ter suffer fer it. I could a' killed meself after what she done, but that there Ellen, enough ter drive a man mad, she were. And Annie, she dain't want me no more. Said as 'ow six childer were enough, an' on'y one livin', so I weren't ter go near 'er. It were more than flesh and blood could stand, so it were, lyin' in same bed an' 'er so cold. We'd bin wed sixteen year.'

Catarina pushed away the thoughts of Dan and his wife in bed, together, but forced to be celibate. At least she and Walter had always occupied separate rooms.

'You had a boy, I think. What's happened to him?'

'Annie's sister took 'im. 'E's got a good job now, errand boy fer a shop in Bristol.'

'So where are you living?'

'Shack. In woods. I've got fellers bring me bread. I'm not poachin' Mr Jeremy's conies.'

Fleetingly Catarina thought that a pity. If he were convicted he would be sent out to New South Wales and might be reunited with Annie. He seemed fond enough of her, deep down. But she could hardly suggest such a course.

'What do you want?' she repeated.

'Could yer 'av a word wi' Mr Lewis? If 'e'd gi' me me job back, I'd work fer lowest rates. I know I don't deserve it, but it weren't my fault Ellen's lad an' 'is friends come lookin' fer me an' started a fight. I'd sleep in barn, I don't want cottage back. It 'ld remind me too much of my Annie.'

'I'll speak to him,' Catarina promised. It had, from what Staines had told her, been

Dan's fault in the first place, and Annie had been provoked. Losing her, and the guilt he felt, was punishment enough.

'Or Master Jeremy might 'av work fer me. I 'eard he were goin' ter enclose common, there'll be men needed ter put up fences.'

'I don't know if he is,' Catarina told him, 'but when he comes down from London I'll ask if he could find you some work.'

'Bless yer, me lady. You was always kind.'

He disappeared into the woods as silently as he had come and Catarina went on towards the marsh soberly. Was Jeremy going ahead with his plans without getting the villagers on his side? Could he make enclosures, legally, without an Act of Parliament? She must try to talk to him when he returned from London. He would probably consider it interference, and resent it, but she felt a continuing responsibility to the people who had once been Walter's.

★   ★   ★

Nicholas was sitting in the library at Marshington Grange. The book he had been trying to read was discarded on the floor beside him. He had dismissed Mr Trubshaw brusquely when the man wanted to ask his advice. After three glasses of wine he had rung to have the decanter taken away. Getting drunk, which he would very much like to have done, would not solve his dilemma.

All night he had tried to decide what to do. Seeing that baby with her olive complexion, dark curly hair, and large eyes, so like Catarina's, had given him a severe jolt. She had contradicted her immediate acceptance that the child was hers, and then spun him some unlikely tale that the baby was her Portuguese cousin's. He supposed it might be the truth, that a cousin had died. Many women did, in childbirth. But she had presumably possessed a husband, so what was he thinking of permitting his child to be taken out of the country and brought to England? Were there not many other cousins in Portugal, married and with families, to whom the child could have gone?

He rubbed his hands over his eyes. Lord, he was tired! In London he could sit up all night at play and feel no ill effects, but now he was spent. He did not know what to do. Yesterday his instinctive reaction was to walk away, to do nothing until he had thought over the implications. He had, fortunately, not actually made Catarina an offer. Did he still wish to?

He wanted her body, he freely admitted to himself. He had spent many nights dreaming

165

of possessing her while she had been away. But there was some mystery regarding that baby, and it seemed as though he did not know the real Catarina at all. Until he did, there was no way he could ask her to be his wife.

There was a tentative knock on the door and his valet came in.

'I said I wasn't to be disturbed,' Nicholas snapped. 'What the devil are you doing here in any case, Chettle?'

'No one else dared interrupt, my lord, so they begged me to tell you.'

'Tell me what, man? I trust it's important!'

'Some of the villagers have asked to see you. Apparently Mr Jeremy has sent orders that the whole common is to be enclosed immediately.'

*　*　*

Mrs Eade was waiting in the drawing room when Catarina returned to the Dower House.

'Please, my lady, I won't keep you a moment,' she said, when Catarina said she ought to change out of her riding habit. 'I have to get back soon, we have one of our daughters coming to stay, but I really had to come and tell you what is happening in the village.'

She paused for breath and Catarina sat down. 'I think I know. It's the common, isn't it?'

'Were you aware of Mr Brooke's plans?'

She sounded accusing and Catarina quickly shook her head.

'I saw Dan up near the woods while I was out, and he seemed to think that was what had been ordered.'

'We thought, the Reverend and I, that Mr Brooke was concerned for the village. He completed the drainage scheme your dear husband started, and the new earl hastened the building of the new cottages. But to rob the poor people of their grazing land, the rights they have held for centuries, is cruel! Most of them will have nowhere else to graze their beasts, and nowhere to grow winter feed for them.'

'Is there no other provision being made for grazing?'

'We have not heard. But there is also the hay that grows there, which has always been allowed to the villagers for the winter feed.'

'Lord Brooke is in residence at the moment, I believe. Can you not speak to him?'

'Will he contradict his brother's orders? As far as we understand he gifted the estate to Mr Brooke, so he may not feel able to overrule him. However, the Reverend and I hope you, as the former owner, might have some influence. Can you not speak to both Mr Brooke and his lordship?'

How could she explain that at the moment she did not know whether his lordship would ever speak to her again?

'I really believe that a representation from your husband would do more good,' she said at last. 'From me it would seem to be interference, as though I were unwilling to relinquish the estate, but you and the Reverend have a duty to care for the village. You have a right to be concerned. And, perhaps, a man speaking to his lordship might be listened to more sympathetically than a mere female.'

Mrs Eade looked at her closely. 'Perhaps you are right. Now, my dear, tell me about this child you have brought home with you. There are all sorts of rumours flying around.'

Catarina tried a light laugh. 'Indeed? People will always gossip, won't they? Maria de Freitas' — she emphasized the name — 'is a cousin's child. It was very sad, she had so longed to have a family, but she died giving birth and, as her husband had died six months earlier, I offered to take the baby in and bring her up. After all, now that Joanna is married and so far away I have no close family. I think you know I do not get on well with my uncle in Bristol.'

She was getting almost as good as Joanna at inventing untruths, Catarina thought in disgust. But what else could she do to protect her sister's reputation?

Mrs Eade sighed. 'Such a pity when families cannot get on. I don't have time now, I must go, but I hope you will soon tell me all about this sudden romance of Joanna's. A Portuguese prince, I heard.'

Catarina did not bother to correct her. To the villagers people from further away than Bristol were considered foreigners, and real foreigners would be singularly exotic, even to people more educated, like the rector and his wife. She ushered Mrs Eade out, and went upstairs to change from her riding habit. Now, as well as her own problem, she had the village concerns to worry about.

★ ★ ★

Nicholas looked at the three men in front of him. They were all elderly and had clearly worked hard all their lives if the gnarled hands and weathered faces meant anything.

'You tell me my brother has sent orders for the whole common to be enclosed? To whom did these orders come?'

'His agent, Mr Trubshaw. He said he were going to tell you this morning,' said the eldest, who seemed to be the spokesman.

Nicholas guiltily recalled how he had dismissed Trubshaw that morning, telling him he did not wish to be bothered with estate business at the moment. He'd been too absorbed in thoughts of Catarina and the child.

'I'll speak to Trubshaw and send a message to my brother. He will have to stop if he does not have the agreement of the villagers. We'll delay doing anything until he is able to come down and speak to you himself.'

Jeremy would fume and accuse him of not wanting to permit him full control over property which had been given to him, of not being willing to let go, but Nicholas decided he had to convince his brother that he could not take away these ancient rights on a whim. Having Jeremy angry with him was preferable to having the whole village so angry with Jeremy he might find life at Marshington intolerable. He was young and impatient, but he needed to understand what his own powers were, and learn how to deal with the people who depended on him for their employment and their housing.

'I'll go and find Mr Trubshaw at once.'

They left, but Nicholas had the distinct

impression they only half believed his assurance that the work would not begin yet. He looked in the estate office where Mr Trubshaw was normally to be found in the morning, but the man was not there. Sighing, he went to change and was soon riding towards the village.

He found Mr Trubshaw standing near the church, surrounded by a noisy group of villagers, women as well as men. The three men who had come to see him appeared to have just arrived and were all speaking at once, presumably telling the agent what he had promised.

Someone saw Nicholas, and the crowd immediately deserted Mr Trubshaw and came hurrying towards him. For a few moments he had problems controlling his horse, disturbed by the noise and the press of bodies around him, but one of the younger men, an ostler from the Bear, grasped the bridle and managed to soothe the horse. Nicholas was irritated, but bit back the sharp rebuke. He was quite capable of controlling his mount, but the man was trying to be helpful and he did not wish to antagonize these people further.

Several of them were talking; he held up his hand for silence.

'I am sure this is a mistake. I will write at

once to my brother to discover what he is about. I do not believe he intends to deprive you of your grazing land, so all the work will be halted until he can come himself and explain what he is intending. Mr Trubshaw, can you come to see me this afternoon, please?'

The three men he had seen earlier nodded, and some of the others appeared to accept what he said. The crowd was beginning to disperse, but a few, younger men, he noticed, remained behind.

'That be all very well, me lord, but your brother wants changes, an' they'll not be good for us,' one said, and the others nodded.

'The drainage of the marsh is good, is it not?'

Reluctantly they agreed.

'But that were the old lord's plan. He'd never have wanted ter steal our grazin' land.'

'My brother has new ideas, to make better use of the land, and breed better animals that will give us all more wool, more milk and meat, but he wants this to benefit everyone. Won't you at least listen to what he wants to do?'

'In some parts, we've 'eard, folk 'ave lost their work from these improvements,' another man said. 'They can't make a livin' if the land they get's too small, the fields too small fer grazin', an' they can't use the common no more.'

'Nor can they get logs ter burn when wood's enclosed.'

'Then they 'as ter sell ter bigger chaps wi' more land already, an' either get work as labourers, or go ter towns an' work in mills or mines.'

'Then they bring in machines ter do the work o' ten men. The on'y ones ter profit be the farmers and men what own the land.'

'There've bin riots,' the first speaker said, with some relish. 'Like them fellers what broke stocking machines. We don't want no machines takin' our work away.'

When Nicholas rode back to the house he was considerably worried. He would write to Jeremy at once and insist he was needed down here to explain what he was doing, not leave it all to his agent to make his excuses.

★ ★ ★

Jeremy arrived at Marshington Grange on Saturday and both brothers were in church the following day. Catarina saw how many of the villagers avoided looking at Jeremy, while others were throwing him angry looks.

She hoped to avoid speaking to them after the service, but Mrs Eade beckoned to her as she was heading for her carriage, so there was no escape. The brothers stood with her and the rector, Mr Lewis and a few other of the more prosperous farmers.

'I will do as I please with my own land,' Catarina heard Jeremy say, as she approached. 'I've explained all the advantages to them, but they refuse to listen. Some of them want to amalgamate the strips, and I will organize that. For now, until I get the power to change it, the rest can carry on in their hidebound way until they see sense!'

'But the common, that's different,' Mrs Eade was saying. 'Catarina, my lady, can you not persuade this stubborn young man that he should at least provide alternative grazing?'

Jeremy frowned. 'I've promised to do that for those who accept my plan of joining their land into compact units.'

'Some of them fear they will be left with just the inferior land,' the rector explained.

'It they would all sit down together and talk we could deal with that. Can you not at least persuade them to do that, Rector? But I'm warning them, if they won't co-operate willingly I'll get an Act and force it on them.'

'I'll do my best, Mr Brooke, but feelings are strong.'

Catarina began to move away, but Nicholas's voice, cold and stern, arrested her.

'My lady, I need to speak to you. May I call tomorrow morning?'

All she could do was nod. She moved on, past Mr Lewis. She could speak to him now and plead for Dan.

'He's truly sorry,' she said, when she had explained about meeting Dan. 'I don't know how he is managing to survive in the woods; it's much colder than usual at this time of year. From what I have heard the fight at the Bear was not instigated by him.'

'You think I've been hard on him?'

'Yes, I do. It would be charitable to forgive him.'

Mr Lewis slowly shook his head. 'I daren't risk having him about the farm. From what I've heard from the other men he's been threatening me with reprisals, even saying he'll burn down the barn. He's a trouble-maker. If you see him again, my lady, advise him to go back to Devon where he came from.'

Catarina could do no more. She climbed into her carriage and went home, to spend the rest of the afternoon wondering what Nicholas would have to say on the following day. From the tone of his voice and his unsmiling face she doubted he wanted to offer for her.

She slept badly, and in the morning,

despite Blodwen's protests that it made her look old and haggard, dressed in one of her black mourning gowns, relieving the starkness with a fichu of white lace. She forced herself to eat a roll and drink coffee, but refused all the other things Staines urged on her, until he asked her if she was developing a cold.

'No, Staines. I just slept badly. I have been able to go outside so little since I came home, it is wearying.'

He said no more, and she settled down to wait. She picked up the latest copy of *La Belle Assemblée*, dropped it again a moment later. She took up some sewing, a dress for Maria, but pricked her finger and had to put the dress down for fear of dripping blood on it. She could concentrate on nothing, and hoped Nicholas would come soon and the wait would be over. She would know what he intended.

It was the middle of the morning before Nicholas was shown into the drawing room. He was curt when he refused wine, and Catarina saw Staines give him a surprised look as he left the room. No doubt they had a tolerable notion of the situation in the servants' hall.

'My lord, will you be seated?' Catarina managed in a calm voice which, she was thankful, did not tremble.

Nicholas shook his head and began to pace the room.

'The baby I saw the other day, is she your own?'

'I have told you, I adopted her.'

'How old is she?'

'She was born in the middle of November.'

He pushed his hands through his hair.

'I do not know what to believe. It's all so confoundedly suspicious! You go off to Portugal for over a year, and just before you went I thought you were putting on weight. Your servants do not have your direction. You don't tell even your closest relatives in Portugal where you are. So how is it you know about your cousin and her baby when even your aunt did not know you were still in the country?'

'I, well, I kept in touch with her,' Catarina said.

If she thought of Joanna as a cousin and not a sister that was true, but she was getting into such a tangle with all these lies. She wanted so desperately to tell Nicholas the real truth, but he would probably never believe her. And for Joanna's sake she could not reveal her secret.

'Very convenient!' Nicholas sneered, and the devilish look was pronounced. 'I understood you had many relatives there, so why do you have to adopt a child? Where was this mythical cousin's husband? Her parents? Other relatives, with families, who might be thought to have a better right to take in such an orphan?'

'I do not have to explain anything to you, my lord. What I do is my business, not yours, and you have no right to question me, especially in such a dictatorial manner.'

'No right? I think I do. While you are there a child appears. A child born roughly eight months after your husband died. A child who looks very much like you. Was it a disappointment it was not a boy, so that you could claim the earldom for him?'

Astounded, Catarina glared at him.

'The child is not mine! I have never borne a child!'

'In eight years of marriage? Yes, indeed it looks very suspicious that you should suddenly do so, that Walter should impregnate you at the last gasp, so to speak. Was it Walter, or did you have a lover? Many people would not have blamed you if you had, for Walter was so very much older than you.'

By now Catarina was on her feet, struggling not to fly at him and tear out his eyes.

'You are insulting, my lord! It ill becomes you to accuse me of such things. If, as you suggest, I had wanted a child in order to challenge your right to the title, and adopted one, why did I not adopt a boy? There must be plenty of orphans in Portugal who would be suitable.'

He swung round towards her and tried to grasp her hands.

'Catarina, I wanted to ask you to be my wife, but how can I when it looks so black against you? Tell me the truth!'

Catarina was pale. 'I have already done so, but if you could not believe my word the first time, I would in no circumstances accept any offer from you, my lord. I have told you the truth: the child is not mine, but you persist in disbelieving and doubting me. Will you please leave? And from now on there will be no connection between us. You will not be welcome here.'

He stared at her for a long moment, then she turned away. She was shaking with fury. All the time in Portugal she had been forced to tell lies, to protect Joanna's reputation, and now, when she was telling the truth, or at least the part of it that mattered, that Maria was not her own daughter, she was disbelieved and her own reputation was being questioned. It served her right. She gave an hysterical sob, and felt Nicholas's hand on her arm.

'Catarina. Can we not sit down and discuss this? I did not mean to distress you so.'

She shook off his hand.

'I am not distressed. I am so angry I could — oh, I don't know what I could do! There is nothing to discuss, my lord. Please go. Leave me alone. I don't want your apologies. I want nothing from you apart from your absence.'

9

For several days Catarina kept to the house and had Staines deny her to all callers, saying she was indisposed. From him she learned that Nicholas had left Marshington Grange the day after he had seen her. Jeremy was still here and had called, but she refused to see him. Staines told her Jeremy was talking to the villagers, and had promised to do nothing about enclosing the common until after the hay was gathered, but, as it continued wet, they expected a poor harvest of that, as well as the corn which was struggling to grow.

She considered going to Bath for a while in order to get away from her problems, so when a letter came from Delphine Pearce inviting her to London it seemed like a miracle.

My husband has to go on some boring mission, and will be away the rest of the Season, which is such a shame, she wrote. *I have many friends in London, of course, so I will not be lonely, and there are all sorts of entertainments, but it would be more pleasant to have someone compatible to go with me.*

Was she compatible? They had got on well

at school, but Delphine was the sort of girl who got on well with most people.

I remembered that you never had the opportunity of a Season when you were young, so I wondered whether you would like to come to me for a month or so? We could have such fun! Do say yes.

Catarina was tempted. Of course, there was always the possibility that in London she would meet Nicholas, and that was the last thing she wanted to do. She could never forget how scathing he had been about the lies told him by Walter's new agent. After his suspicions of her, and the lies she had been forced to tell him, that would be unpleasant. Perhaps, she thought hopefully, he and Delphine did not move in the same circles. She would know the military, while he might be more involved with politicians, since he was now in the House of Lords.

Why, she then wondered, was she concerned? Was she always to govern her actions by the fear of meeting him? He was the one, after all, who had thrown unjustified accusations at her. Was that worse than telling lies to protect Joanna? He should be ashamed of that. She would not allow herself to be intimidated. She had been longing to escape from the Dower House.

What about Maria? She could not take the

baby to London, but in Clarice she had a reliable wet nurse who loved the child as though she were her own. The rest of her servants, Liza, the new cook, and the others, were to be trusted absolutely. Most of all, she had Staines, who was more capable of controlling the household than she was herself.

Before she could change her mind she sat at her writing desk and dashed off an acceptance. Delphine had said to come at any time, as early as she could make arrangements, so she told her friend to expect her in a week.

She had a sudden spurt of energy, sorting out what she intended to take with her, and changing her mind almost daily, so that Blodwen, in desperation, finally suggested they take her entire wardrobe.

Catarina laughed, for the first time since the argument with Nicholas.

'I will replenish my wardrobe in London,' she decided. 'I don't want to take any mourning clothes, I'm done with that. The rest of my clothes are sadly out of fashion. Before Walter died I used to depend on the modistes in Bath, as we so rarely went to London. So I will take as little as possible, just enough to manage until I can buy more.'

'I can alter some of the gowns, my lady, to

make them more fashionable. Why don't you leave them to me?'

Catarina was happy to do so. Blodwen was clever with her needle, and she would trim the gowns so that they were in the latest mode.

They would take two days for the journey, travelling post. Catarina saw no one and told no one in the village she was going.

'I cannot abide farewells,' she said to Staines, 'so please tell everyone who calls I am still indisposed. After I have left you can inform them I have gone away for a change, but let them think I have gone to some watering place. Mrs Eade will not consider going to London of any benefit to health.'

How easy it was becoming to tell more lies, she thought, as she lay in bed on the last night before they left. If she had ever been a truthful girl and woman it seemed a long time ago. Or was it that circumstances had never before been such that lies were better than the truth?

★   ★   ★

Delphine welcomed her with her usual enthusiasm to the house in Hill Street she had hired for the Season, and soon Catarina was enjoying all the entertainments. Delphine

184

took her to her own favourite modists and milliners, and Catarina bought gowns and hats and shawls, reticules, gloves, scarves, shoes, fans and everything else with abandon. She was wealthy; she had spent comparatively little on clothes during her time with Walter, and almost nothing in the dreadful time since his death, so she felt she deserved to pamper herself. This orgy of spending did not, however, cure the depression she suffered whenever she thought of Nicholas and the lost opportunity of being his wife.

Did she want to be, she asked herself? If he was the kind of man who harboured unjustified suspicions, accused her of deceit and calculation, refused to accept her word, was he the sort she would be happy with if married to him? Dejectedly she reminded herself of all the lies she had told for Joanna's sake. Why should she expect anyone to believe her?

She spent many hours during sleepless nights arguing with herself, going over every word she and Nicholas had ever exchanged, trying to see what sort of man he really was. Had his suspicions of her seemed justified to him? When she considered the facts he had thrown at her she had to admit they could be interpreted as he suggested.

She had gained weight just before she left

for Portugal, it was true, but it was regaining what she had lost in the weeks after Walter's death when she had been too devastated to eat properly. Nicholas had probably not looked at her very closely when they first met at the funeral, swathed as she was in her blacks, and he had not known her before.

If she had conceived a child just before Walter's death in March it would have been born in November or December. No one but themselves knew that they lived apart, Walter had still been vigorous though in his sixties, and in good health. His death had been a sudden accident, not the result of a long illness. The timing was, she admitted, suspicious.

Hiding away in Portugal, out of touch with all their friends and relatives, had been for Joanna's sake, but could equally have been for hers. However much Catarina thought about it, she had to admit there were grounds for Nicholas's suspicion that Maria was her child.

What had hurt most, though, was his suggestion she had wished for a son so that she could claim the earldom back from him. The very fact she had not adopted a boy child tended to reinforce the notion that Maria was her own, and no threat to Nicholas.

Delphine commented on Catarina's pallor,

but put it down to the continuing cold and wet weather, which on many days prevented them from walking or driving in the Park.

'We even have to go shopping in a closed carriage,' she grumbled one morning as they were sitting over breakfast.

Catarina laughed. 'You only want to be able to walk in Bond Street to be seen,' she told her friend.

Delphine grinned at her, the impish grin Catarina recalled from their schooldays.

'Of course I do. And to see what new fashions are being sported. But the skies are clearer today, so perhaps we can walk to the circulating library and change our books. I gave up on the one I chose last time, it is so tedious. Have you finished yours?'

Catarina had, so later in the afternoon, when a fitful sun was peeping from behind some fluffy white clouds, they set off. Delphine's house was only a short distance away, and they were soon at the circulating library. Catarina selected another volume, and sat down to wait for Delphine. She looked round at the other borrowers and froze. Coming straight towards her, accompanied by an older woman, was Olivia.

'Catarina! Oh, I beg your pardon, I should say my lady! I didn't know you were in Town. How marvellous! I was about to send you an invitation to my ball, but I thought you'd be in Somerset. Now you are here, there is no excuse for not coming.'

'Will you present us, my dear?' the older woman said gently, and Olivia blushed.

'Oh, I do beg your pardon, Cousin Jane, but I was so excited to see dear Catarina.'

Olivia's companion, Catarina discovered, was Lady Mortimer, a connection of her late mother's, and her chaperon for the season.

Delphine then joined the group, was introduced, and Olivia promptly said she would send her an invitation to the ball as well.

'You must promise to make Catarina come. I see she is out of mourning now, and I do long to see her.'

Delphine was always willing to enlarge her circle of acquaintances, and suggested that Olivia and Lady Mortimer called for tea one day soon, so that Catarina and Olivia could have a longer gossip.

Lady Mortimer laughed. 'Gossiping seems to be all we do. But come, Olivia, we need to go back to Grosvenor Square soon when you have chosen your book. Nicholas promised to drive you in the Park on the first fine day we had, and tomorrow he is going down to Brooke Court.'

Catarina scarcely listened to Delphine's

chatter as they walked back home. She knew Nicholas Brooke, had met him occasionally at large affairs before her husband went to Lisbon, but had not known he had succeeded to Walter's title. She wanted to know more about it.

'How exciting for you,' she said. 'He's such a handsome man, so sought after by the debutantes. I'd be tempted to flirt with him myself, but I heard a rumour the other day that he was paying attention to Arabella Forster. Her husband is something in the army of occupation in France, but she refused to go with him. He would make you an admirable second husband, and you would not even have to change your name!' She giggled. 'We must see what we can do to forward a match. I must arrange a small evening party.'

Catarina escaped to her room as soon as they reached Hill Street. How could she avoid meeting Nicholas? It would be too painful to see him again, to have to make polite conversation, and particularly watch him flirting with other women. At least she knew he would be away from London for a short while, so she could breathe easily again.

★ ★ ★

Nicholas spent a few days at Brooke Court, then he and Jeremy, who had come down from London with him, went to Marshington Grange. A few of the villagers had been persuaded to consolidate their scattered strips of land from the three big fields, but it was a complicated and time-consuming matter to allocate the others in a way the men who still wanted to follow the old system found acceptable.

'Me and Pa and Grandpa before 'im allus 'ad that strip,' was a frequent objection.

'If I 'as that 'un, it's ten more minutes fer me ter walk in mornin's.'

'It's not such good land, like the one yer wants us ter give up.'

Jeremy became more and more exasperated. He was telling Nicholas, as they sat over their port after dinner, of the many excuses he had been offered, as well as outright refusals even to consider his suggestions.

'I've promised to build cottages on the consolidated farms, and charge low rents for the first few years, but even that won't persuade the others of the benefits. Now they are saying they can't afford to keep the same number of oxen for the ploughing. They complain the ones with the farms will acquire their own and won't want to share them like they did in the past.'

'Patience,' Nicholas advised. 'In a few years the rest will see the benefits and want to leave their old ways.'

He was finding it difficult to contain his own impatience. He wanted to see Catarina, but he was not at all sure why. How could he ask her to be his wife when this cloud of suspicion still hung over him? Had he mistaken the matter? Had she told the truth? How would she behave when, as seemed likely, they met after church on Sunday?

One way had suggested itself for him to discover the truth independently. Brooding over the quarrel when he first went back to London, he suddenly thought he could ask Thomas Winterton to enquire about the death of a cousin in childbirth. No sooner had he decided than he sent a letter, and was now eagerly awaiting a reply. Thomas knew the family, he could say he'd heard a rumour, and surely they would either confirm or deny it. Then he would know how to approach Catarina, whether he could try once more to make her an offer, or whether he would have to abandon hope of making her his wife.

Their discussion was cut short when the butler came in to say that Mr Trubshaw, together with Mr Lewis, was anxious to see Mr Brooke.

'At this time of day?' Jeremy asked the

apologetic butler. 'Oh, well, show them in. They can sit and have a glass of port with us. I'm not moving.'

He had been drinking too much of late, Nicholas thought, and was now afraid of not being steady on his feet. He would need help getting upstairs. He was concerned. This was a new departure for his younger brother, but, after one angry retort the previous day, when he suggested Jeremy had drunk enough, he restrained himself from interfering.

Trubshaw looked frightened, Mr Lewis furiously angry, but Jeremy bade them sit opposite and held up his hand to stop them speaking until he had poured them both glasses of port and pushed the bowl of nuts towards them.

'Well, gentlemen, what's so urgent it can't wait till morning?'

Mr Lewis was truculent, leaning forward and wagging his finger at Jeremy.

'You may think it unimportant, Mr Brooke, but I don't when my barn's set alight.'

'Your barn? Fired? When?' Nicholas asked.

'Earlier today. Luckily one of my lads saw it. If it hadn't been raining so much yesterday, so the ground was too sodden for planting, we'd all have been in the far field, with only my wife at the house. Then the whole lot, and the hay we've managed to save, would have been lost.'

'Were you able to save it?'

'Most of it, my lord. Part of the roof thatch has gone, and the posts and wall at one end aren't safe, they'll have to be pulled down and rebuilt.'

'Do you know who did it?'

'I have my suspicions. Dan, whose wife killed that lass at the Dower House, has been seen living rough in your woods. I wouldn't give him his job back and he resents it. I've no doubt it's him.'

'I've tried to find him, before now,' Mr Trubshaw put in anxiously, 'but I suspect he moves from place to place. I've found a couple of shelters he seems to have built from branches, but they'd been abandoned before I got there.'

'Never mind that,' Mr Lewis interrupted. 'What we want's a full manhunt in the woods. They're too big for one man to search. Then we can give him up to the constable. Mr Brooke, will you let us do it, tomorrow?'

Jeremy raised his glass, found it empty, and refilled it. 'Tally ho! It'sh off to hunt we go! What time in the morning can you get your hunt together?'

'By eight. All my own lads are eager; they're down in the village now telling the others.'

'Has Dan any friends who might warn him?' Nicholas asked. 'Lady Brooke once met him, and she told Staines, who told me, he claimed he had friends who took him food.'

'They know if they warn him they'll have me to deal with! So we have your permission, sir?'

Jeremy, slurring his words, nodded. 'Shure you do, Mr Lewish. Where do you shtart?'

'West side. Then he can't make a break Devon way. Though I wish he'd go back there.'

★ ★ ★

Catarina and Delphine were at a small musical evening where the latest sensational soprano, according to their hostess, would be performing. They had arrived early and been ushered to seats at the front. Delphine sat sideways on her chair and kept commenting to Catarina about the guests who followed them. Catarina resisted looking round, not wishing to know whether Nicholas might be there. She had no desire to meet him.

At the interval, after politely applauding an uninspiring performance by a very attractive but not very talented singer, they were invited to another room where a buffet had been laid out.

'Let's hope the trio we've been promised for afterwards is better,' Delphine muttered into Catarina's ear, as they rose to move. 'We can't leave, sitting right at the front.'

Catarina nodded. She had suffered so many sleepless nights lately she had almost fallen asleep, and only by pinching herself hard had she managed to stay awake. She turned towards the door and gasped. Looking straight at her was Sir Humphrey Unwin.

There was no way to avoid him. She had not seen him since she had refused his offer, and to meet him here in London was most unfortunate, as he rarely visited. For a dreadful moment she wondered if he had somehow discovered she was here and had followed her. He stood aside to let the rest of the small audience leave the room and, when he could, moved towards Catarina.

'My dear Lady Brooke. What a pleasant surprise to see you here. Staines gave me the impression you had gone to Bath, but the man looked so shifty I rather doubted him. I wondered whether you had come to London, but you have not opened your town house; your tenants are still in residence.'

So the man had checked up on her, had he? Why did he think he had the right to do so?

'Sir Humphrey,' she managed. 'What a

surprise to see you here. Do you stay in Town for long?'

'That will depend,' he said, and gave her a speaking look. 'Won't you introduce me to your charming companion?'

As they moved on to the supper room, Sir Humphrey between them, Delphine kept up a flow of inconsequential chatter, allowing Catarina to regain her composure. They found a small table laid for three and Catarina, whose appetite had vanished, tried to bear her part in the conversation while she nibbled at lobster patties and sipped champagne.

'I hope I may be permitted to call,' Sir Humphrey said, as they rose at the signal and started back to the temporary auditorium.

'Of course, Sir Humphrey. I receive on Wednesdays.'

'Who is he?' Delphine hissed, as they regained their seats. 'He was looking at you as though he could eat you.'

'Walter's friend. Hush now, they are waiting to start.'

'I will not accept any more invitations to musical evenings,' Delphine declared as they were driven home. 'I don't know which was the worst, the soprano or the violinist whose instrument was out of tune. Now, your very attentive Sir Humphrey: tell me all.'

'Let's wait until we are back at home,' Catarina said, conscious of the coachman, even though he might not be able to hear anything.

Delphine did not permit her to escape. She led the way into her boudoir and dismissed her maid.

'Tell.'

Catarina bowed to the inevitable, praying that Delphine would not spread gossip, but unable to avoid telling her.

'He lives a few miles from Marshington Grange, has been Walter's friend for decades, lost his wife a few years ago, his children are all married and away from home. He is lonely and wants another wife.'

'He wants you for wife. Catarina, my dearest friend, you won't marry another old man, will you?'

'Of course I won't. I don't suppose I'll marry again.'

'Has he offered?'

'Yes, and I refused him, very decidedly, but like many men he cannot accept that what a woman says might be what she means. I'm horribly afraid he intends to ask me again. He implied as much when I refused him.'

'And means to ask you while he's here, if I read him aright.'

'He'll keep on asking until he wears down

my resistance. He is that kind of stubborn man. But I swear I won't give way.'

Delphine, to Catarina's annoyance, laughed.

'Poor man. He'll come and make sheep's eyes at you. We will have to provide you with a more suitable cavalier. That would perhaps deter him. I know just the right one. My brother-in-law George is a few years older than we are, a confirmed bachelor, but also a confirmed flirt. He will be in town in a few days. I must ask him to play the suitor and guard you from old *roués* like Sir Humphrey.'

Catarina began to deny Sir Humphrey was a *roué*, then wondered why she need defend him. If Delphine considered him in that light it might make her more willing to aid Catarina in avoiding or rejecting his offers. She was able to face seeing him again more calmly.

★   ★   ★

The search of Marshington's woods found traces of Dan's occupation, but no Dan. Jeremy had woken with a sore head and refused to take part, saying he'd hear soon enough if the man were caught, but he had no desire to spend the morning tramping through wet undergrowth.

'Let's hope he has left the district,'

Nicholas said, when Trubshaw brought the news.

He planned to go back to London on Monday, in two days' time and, after a good deal of persuasion, Jeremy agreed to go with him. Nicholas was relieved. He wanted to distract his brother from the difficulties he was encountering trying to introduce his ideas to the conservative villagers. Jeremy was young, too impatient, and liable to offend people by not taking their views into consideration.

On Sunday he hoped to see Catarina, but she was not in church. When he asked Mrs Eade, hoping she was not ill, the rector's wife said she had gone to some watering place.

'She has been indisposed for the past few weeks, so I believe a change will be good for her, but I do not know which spa she has gone to. I don't believe it is Bath, for I wrote to enquire from a friend who lives there whether she had been seen. Besides, she has her own house in Bath, and could have taken the baby, but she left the child behind. So I assume it was a longer journey, and she would be staying in lodgings. The only servant she has taken with her is her maid. She did not even go in her own carriage, which is another reason I believe she has gone some distance.'

'What a gabblemonger!' Jeremy exclaimed, when they were barely out of Mrs Eade's hearing. 'What business is it of hers where Catarina is? Why does she need to check on her?'

'She was probably trying to help, assuming we needed to speak to Catarina about the estate,' Nicholas said.

'Apart from asking her if she knows how I can make these people listen to me, there's nothing.'

They made an early start and reached Grosvenor Square late the same evening. Olivia, they were told, was at some debutante's ball, and would not be back until late, so for once they went to bed early, though it had been suggested on the journey that they might look in at White's for a few hours.

Nicholas had to remain in London for the next few weeks to oversee Olivia's own ball, and there were a few debates he wanted to attend in the House. It would be a long time before he saw Catarina again. He would have to do his utmost to forget her.

10

'Nearly everyone has accepted,' Olivia told Nicholas the morning after he reached London. 'It will be such a crush! How wonderful!'

He smiled at her. His little sister had blossomed during the past few weeks. She had changed her hairstyle and she wore more fashionable gowns. She was acquiring some town bronze. Though still appealingly shy, she was not looking scared most of the time as she had when with Lady Keith. He seemed to have chosen wisely in asking Lady Mortimer to be her duenna.

'So what have you been doing while we were out of Town?'

She reeled off a list of balls and receptions and morning calls.

'I wanted to go to Vauxhall Gardens, but Lady Mortimer said it was not suitable, too many cits went there, and we had no male protectors. Nicholas, now you and Jeremy are back, could we not go?'

'We'll see.'

'That's what you always say when you don't wish to do something. I suppose you will say it when I ask to go to a masquerade. Louisa told me they are great fun.'

Nicholas made a mental note to tell Lady Mortimer to avoid Louisa, whoever she was, as a bad influence.

'I'll refuse permission entirely for that!' he said now.

'Vauxhall is bad enough, but for you, or any respectable girl, to go to a masquerade is out of the question.'

'Why? People just go masked, don't they?'

'They — ' He paused. How could he explain to his innocent young sister that these affairs were licentious, that unsuitable, even disreputable people attended, and most of the men and women who patronized them were seeking particular unsavoury pleasures?

'They what?'

'A masked ball in a private house, with invited guests only, is acceptable,' he said slowly. 'But at public affairs one does not know who might be there, anyone with the price of a ticket.'

Olivia looked unconvinced. 'I think that's odiously toplofty! Why should we mix only with the *ton*? I like being with some of the villagers at Brooke Court, they are friendly and helpful.'

'Our own people are different, we've known them all our lives. But there are some unscrupulous characters at public masquerades.' He paused for a moment, and then decided it would do no harm to frighten her a little. 'If they knew you had expectations from Grandmama, for example, or that I am your brother, they might attempt to kidnap you and hold you for ransom.' Or worse, he thought, but it would destroy all Olivia's new-found confidence to spell out the other dangers. At private functions she was safe, protected.

'Oh. Then of course I won't ask to go,' she conceded. 'Perhaps we could arrange a small masked party here, after my ball, then?'

He was happy to agree.

'Have you met anyone interesting?' he asked, wondering if any of the young men had attracted her notice.

'Oh, yes. But can you guess who is in Town? Lady Brooke, Catarina. She is staying with a Mrs Pearce, who used to be at school with her. Lady Mortimer and I went to have tea with them, and their cook had made some delicious cakes. They weren't from Gunter's. Some I had never tasted before. I think one was a Portuguese receipt Cat — Lady Brooke had taught her.'

For a few moments Nicholas was incapable of speaking. Catarina was here, within his reach, and they were likely to meet. How should he behave towards her? Did he wish to renew his offer? He was undecided. He still longed to possess her, but did he wish to have her as his wife?

'Are they coming to your ball?' he asked eventually. 'Have you sent invitations?'

'Oh yes, and I have also asked Mrs Pearce's brother-in-law, George Pearce. He is in the 10th Light Dragoons, the Prince's own regiment, and he looks so smart in his uniform. And Nicholas,' she said, giggling slightly, 'I think he is in love with Catarina; he could not take his eyes from her. When he was leaving he held her hands for far longer than he did Mrs Pearce's.'

Nicholas had a great deal to consider when Olivia left him to go with Lady Mortimer to purchase new evening sandals. Catarina was here in London. He would meet her soon, and apparently she had a new admirer. The thought infuriated him, and eventually decided him that he wanted Catarina sufficiently to make her an apology and an offer.

★ ★ ★

Catarina meanwhile was attempting to deflect another offer. Sir Humphrey had arrived in Hill Street that afternoon in a barouche and she had been forced to drive out with him. Delphine had, she learned with disquiet, accepted the invitation on her behalf.

'You have to make your refusal firmer,' her friend admonished. 'If you decline and make it absolutely clear you do not wish him to repeat his offer, perhaps he will go home and you will be free of him.'

'And perhaps not. Delphine, you do not know the stubbornness of the man! I can refuse him a score or more times and he will still regard it as maidenly reticence.'

'Well, talk about George all the time. I could see young Olivia's eyes grow even bigger when they were here, he was ogling you so blatantly.'

Catarina giggled. 'He was behaving like the lover in a ridiculous farce.'

'I will get him to ride in the Park and meet you there. If that does not signal to your ancient Sir Humphrey that his suit is hopeless, nothing will, until you become betrothed to someone else.'

Not at all sure that meeting George in the Park would deter Sir Humphrey, who seemed to have grown in his own self-esteem as he became older, Catarina joined him in his hired barouche with great foreboding. It was a staid conveyance, and she longed to be driven in a high-perch phaeton, such as she saw the young men and their fortunate companions enjoying. Might she regard him more kindly if he provided her with that pleasure? She shivered at the thought. Though he was a competent driver in the country, she had never seen him drive anything but a gig or, occasionally, when the roads were dry and easy to negotiate, a curricle. But all his horses were sluggish, far from excitable. He would never be able to control high-spirited teams with the same skill as was shown by many of the more sporting young men.

They reached the Park at a steady trot, and for the first round Sir Humphrey confined his remarks to news from Somerset and comments on how life in London was becoming more unpleasant.

'I shall be glad to return home,' he said, and paused. 'I shall be even happier, my dear, if you will consent to become my wife and come with me to prepare for our marriage. I envisage a simple ceremony, conducted by the Reverend Eade. As a widow you will not wish for a great show, or to spend months preparing a trousseau. From the many new gowns I have seen you wearing up in Town I assume you have been shopping and have sufficient. Nor is it as though we were setting up home together. I imagine that between us we have everything of a household nature that we need.'

Catarina had been attempting to break into this flow of eloquence. At last, when he paused for breath, she was able to speak.

'Sir Humphrey, you go too fast. I have not and will not, ever, agree to become your wife. I have already refused you once, and it distresses me to have to listen to you when there is no hope. Please take me back home now.'

She could swear the coachman's shoulders were shaking, and she could not blame him. Without waiting for Sir Humphrey's order he turned the barouche towards the Park entrance. Just at that moment George Pearce rode up and saluted them.

'My dear Lady Brooke, what a surprise to meet you here,' he sang out, winking outrageously at Catarina. 'It was such a pleasure to dance with you last night. I am looking forward to doing so again, tonight and many other times.'

Catarina smothered a grin. They had been to no ball on the previous day, nor was one planned for tonight.

'Mr Pearce. Sir Humphrey, may I introduce my good hostess's brother-in-law, George Pearce. He has been so assiduous in escorting us ladies around Town. Mr Pearce,

Sir Humphrey Unwin lives in Somerset and was a good friend to my late husband.'

The men bowed coldly to one another, and Catarina was startled to detect the creak of corsets from Sir Humphrey. He had been growing corpulent over the past few years, but she had never suspected him of the vanity which would make him adopt such a fashion.

George rode alongside for a while, chatting eagerly to Catarina about mutual acquaintances, and occasionally, seeming to recall Sir Humphrey's presence, tossing a few remarks to him. Then he bowed, brazenly lifted Catarina's hand to his lips, and took his leave, again reminding her she had promised to reserve the waltz for him that evening.

'H'm. Just the sort of fortune-hunting scoundrel I wish to protect you from, my dear lady!'

Catarina stiffened. 'George Pearce has an independent fortune, and I like him. I consider him a good friend, Sir Humphrey, and would be grateful if you do not abuse him.'

They drove back to Hill Street with him keeping an offended silence. Catarina hoped she had done enough to prevent future proposals, but she was sorry if he had been hurt, for he had been a good friend to Walter. He allowed the footman who came out of the house to assist her from the barouche, merely nodding farewell, and ordering the coachman to drive on before she had gained the house.

★ ★ ★

Lady Mortimer received on Tuesdays, and Nicholas was sitting with them when Sir Humphrey was announced. After paying attentions to the ladies, Sir Humphrey moved to sit next to Nicholas.

'My lord,' he said, 'may I have a private word with you?'

'Something to do with Marshington Grange?' Nicholas asked. 'Let us go to the library.'

When they were seated and drinking glasses of wine, Nicholas looked enquiringly at his visitor. 'How may I help you, Sir Humphrey?'

'It's about Lady Brooke. I fear she is getting into unsuitable company,' Sir Humphrey said. 'When I drove her out yesterday we were accosted — I put it as strongly as that — by some whippersnapper who thought, because he wore some fancy uniform, that he could insult us both with impunity. Why, the fellow was making love to her right under my nose!'

Nicholas suppressed a smile. He had only

met Sir Humphrey a couple of times, but had put him down as a rather pompous provincial. He discounted Sir Humphrey's wider assertion, but none the less the intelligence that Catarina seemed to have acquired an admirer, and a military man at that, caused him some unease. Was it at all possible this man was someone she had met in Portugal? Was their acquaintance of long standing? Could that be why she had stayed in Lisbon for so long? Was this why she had come to London?

'Who was the man?' he asked.

'He called himself George Pearce. He's some connection of the friend Catarina is staying with, but he's an impudent dog.'

'Lady Brooke is of age, independent, able to choose her own friends,' Nicholas said. 'I do not see what it has to do with either of us.'

Sir Humphrey huffed for a moment.

'I can see I need to put my cards on the table. I have expectations that Lady Brooke will soon become my wife.'

That did startle Nicholas. Why, after so many years with Walter, would Catarina want another elderly husband? It was not for acquiring another wealthy husband who might be expected to die long before her. From what he had heard Sir Humphrey's fortune was modest, as was his estate. He would benefit more from such a marriage, if he acquired Catarina's much larger fortune.

His throat was dry and he had to clear it before he spoke.

'Has she accepted you?'

'Not yet, but, as you know, ladies are reluctant to be brought up to scratch. They like to keep us in suspense. However, I'm not the sort of man to be put off by a couple of refusals. I've no doubt she'll come round to it in time. But as a member of her family, or rather of Walter's, I would be grateful if you would drop a word in her ear that consorting with fellows like George Pearce will harm her reputation. She would listen to you.'

Nicholas very much doubted it. He was tempted to throw Sir Humphrey out of the house. How dare the old reprobate even think of offering for Catarina? The only welcome information was that she had twice refused him. Catarina was no coquette; she would not refuse a man simply to tease him. But George Pearce might be a different matter. Suddenly he was certain he wanted her for his wife. He must capture her before she was stolen from him.

'Come back to the ladies,' he suggested, managing to avoid making any promises to speak to Catarina on Sir Humphrey's behalf.

An hour later he was condemning himself

for taking the man back upstairs, for Olivia had, hearing he was a neighbour at Marshington, issued an invitation to her ball in a few days' time.

* * *

Catarina, back in Hill Street, fumed, but she had to laugh when she told Delphine what had happened.

'George was superb, but I felt rather sorry for Sir Humphrey. He was quite out of his depth.'

They spoke no more of the encounter, and Catarina became absorbed in deciding what she wanted to wear to Olivia's ball. As a widow, she felt she ought to wear something sober. She told Delphine she had no intention of dancing, but her friend ridiculed the suggestion.

'My dear Catarina, you do not, I hope, intend to wear a train and a turban and sit for the entire evening amongst the dowagers, do you? That would be a wicked waste. And you've danced at other balls. It would be noticed and remarked upon, cause gossip and speculation. I intend to dance. I am determined to capture your handsome new earl for at least one.'

There was no stopping Delphine, so

Catarina was persuaded to wear her most attractive gown, of rose silk, low cut and with tiny sleeves, with deeper shaded embroidery and rouleaux decorated with silk roses round the hem. With it she had beaded satin slippers and white silk gloves. She wore the diamond parure Walter had given her when they were first married, which she had had few occasions to wear and which reflected the colour of the gown in a million shimmering gleams. To her surprise she had received a posy of white rosebuds from George, and she smiled as she pinned it on to her gown. It was a new experience for her to have a handsome young man pay her such attention and, even though she knew they were both playing a part, it was enjoyable and gave her courage to face the inevitable meeting with Nicholas.

They set off for the ball early, Delphine predicting a crush of vehicles converging on Grosvenor Square. Catarina, waiting for the carriages to disentangle themselves and disgorge their passengers outside Nicholas's house, thought it would have been much faster for them to have walked, but when she said this to Delphine, the latter laughed.

'In these pumps? Catarina, they would be ruined before we had walked halfway. By the dirt, if not by being worn through.'

At last, after what seemed like an hour of

waiting, they drew up before the portico and were handed down by a liveried footman on to a red carpet leading to the open front door. Other footmen lined the path, keeping back the crowd of people who, Delphine whispered, always gathered outside houses where Society balls were taking place.

'Some of them look as though they are starving!' Catarina exclaimed. 'They are thinner even than Dan was.'

'Who is Dan? Never mind, tell me later, we haven't time now.'

Lady Mortimer and Nicholas were at the top of the stairs, flanking Olivia, greeting their guests. Olivia looked enchanting in a white silk gown, gently ruched all down the skirt, embroidered only with white flowers. Her dark hair was cut in the latest style to frame her face, and she was wearing a delicate gold chain with a heart-shaped gold locket. She had shown Catarina the locket, opening it to reveal miniatures of her parents. Catarina thought how sensible of her, or perhaps it was Lady Mortimer's influence, to wear only simple jewellery.

They exchanged greetings and then, to Catarina's confusion, Nicholas leant closer to her, speaking so that none of the others could hear.

'Please keep the first waltz for me.'

The first person Catarina saw when she entered the ballroom was Sir Humphrey Unwin. He was standing sideways towards her and seemed to be staring hard at someone just out of her sight behind a bank of greenery. She hesitated. She had not known he was coming and, after their drive in the Park, she had no wish to see him again.

Then the object of his fixed regard moved forward. It was George Pearce. He saw her immediately and strolled towards her, nodding affably to Sir Humphrey as he came. Sir Humphrey swivelled round to watch his progress and saw Catarina. He started towards her as well, almost running, and the two men reached her simultaneously.

'My dear Lady Brooke, how delicious you look. And I see how well my little gift goes with your gown.'

'Good evening Catarina.'

'Sir Humphrey, Mr Pearce.'

Delphine, who had paused to greet an acquaintance, was slightly behind Catarina. Catarina heard her smother a chuckle before she spoke.

'Sir Humphrey, how elegant you look. George, not in your regimentals? I'm disappointed, you look so dashing in them.'

'I've decided to join the Dandy set, now the Beau has left us and made room for others to shine.'

'The Beau? Mr Brummell, you mean? Where has he gone?' Delphine asked.

'Haven't you heard? Alvanley told me. It's all they can talk about in the clubs. His debts have finally caught up with him and he has decamped to France. They are auctioning all his possessions in a day or so. I may try to secure one of his snuffboxes. He's reputed to have hundreds, at least one for every day of the year. He always used them with such style.'

'Foppery! All the man ever thought of was clothing and fashion!'

'Oh no, Sir Humphrey; he enjoyed the play and opera, and his debts are mainly due to his losses at the tables,' George contradicted gently. 'But no doubt you are unaware of that down in the country.'

Sir Humphrey snorted. There was no other word for it, Catarina thought, and was suddenly reminded of Mr Lewis's pigs. When George asked her to partner him in the country dance just forming, she thankfully escaped before she disgraced herself by laughing.

'That was unkind, suggesting he is a country bumpkin,' she said.

George laughed. 'Isn't he?'

'He was been a good friend of my husband, but I do wish he would accept that I have no wish to marry him!'

The movement of the dance separated them, and there was no more opportunity for much conversation. Sir Humphrey was standing at the side of the room, glowering, but Delphine had been drawn into another set and he was alone. Catarina felt a moment's sorrow for him; he looked and no doubt felt out of place. She had to remind herself firmly that she could not afford to be kind as he would assume her resolve was weakening and pursue her even more ardently. He had never spent a great deal of time in London, even when his wife was alive. She did not think his daughters had been given Seasons here. Most probably they had been sent to Bath until they found husbands similar to himself. Both of them had married unremarkable men, small land-holders like himself, and his sons had both married the daughters of clergymen and had to earn their own livings, though she was unsure whether both were attorneys, or whether one was a doctor.

When the dance ended she and Delphine found seats together near one of the tall windows opening into the garden. It was a cold night, so the windows were closed, but the garden, decorated with flambeaux and coloured streamers, looked enchanting.

They were no sooner seated than Sir Humphrey approached.

'Catarina, I am surprised to see you dancing so soon after poor Walter's death. It does not strike me as seemly, but no doubt your fashionable new friends do not mind.'

All her gentle feelings for him vanished.

'Sir Humphrey, you appear to consider it soon enough, and seemly, for me to contract another marriage. You have no jurisdiction over my behaviour. I shall determine what is seemly. I beg you not to embarrass me in front of my friends by chiding me as though I were a child!'

He gave her a hard look, then, without a further word, turned and walked away. Catarina gave a deep sigh.

'Oh dear, now I have offended him.'

'He deserved it, the pompous old fool,' Delphine comforted her. 'You must not permit it to spoil your enjoyment. Listen, they have started a waltz and here comes your partner.'

★ ★ ★

Catarina was stiff with apprehension when Nicholas bowed before her, but she managed to rise to her feet and accompany him on to the floor. When he put his arm round her waist she trembled violently.

'I'm not about to harm you,' he said, and she detected a hint of amusement in his voice.

She swallowed. 'No my lord. I did not think you were.'

For some time after that they did not speak. He was an excellent dancer and, though Catarina had only danced the waltz occasionally during the last year of Walter's life, at local assemblies, she had no difficulty in following his lead.

Eventually he broke the silence.

'Are you enjoying your stay in London?'

'Yes. Yes, my lord, it is very pleasant. Delphine, Mrs Pearce, has made me most welcome.'

'She is an old friend?'

'We were at school together.'

'And you know her brother-in-law well?'

'I only met him here. Although Delphine and I have corresponded over the years, since we left school, I have only met her husband once, and George not at all previously.'

'He seems very attentive.'

'He is kind.'

'And Sir Humphrey? I understand he was surprised to find you here. Mrs Eade seemed to believe you had gone to some watering place for your health. I was sorry to hear you had been indisposed.'

'It was not serious, my lord.'

Just hurt and disappointment after he had rejected her. Catarina raised her chin slightly, then had to blink hard. She looked round the room and saw that Olivia was dancing with a young man she did not know.

'Your sister is permitted to waltz?' she asked. 'I understood it was not the thing for debutantes.'

'She luckily pleased the patronesses at Almack's, and they gave her permission two weeks ago. I think she would have hesitated to waltz even at a private ball if they had not.'

'She looks lovely tonight, and is clearly enjoying herself.'

'Catarina.' He paused, then started again. 'Catarina, we parted on difficult terms, and I would like an opportunity to talk to you. Will you drive out with me tomorrow, if the weather is clement? It has been such a cold and wet few months it is difficult to make arrangements.'

Catarina hesitated. Did she want to be alone with Nicholas? But if she refused she might lose her last opportunity of talking to him, and perhaps trying to convince him that Maria was not her child.

'Very well, my lord.'

'I will call for you at four.'

11

Nicholas had still not decided what he wanted when he called for Catarina the following day. She eyed the high perch phaeton and four horses, smiled in delight, then lifted her skirts and scrambled up beside him before his groom could go to her assistance.

'I've always wanted to ride in one of these carriages; they look such fun,' she said, as she settled herself.

'Allow me to put this rug around your knees,' he said, smiling at her enthusiasm. Many ladies were terrified of sitting two yards above the ground. 'It's unseasonably cold.'

'But not, for once, raining. Thank you, my lord.'

She did not speak again as he negotiated the traffic and turned into the relative peace of the Park. He wondered whether she thought he would be unable to talk and drive at the same time.

'I hope you enjoyed the ball.'

'Yes, indeed, it was most pleasant. Was Olivia happy?'

'The child is overwhelmed with flowers,

messages of thanks and invitations to so many events she will have to attend three at least every day. I shall be glad that the Season will soon be over and we can all get away from London.'

'Will you go to Brighton? I believe most of the *ton* retreat there in June and July. Some have gone already.'

'Have you ever been?'

'No. Walter did not approve of the Prince Regent's folly, as he called the Pavilion. Besides, we did not come to London above two or three times in our entire married life.'

Nicholas detected no trace of regret in her tone. Suddenly he wanted to know more about her first marriage.

'What in the world made you marry a man as old as Walter, when you were so young?' he demanded.

She glanced at him.

'*Because* I was so young. My uncle arranged it. Sir Ivor became our guardian when Papa died when I was fifteen. I was still grieving for him a year later. I had been told so often that girls were supposed to obey their parents, accept any match arranged for them, that I never questioned it, let alone objected. Besides — '

'Besides what?'

'Uncle Ivor was a very strict disciplinarian.

He took me away from the Bath seminary, told me I had to help Aunt Hebe, learn how to run a house. But he was never satisfied. I was always being punished, often for things I did not know I had done, or not done when I was supposed to have. I looked on marriage as an escape. And Walter was gentle, always kind to me.'

Nicholas tightened his hands on the reins and then had to bring his team under control as they broke into a canter. If he could have met Sir Ivor Norton just then the man would have been sorry.

'What about your sister? I believe she is eighteen. Has he not tried to arrange a marriage for her?'

'Joanna was stronger than I, and refused two matches he tried to force on her. Uncle beat her and starved her, but she would not obey him. When she could endure it no more she came to me; that was one reason we went to visit our Portuguese family then.'

'And that turned out happily, since she married a man she loved.'

'Yes.'

Now she had mentioned Portugal herself Nicholas felt able to mention the child.

'Catarina, I have to apologize for the way I spoke to you the last time we met at Marshington. I have no excuse, other than being taken by surprise. I had not known there was a baby in the house.'

'I understand, my lord.'

Her voice was so low he scarcely heard the words. He halted the phaeton and motioned to the tiger to go to the horses' heads.

'Shall we walk for a while?'

Without waiting for her reply he sprang down and was ready to lift her before she had disentangled herself from the rug.

She gasped as he seized her round the waist and for a moment Nicholas stood there looking deep into her eyes. Then she lowered her gaze and moved away from him. He let her go, but his mind was made up. He wanted her; whatever the truth about the child it made no difference to him.

There was a gravel walk nearby. He drew her hand through his arm and led her along it.

'What I have to say, Catarina, is not for my tiger's ears. I told you before that I had been about to ask you to be my wife. I was a fool to allow my surprise to deflect me, and even more of a fool to disbelieve you about the child. I made some wild accusations. Will you forgive me?'

She bowed her head and again he had to struggle to hear her words.

'I understood. Yes, I was hurt you did not

believe me, but afterwards, when I considered the facts, I realized they could be interpreted as you had done.'

'Then can we go back? Will you forgive me enough to accept my hand? Will you be my wife?'

Catarina slowed to a halt. He turned her to face him, but she kept her head lowered. After a few moments she spoke.

'My lord, I am honoured. I forgive you your suspicions, the facts looked damning. But I have no wish to marry again. I'm sorry, but I cannot accept your offer. Now, please, can you take me back home?'

* * *

Delphine had just arrived home when Catarina entered the house and, taking one look at her friend, she dismissed her maid and led Catarina to her boudoir.

'My love, what is it? Have you had bad news?'

Catarina laughed, a wild, broken sound, and buried her face in her hands.

'Delphine, I don't know if I have been a fool or not. Nicholas made me an offer and I refused him.'

'Nicholas Brooke? One of the most sought after bachelors in London, the despair of all the mamas, has proposed to you and you have refused him? For heaven's sake, why?'

Catarina suddenly realized there was no way she could explain her real reasons to Delphine, a noted gossip. Once more, she thought wryly, she was reduced to telling lies.

'I don't love him, and I do not wish to marry again.'

That was two lies, she told herself, weary of all the pretence. How many more would she have to tell before she could escape back to the peace and safety of the Dower House?

Delphine was disbelieving, but when Catarina begged to be left alone, as she had a raging headache, which was the truth, she thought wryly, her friend left her, saying she would have a light supper sent up later.

'You must go to the reception,' Catarina managed, as Delphine drew the curtains closed and was leaving the room. 'If I need anything Blodwen can look after me.'

Left alone, she allowed the tears to fall. She could not tell Nicholas the truth, that Maria was Joanna's child, and she could not marry him without there being complete truthfulness and trust between them. Bleakly she wondered whether he would ever speak to her again. Would he think she had refused him in retaliation for the hurt he had caused her? But that did not make sense. If she had never wished to marry him, she would have refused him. There would have been no thought of revenge. She gave up trying to puzzle it out, submitted meekly to Blodwen's anxious attentions with eau de cologne and a tisane of rosemary and honey, rejected the offer of cucumber slices on her forehead, and announced she meant to try and sleep.

Sleep would not come, but when Blodwen peeped into the bedroom two hours later she pretended to be so. She knew her face was ravaged with tears, and felt utterly unable to look at food. Blodwen withdrew. Soon afterwards Catarina did fall asleep, emotionally exhausted.

She woke early and for a while lay there in a dazed state, wondering why she felt so despondent. Then it all flooded back, Nicholas's apology and proposal, and her own inability to accept the latter.

Getting out of bed she looked at her face in the mirror. Her eyes were red with weeping, there was puffiness around them. Even after she bathed them in cold water the evidence of her tears remained.

Delphine was unusually tactful. She brought Catarina some breakfast herself, tea and toast, and gently insisted she eat and drink.

'Then you shall stay in bed all day, tomorrow as well, and be made to see no one.

Would you like a book to read?'

Listlessly Catarina agreed. 'I left my library book in the drawing room. I have only just started it.'

It would perhaps distract her thoughts, prevent her from thinking of what might have been.

★ ★ ★

The following day Catarina felt better and insisted on getting up. Her eyes were suspiciously pink still, but she would stay quietly at home, reading. Delphine offered to stay with her, but Catarina said she would be perfectly content on her own. If Delphine gave up her plans she would feel guilty.

'And you'll be all the better without my fussing, no doubt. Very well, I will do the shopping I had planned, and pay visits. You won't be disturbed.'

Blodwen seemed to be the only servant allowed to come near her, and she was careful only to come into the room to bring Catarina a nuncheon on a tray, or to make up the fire.

'It's dreadful, it is, having to have fires in June,' she said. 'My lady, there's a letter come for you.'

She fished in her pocket and brought out the letter. Catarina hoped it was from Joanna, but she recognized the handwriting of her butler. Quickly she scanned the contents and frowned. He reassured her that all was well at the Dower House, told her they had organized a big search for Dan but had failed to find him, then came to the real point of the letter. Jeremy, Staines had written, had ordered the common to be enclosed now the hay had been gathered.

There'll be trouble, my lady. I cannot write to Mr Brooke myself, it wouldn't be seemly, and unless Mr Trubshaw has done so, which is his duty, Mr Brooke will not know the deep feeling there is in the village against him. I doubt if Mr Trubshaw will make it clear to him, which is why I am venturing to ask you, if you would be so kind, and can speak to Mr Brooke, that is, if he is in London, and let him know of our concerns.

After some thought Catarina wrote a note for Jeremy and sent it with one of the footmen, asking him to call on her. She did not expect to change his mind, but the least she could do was remind him of his legal rights and inform him of the unrest his enclosure was causing.

Somewhat to her surprise he came at once.

'To tell the truth, Catarina, I'm glad to be out of the house. Nicholas has been in a foul mood for a couple of days. He even snapped at Olivia when she mentioned Vauxhall, and told her she could forget the idea. And he'd virtually promised to take her.'

Catarina felt guilty. It was most likely her refusal of his offer which had put him out of countenance.

'I've had a letter from Staines,' she said abruptly. 'He says you have ordered the enclosure of the common. Don't you need an Act of Parliament to do that?'

Jeremy sighed. 'I'm merely putting a fence round it so that the animals don't stray. The people will still be able to graze them there. Why, has Trubshaw not told them this?'

'I don't know. Is he in charge while you are in London?'

'Yes. But the man seems incapable of explaining things in simple enough terms for the villagers to understand.'

'Staines says there is a good deal of ill feeling in the village against you. Can you not go down and reassure them?'

Jeremy frowned. 'I won't be at the beck and call of a pack of disgruntled villagers! Some of them resent me so much they'll not believe anything I tell them. Besides, I have plans for the rest of the Season, then I'm going to

Brighton, and afterwards to visit an army friend for some shooting up in Yorkshire. If it weren't for this wretched leg of mine I'd be glad to be back in the army, and Nicholas could deal with Marshington.'

He left soon afterwards. Catarina decided she had had enough of London. She dreaded the thought of seeing Nicholas again, was tired of parties and balls and polite conversation. She was also missing Maria, and looked forward to seeing how the baby had changed during the few weeks she'd been away. Perhaps, if she were back at the Dower House and could explain the position to the villagers, they would understand.

★ ★ ★

Delphine was reluctant to see her leave, but assured Catarina she understood how difficult it would be for her to be always fearing seeing Nicholas again.

'I hoped you might come to Paris with me. I'm thinking of going there instead of Brighton, but I will write and tell you all the news,' she promised, 'and you must write back. I want to know how Joanna fares in Brazil, and what happens in Marshington.'

Three days later Catarina was home and breathing a sigh of relief. Maria had grown, could sit up by herself, and had produced two teeth. At first she was shy of Catarina, but she was such a happy and contented child she soon accepted her once more. Catarina praised her servants for the excellent care they had taken both of the baby and the Dower House. Even though she had not been able to warn them of her return everything had been in perfect order and it only needed dust sheets to be removed from the drawing-room furniture for the house to return to normal.

Conditions in the village were not happy, though.

Catarina, driving her gig, and looking at the changes to the trees and flowers since she'd been away, went first to see Mr Lewis, to tell him what Jeremy had told her, and ask how she could convince the villagers they could still use the common for grazing their animals.

'That wasn't what Mr Trubshaw was telling them.'

'He must have misunderstood Mr Brooke. From what he told me he means to leave the common for them to use, both for hay and grazing. He thought a fence to keep the animals from straying all over the village would please them. He would need an Act to take the land away from common use.'

'He offended a good many people trying to force them to accept his new ideas. Country folk need time to absorb them and see the benefit, but there, young men are always in a hurry.'

'Has there been much resentment?'

'Folk are worried. The hay was poor, and it was so wet we couldn't dry it properly,' Mr Lewis told her. 'There won't be enough to feed all the animals during the winter. We'll have to slaughter more than usual, and they won't be full grown and have enough flesh for meat.'

'Can't they be sold at market?'

'No. Everyone is suffering; no one has the spare hay to feed them up or keep them. Besides, the way the weather is, the rest of the harvest will be poor. It's going to be a lean winter for everyone as well as the animals.'

'I see. There was something else I wanted to ask you. Is Dan still around? Did he evade that manhunt and return?'

'I think he did, though he's not seen in the village now. But Trubshaw says he's found more shelters built in the woods, and we don't know of any other vagrants living rough.'

Catarina drove home wondering who to see next. Would the Reverend Eade be able to convince the villagers that Jeremy intended them no harm? Or ought she to talk to Mr Trubshaw and discover exactly what he had been telling people?

★ ★ ★

Nicholas was unsure whether to be sorry or pleased when he heard Catarina had gone back to Somerset. Meeting her would have been awkward and, as neither Jeremy nor Olivia knew of his offer, they would continue to see her and invite her to their parties. In particular, repenting of his brusqueness towards Olivia he had agreed to her holding a masquerade, instead of taking her to Vauxhall.

It was on the morning of the masquerade, when the entire house was in an uproar of preparations and he had retreated to his library, that a letter from Portugal was delivered to him.

Thomas had news for him. Nicholas was reluctant to open the letter. It could matter little to him now. Catarina's refusal had been so decided he doubted whether she would ever again agree to listen to him, and he was at a loss to find a way of making her do so.

He wanted her more than ever, whatever the truth about Maria, he acknowledged to himself. Was this simply because she had refused him? He had been aware from an early age that he was a major prize on the marriage market. He had wealth, birth, looks, and the prospect, now realized, of a title. He had assumed, arrogantly, it seemed, that any girl he honoured with an offer would gladly accept him. To be refused had been a shock to his self-esteem, as well as a more personal disappointment. No, that was too mild a term: he was devastated. From the first moment he had been able to think coherently after driving back home he had known he would never offer for anyone else. Other women might match the beauty and allure of Catarina, but he did not love them.

Eventually he opened the letter, which he had been turning over and over as he sat ruminating, wondering what he could have done differently to make Catarina accept him.

Thomas came straight to the point.

'I have spoken to several members of the de Freitas family in Oporto,' he wrote, 'including Senhora Madalene de Freitas, who seems to be the leading member of the family. They all assure me that none of their relatives, however distant, has died recently, within the past year. Nor have any of the ladies been delivered of babies. It occurred to me that the child who is now in England might have been born to a girl who was not married, but from what I can discover, all the members of the family in Portugal were at some family celebration at the end of October, a wedding anniversary, I believe, and any late pregnancy would have been obvious and commented on. I was able to speak to one of the senior servants who was present on that occasion, some sort of major domo, whose wife is housekeeper at the quinta where the celebration took place, and they were both sure no lady present was on the verge of giving birth.'

Nicholas put down the letter and stared across the room. What did this mean? Catarina had told him the child had been born to a cousin who had died. According to Thomas no cousin had given birth at the right time, and none had died. So Catarina must have lied to him. Why? Either the baby was her own, after all, or belonged to some unknown woman and Catarina had adopted her. All his doubts came flooding back.

Supposing the baby was hers, had Walter been the father? Given that he and Catarina had been childless for eight years, it seemed unlikely. Had she taken a lover? A sudden surge of jealousy made his hands shake. He made an effort to calm himself and think clearly. In some ways, tied to an elderly husband, it would not have been surprising had Catarina wanted romance with a younger man. How long might she have been involved with him? Had they been careless, allowing the pregnancy?

That led to even blacker thoughts. Walter had died from a fall and not been found for hours. Might he have survived if he had been found earlier? No one had essayed any thoughts on that. But how had the fall happened? Was it at all possible that Catarina or her lover had engineered an accident? But no lover apart from George Pearce had been noticed, and Nicholas, who had known him for years, felt that George was not serious about any woman.

His instincts made him reject the notion. He did not want to believe Catarina could have been a party to murder, but a niggling doubt remained. Who might her lover have been? Would he have been less scrupulous? Would they, at some time, marry? Was that the reason for her rejection of his offer? Who the devil could it be?

Suddenly Nicholas could bear his thoughts no longer. He tore Thomas's letter into a hundred tiny pieces, rang for his valet and left the house. He would seek some congenial company at White's, order wine and try to forget Catarina and his suspicions.

★ ★ ★

Catarina was aware of continued unrest in the village, as people speculated on what their new landlord would do next. They had treated with considerable reserve the fact they were allowed to graze their animals still, and openly asked for how long this concession might last. They treated it as a concession, and all assumed it would not continue.

The harvest was as bad as Mr Lewis had predicted. The cold and wet weather earlier in the year had damaged the crops, and often what had survived was barely worth the harvesting. The villagers faced semi-starvation that winter, many of them blaming Jeremy. Especially they blamed him for not being there to listen to their complaints. Many of them approached Catarina.

'We can't be doin' wi' that Trubshaw,' one of them said to her. 'He don't listen; all 'e can say is that Mr Brooke will be told, but 'e never comes back to us wi' any replies. 'Tis my opinion 'e never tells Mr Brooke.'

'He tells 'im, but the young feller don't care. Enjoyin' 'isself in Lunnon, or that there seaside place where the Prince teks all 'is wimmin.'

Catarina did what she could. She still had

238

friends in Bath and some acquaintances in Bristol, and she begged them for promises of help in providing money, or finding food later in the year when conditions would be worse. She wrote to her family in Portugal, but was told that all Europe suffered in the same way, and they could not help. Rather ruefully she wondered whether supplies of olives would have been acceptable to the villagers in any case. She even wrote to Joanna, without knowing what her sister might be able to do, but she received no reply, just another ecstatic letter saying what fun it was to be living in Rio, and how much she enjoyed life as a married woman. Eduardo was apparently still infatuated with her, loading her with fabulous jewellery, the Brazilian and Portuguese aristocracy were delightful, so attentive, and she had absolutely no regrets at leaving England and Portugal behind her.

In that last sentence, Catarina read an unspoken reference to Maria. Joanna had never once enquired after her daughter, and this remark seemed to imply she had no regrets at abandoning her. She had always known Joanna was tougher than she was herself, but this showed her sister was hard and selfish.

Though keeping Joanna's secret had

involved Catarina in so many lies and caused her to reject Nicholas, she delighted in the baby. Maria was an enchanting little girl. That was the one joyful outcome of the whole miserable business, and made life bearable.

12

Olivia enjoyed her stay in Brighton, but confessed to Nicholas she would be glad when they returned to Brooke Court.

'I want to see everyone again. Of course it has all been exciting, but I think I prefer living in the country most of the time.'

She had received two offers, both from unexceptional young men of good family and adequate income, but she confessed to her brother that she did not think she would like to live with either of them for the rest of her life, as they bored her.

One was concerned only with the fit of his coat and the correctness of his necktie, while attempting to set some new fashion by sporting violently patterned waistcoats and coloured pantaloons. Nicholas privately suspected he was aiming to replace the Beau, now Brummell had been forced to flee to Calais.

The other was a hearty young man dedicated to all forms of sport, who had confided in Nicholas that his family wished him to marry and provide an heir before he was killed in an accident on the hunting field, as they did not wish his very insignificant title to go to a detested cousin. Nicholas had taken a strong objection to having his sister used for such a purpose, and was thankful she did not favour the fellow.

She was still very young, and he hoped she would in time meet a man she could both respect and love. In late August he took her back to Brooke Court, but asked Lady Mortimer to stay with them for a longer time, as he himself needed to be elsewhere.

He did not enlarge on his plans apart from saying he meant to go to Paris for a few weeks. He was much too restless to stay at home. Jeremy was somewhere in the north, and had written that he would be visiting the lakes before returning to Marshington Grange. Trubshaw, he reported, wrote that all was well there, so Nicholas did not have to worry.

Nicholas reflected that he would have needed a strong reason to go back to Marshington, where he would be bound to meet Catarina. He was torn, his emotions in turmoil. He still desired her, but could not rid his mind of suspicions about the child. She must have lied to him when she said the baby belonged to a dead cousin. Thomas was reliable and had a knack of drawing information out of people. When he'd been in the army he had often been used as a scout. Since he spoke the language, he had been able to talk to the natives and discover more about the enemy's movements than others who had been forced to rely on interpreters. His information would be accurate, and it was damning for Catarina.

He went to Paris and enjoyed a flirtation with a beautiful young Parisian, the wife of a French diplomat who was currently in Austria. When she intimated she would not object to something more than a flirtation, however, he discovered he had no appetite. The only woman he could envisage taking to bed was Catarina.

Was he to be celibate for the rest of his life, he wondered? Perhaps the repugnance he had felt on contemplating her invitation would lessen in time. He threw himself into all the entertainments Paris offered, visited the country château of an old friend and, when his conscience urged him to go home and make sure all was well there, he quietened it by telling himself that any bad news would come to him quickly. He was not yet ready to face life in England without the prospect of having Catarina by his side.

★　★　★

It was Mrs Eade who told Catarina of the trouble in the village. To occupy herself and try to forget Nicholas she had joined the weekly sewing circle. Half-a-dozen women were sitting round the rectory dining-room table with a heap of clothes they were sorting to find material suitable for turning into smocks for the poorer children of the parish.

'Mr Lewis had several hens stolen two nights ago and his old dog was killed. It is supposed to have been to prevent him giving the alarm.'

The women looked nervous.

'How shocking!'

'The poor man. He might have been killed in his bed.'

'That's not all. It seems as though during the night someone has been milking one of the cows on the common.'

'That sounds like vagrants, someone living rough.'

'Are any of us safe in our beds? They'll be breaking into houses next, in search of food.'

'Is Dan still living rough in the woods, does anyone know?' Catarina asked.

'I'm sure some of the younger men know, but they won't admit it, not even to the rector, and he has spoken very firmly to them. He means to make it the subject of his next sermon.'

Briefly Catarina contemplated the vision of a dozen repentant young men rushing forward to confess knowledge of one of their former drinking cronies living wild in the woods, and suppressed a smile. If they were in church, which she doubted, they would hardly be moved by one of the Reverend Eade's sermons. Though he very occasionally raised his voice, he was usually too academic for them, inclined to pepper his discourse with quotations from the classics, in Latin or Greek, and wander off into abstruse philosophical reflections. Now if Mrs Eade were to deliver it, she would at least be listened to with attention, as she had a very forceful way of stating her opinions.

Her amused reflections were interrupted and she paid attention to Mrs Eade once more.

'Mr Lewis is setting up a guard. One of his men will sit up every night. Remember his barn which was set alight earlier in the year? He doesn't want that to happen again.'

'But don't we all need protecting?'

'What is the constable doing about it?'

'They should have men patrolling the village every night.'

Catarina stopped listening. She felt sorry for Dan, even though he had brought his misfortune on himself. If it were he stealing the hens it would be in desperation. She wondered whether he would come to her if she rode near the woods, like he had on a previous occasion. He trusted her, she thought, and she might be able to help him. What he needed was to get away from the area. Perhaps if she could give him some respectable clothes and some money he would be able to leave and find himself a job somewhere he was not known. He might even be able to sign on to a ship going to New South Wales and try to rejoin Annie.

★   ★   ★

In Paris Nicholas was getting restive. He was tired of the parties, and the people. When he was invited to the embassy to a reception for some visiting diplomats he almost sent his apologies, but at the last minute, suddenly impatient with the book he was trying to read, he decided he might as well be bored somewhere other than in his hotel suite.

The reception rooms at the embassy were crowded, but Nicholas knew many of the people there. Rather to his annoyance he found his Aunt Clara had been invited and, as soon as she saw him, she broke off her conversation with a timid-looking Frenchwoman and came straight across the room to him.

'You still here, Nicholas? I thought when you called you were only going to be here for a couple of weeks. It would have been courteous to have let me know your movements.'

Nicholas ground his teeth together.

'Aunt, I told you I was unsure how long I would stay.'

'Still flirting with that French jade, are you? Be warned, Nephew, her husband's reported to be excessively jealous, has fought two duels over her already and he's reputed to be a crack shot.'

'Did he kill his men?' Nicholas asked, intrigued. His interest in the lady had waned weeks ago. When he rejected her advances she had made it clear she was no longer willing to tolerate his company. But he had not realized she was such a fatal attraction.

'I expect so. I don't pay much attention to these affairs. They are so vulgar. But I would hate to know a member of my own family had been killed by a jealous husband.'

She would not, he noted with some amusement, appear to regret his death, merely the manner of it.

Somewhat to his relief she saw another victim just entering the room and, with a parting recommendation to behave himself, almost as though he were still a schoolboy, she sped away. He looked round for more congenial company and saw two men he knew from his days in the army the previous year. It was only when he had approached the group and been made welcome, he saw Delphine Pearce was amongst them.

What did she know about his offer to Catarina? They had appeared to be good friends, and when Catarina had left him on that fateful day she had looked pale. Delphine would have been bound to ask her what was the matter, and in all likelihood Catarina would have told her. Women liked to have confidantes, he understood, and were likely to choose girls they had known at school. He knew Catarina had left Town a few days later, for Olivia had been so disappointed not to have her at her private masquerade. Had she left London, gone back to the Dower House because of his proposal? In which case Delphine Pearce would almost certainly know at least the bare facts.

When the group split up Delphine remained, smiling at him. He moved across to speak to her.

'Let us find somewhere more private,' she said, before he could say anything, and turned to lead the way to a small alcove at the side of the room. She sat on one of the sophas and patted the seat beside her.

'How is Catarina?' he asked, unable to prevent himself.

'I have only received one letter, but she says she is well, though there is a good deal of unrest in the village. The harvest was exceptionally poor and the villagers are facing a bad winter.'

'My brother has not yet returned?'

'He had not when she wrote. Why do you not go down there to see for yourself?'

Nicholas shook his head.

'I don't plan to go down there. Marshington Grange belongs to Jeremy now; it would be interference on my part.'

'Then he should be looking after it himself. Ah, Senhor Gomez, how pleasant to meet you again. It seems such a long time since I was at your party. My lord, may I introduce Senhor Fernando Gomez, one of the Brazilian delegation currently visiting Europe. Senhor, the Earl of Rasen.'

Nicholas stood up and offered his hand to the Brazilian, a flamboyantly handsome man with dark, curling hair and brilliant green eyes. The other bowed, lifted Delphine's hands to his lips, complimented her on her gown, then turned back to Nicholas.

'I am honoured to meet you, my lord. I have heard your name on the lips of Joanna, my friend Eduardo's wife. I understand she met you — now, where did she say? Not in Lisbon, I think, where she met Eduardo. It was something to do with her sister. I am hoping to meet the lady when I go to England.'

Delphine was smiling at him rather coquettishly, Nicholas thought sourly.

'I was so sorry not to meet Eduardo Goncalves myself,' she said, 'but unfortunately we left Lisbon in November, before he arrived. His romance with Joanna was rather a whirlwind one, I understand from Catarina, her sister.'

'Catarina, yes. The pretty young widow. Joanna told me how sad it was that she was left with a young child.'

Nicholas stopped listening. He had not known Delphine had been in Lisbon, but from her words it appeared she had been there just before the time Catarina, if Maria were her child, would have given birth. Surely she must have known about it. Perhaps she did and was keeping her friend's secret. Joanna seemed to have mentioned it in such a way that Senhor Gomez took it for granted Maria was her sister's child.

Before he could demand information, Senhor Gomez was excusing himself to Nicholas, saying he had promised to introduce Delphine to another of his friends, and drew her away. Nicholas left the embassy soon afterwards and spent the rest of the night juggling with dates. He did not know enough. He knew roughly when Maria had been born, and when Catarina had returned home. He must speak to Delphine again.

* * *

Catarina was walking in the village near the rectory when she saw Mr Trubshaw driving a gig along the main street. He was lashing the pony into a gallop and apparently talking to himself, as his mouth was opening and shutting and he kept shaking his head. He drew to a clattering halt outside the small house belonging to the village constable, and without bothering to tie up the pony which was blowing so much it would hardly be likely to run away, he ran up to the door and pounded on it. A few minutes later both he and the constable were clambering into the gig. Mr Trubshaw turned it and set off back towards the Grange.

Wondering what had made the usually calm agent behave so oddly, she strolled back to the Dower House. Blodwen came into her bedroom as she was removing her hat, and was clearly excited.

'My lady, there's been a robbery at the

Grange. One of the footmen came down here, sent by Mr Trubshaw, he was, to ask if we'd had any trouble ourselves.'

'You mean someone broke into the house?'

'Yes, indeed, through one of the dining-room windows. None of the servants heard a thing; they only discovered it this morning when one of the gardeners saw the broken window. I suppose, with none of the family there, the dining room would not be in use.'

'What did they steal? Do you know?'

'Small pieces of silverware, they say. Easy enough to carry away in their pockets, but worth some money. I wonder if it was thieves from Bristol? Perhaps they think it's easier to break into country houses where there are no neighbours to see them like in a town.'

That made sense, but Catarina was suspicious. After the trouble Mr Lewis had encountered she suspected the culprit came from nearer home. She hoped it was not Dan. Despite everything she had a sneaking sympathy for him. There was also a mild feeling of guilt, which she knew was irrational, but which persisted, that it had been her own cook Ellen who had tempted him to betray his wife, which had led to Ellen's murder.

Blodwen was still talking, a scarcely concealed excitement beneath her scandalized tones.

'Mr Staines has looked all round the Dower House and now he is checking the garden. He said there are no signs anyone has entered the house and nothing is missing. He had me check your jewellery, my lady, but I told him, I did, that no one could have come into your bedroom without your being aware of it. My lady is a light sleeper, I told him; she always wakes if the baby cries during the night, but 'Better safe than sorry', he says to me.'

Catarina was not listening. Mr Trubshaw would be bound to report the theft to Jeremy who would probably come down to Marshington. She shivered. She could face seeing Jeremy, but if Nicholas came too she would probably see him, and that would be unbearable.

She had schooled herself to bury her thoughts deep in her mind. It did no good to brood over their encounters, or regret what might have been. At some time she would no doubt have to see him again, for he would occasionally visit his brother here. She hoped it would not be soon, she needed time to regain enough composure for when she once more came face to face with him.

★ ★ ★

Nicholas had to go to the embassy to discover Delphine's direction. The young man he saw

253

who gave it to him smiled knowingly, then blushed and stammered an apology when he encountered Nicholas's most arrogant look.

Nicholas nodded and turned away. Fortunately the house where she was staying was not far away and he decided to walk there. To his frustration he found that Delphine had gone out of Paris with friends for a few days, so he left a message asking to speak to her as soon as she returned, then went back to his own rooms.

By the time she replied to his message he was fretting with unconcealed impatience. Chettle, normally chatty, was careful not to make a sound or utter any but the most essential words when in his master's presence. Nicholas neither noticed nor, if he had done so, would he have cared.

He felt an enormous burden lift from his spirits when a note came from Delphine, inviting him to call on her that afternoon. It was irrational, he told himself, it didn't change anything, but it brought him closer to discovering more about Catarina's time in Lisbon. He had almost reached Delphine's address when it suddenly occurred to him that he could hardly walk straight in and demand to know whether Catarina had been pregnant when Delphine knew her last November in Lisbon. Besides, if she were in

Catarina's confidence, she might not tell him.

Delphine welcomed him with a slightly puzzled air.

'My lord, how can I be of help?' she asked, when he was seated in her drawing room.

'I believe you were in Lisbon last year. Did you meet Joanna and her husband, Eduardo? Was it a good match? Catarina told me she was happy, but she is so far away and, I understand, not a very satisfactory correspondent. Do you believe the man will treat her well?'

Delphine shook her head. 'I didn't see Joanna in Lisbon. In fact, I only knew she had been there when I met Catarina again in England. Catarina never mentioned her and I rather assumed she had been staying elsewhere. We left Portugal in November, before Eduardo and the other Brazilians arrived, so I never met him.'

'Catarina was living there alone? I find that rather odd.'

'Joanna may have been with her, but I saw Catarina briefly one day, just long enough to invite her to the farewell dinner we were giving our friends. At the dinner itself, we were only able to exchange a few words.'

'And you left in mid-November, I believe?'

'Yes. My lord, why these strange questions?'

Nicholas thought quickly.

'Something Catarina said to me once, which rather puzzled me. She was not staying with her family, then?'

'I don't think any of them live in Lisbon. But why don't you ask her yourself? You will be visiting your brother in Marshington soon, no doubt, and will meet her there.'

It was a question, and suddenly Nicholas was certain Delphine knew about his proposal and was encouraging him to renew it.

'I will be going back to England soon, but I will have to visit my own home first. I have been away rather longer than I expected.'

He escaped, but with much to ponder. He sat in his rooms toying with a glass of brandy and tried to work it all out. Ladies of Catarina's class did not go to parties when on the verge of motherhood, and Delphine's dinner party had been very close to the date of Maria's birth. Neither would they attend such a party for at least three weeks after giving birth. Therefore it seemed conclusive that Maria was not Catarina's own child. Yet Joanna seemed to have told the Brazilian the child belonged to her sister.

She could not, however have been telling the truth about a cousin dying. Thomas was adamant no such cousin existed. He had once thought the cousin may have given birth to an illegitimate child, and quite possibly a strict Portuguese family might have disowned her, but he trusted Thomas to have discovered that. The old housekeeper he had talked to would, he was sure, have said something when he was asking such specific questions. If there was no cousin, why had she adopted a child? A glimmering of a possible solution to the mystery began to form in his thoughts.

Suddenly making up his mind, he called for Chettle, gave orders for his bags to be packed immediately, and sallied forth to settle all his bills. He would go first to Brooke Court, send for Jeremy if his brother were not there, and discover what he could of Catarina's present whereabouts. Then, if she was at the Dower House, he would go to Marshington and make her tell him the truth.

13

It was October before Jeremy returned to Marshington Grange. Mrs Eade had learned from Mr Trubshaw that he was staying somewhere in the north, but had omitted to tell any of his relatives exactly where. It was only when he appeared one day at Brooke Court that he could be told about the theft.

'What the devil they expected me to do about it, even if I had been here, I can't imagine,' he said to Catarina, when he called on her the day after he arrived.

'There have been several more incidents, despite the watch people are keeping,' Catarina told him. 'Most of them are small, and from gardens only, not from inside houses.'

'What kind of thefts? Things they can sell, like my silver?'

'No; food, such as thefts of eggs and the occasional chicken, or winter vegetables dug up from gardens. Mr Trubshaw keeps suggesting another manhunt through the woods; he is convinced it is Dan living there.'

'I thought they'd driven the fellow away last time.'

'Apparently not. But he cannot find enough people to make it worth while. Only the better off men who have been robbed show any enthusiasm for it. The villagers tell him it was unsuccessful last time, Dan managed to elude the searchers, so why should they bother, especially as he would be unable to offer them payment.'

'If I catch him, or anyone else robbing me, I'll make sure he is transported. It doesn't do to show weakness, or others begin to take advantage.'

'Many of the villagers are already short of food,' Catarina said, 'I and a few more do what we can; we give them money, but even when there is money there is little to buy.'

'There's plenty of work in the towns,' Jeremy said. 'I'm told many countryfolk are leaving the land, so there must be. If they are not able to support themselves here they should move. Of course, if they had listened to me and been willing to amalgamate their old-fashioned strips, they might be faring better now.'

'Even the ones who did that are suffering,' Catarina said sharply. 'No one can do well with the sort of weather we've had this summer, when the crops won't ripen and there are shortages of everything. My own gardeners complain that the vegetables are poor quality, small, and in some cases they rot before we can save them. It isn't the fault of the farmers.'

Jeremy grinned at her and for a fleeting second she could have imagined it was Nicholas sitting opposite. It had been bad enough anticipating the embarrassment of meeting him again, but to have his younger brother living here, constantly reminding her of him, would be torture.

'You always appear willing to support the weak and unfortunate,' he said, 'and that's probably why all the villagers love you. Oh, don't blush, you should hear the compliments they heap on you. Whenever I am in the village it's Lady Brooke helped someone, or gave them some food or money, and I swear, if the Church of England had saints you would be in the running for canonization!'

Catarina laughed. 'What nonsense! Who else is to help them? Walter was always generous, especially when times were bad, or someone had suffered some misfortune. I can give them money, but there is little point when there is almost no food to buy.'

Soon afterwards Jeremy left her, saying he intended to ride round the estate and visit his tenants to talk with them to see what could be done to help matters.

'I'm not heartless, Catarina. I will help

wherever I can. I have to carry on Walter's traditions, don't I?'

She had a suspicion he was mocking her, but surely he would listen to the villagers and his tenants, and if he did not try to help he would be utterly unfeeling. She did not believe he was.

It was several hours later, almost dusk. She was up in the nursery playing with Maria, who was approaching her first birthday and trying to walk, when she heard a commotion outside. She looked up and went to peer out of the window which overlooked the small front garden. She could hear several men shouting, but could see little. Then there was the sound of a shot, and two men on horseback galloped past the Dower House.

'My lady, what is it?' Clarice asked nervously. Her English had improved, but she now spoke with the local accent.

'I don't know, but we had better not venture out.'

She stayed watching. The shouting had ceased and she sensed the men making the noise had departed. Then she saw a man running up the path to the front door to hammer on it.

Catarina went swiftly from the room and leaned over the banisters.

'Staines,' she called to the butler who was approaching the door. 'Don't open unless you know who it is and what they want!'

'No, my lady, of course not. We heard the shot from the kitchen.'

He pushed home the bolt on the door before shouting through the thick oak to ask who was making such a noise. Catarina could not hear the reply, but suddenly Staines was pulling back the bolt and dragging open the door. Before she could ask what was happening he ran outside.

Puzzled, apprehensive, she ventured down the stairs and reached the front door just as two men came through the gate and up the path. One of them was Staines. They were carrying another man between them. Staines, looking across to her, spoke.

'It's Mr Jeremy, my lady. He's been attacked and has a nasty wound to his head.'

★ ★ ★

Liza and Blodwen were standing at the back of the entrance hall, looking apprehensive.

'Go and make sure everything in the green bedroom is ready, Liza. Blodwen, get a warming pan and some hot bricks wrapped in flannel. Send one of the men to fetch the doctor. Can you carry him upstairs?' Catarina asked. 'The room at the back, on the left, is ready.'

The second man helping to carry Jeremy was Mr Lewis.

'My fellow's already gone for Dr Holt,' he said. 'Can you get some hot water and plenty of rags, and something for bandages?' he added, as he and Staines carefully began to negotiate the stairs. 'He's bleeding badly.'

Catarina went to organize this and, by the time she went to the bedroom, the men had stripped off Jeremy's boots, breeches and coat and laid him in the big bed.

She could see he had been viciously beaten about the head. A large swelling had risen on one side and he was bleeding from a severe cut on the other. One arm hung at an odd angle and seemed to be broken.

Mr Lewis took control, smiling at her briefly and taking some of the sheeting she had torn to strips to serve as bandages.

'I've had a fair bit of experience tending my men when they've had accidents,' he said, as he dipped the sheeting in the water and began gently wiping away the blood. 'He's been knocked unconscious, poor lad.'

'Who was it?'

He seemed willing to talk as he worked gently on Jeremy's head.

'We didn't see. They scattered when I fired

263

my gun in the air. But I've a fair idea who they are.'

'How many were there? We heard several voices.'

'Half a dozen, at least, maybe more. I'll hazard they lay in wait for him just inside the gates, where the trees give some cover. I told him to take care and always have a groom with him when he went out, but these young 'uns always think they know better. It was a fortunate thing for him I was riding back from the village, or it might have been even worse.'

Staines, who had gone downstairs, now came softly into the room followed by the doctor.

'My lady,' the doctor nodded a greeting. 'So, Mr Lewis, you'll be doing my job, will you?'

'Not now you're here, Dr Holt. I'd far rather you set this arm, then if it's crooked I won't be blamed.'

How could he jest when Jeremy lay comatose in front of them, Catarina wondered.

The doctor trod over to the bed.

'Nasty. Your man explained what had happened. I'd better have a good look at him. My lady, perhaps you would excuse us?'

Realizing she was tactfully being got rid of,

Catarina went out of the room and back to the nursery, where she found Blodwen and Clarice talking softly together.

'Is Mr Brooke dead?' Blodwen asked.

'No, but he's seriously injured. Clarice, put Maria to bed and try not to let her sense there is something wrong. Blodwen, I'm going to write a note to tell Mr Brooke's people he is here. Can you ask one of the men to be ready to ride up to the Grange with it?'

Before this could be done, however, a groom from the Grange arrived, saying Jeremy's horse had arrived back in his stable, cut about the legs and in a frightened lather.

Catarina waited in the drawing room for the doctor to finish whatever ministrations he had to do for Jeremy. With no urgent tasks to occupy her, she began to tremble. The shock had been so sudden. She found it hard to believe any of the villagers would have attacked Jeremy. Would he recover?

When Staines appeared and handed her a glass of brandy she smiled her thanks.

'I know you don't normally drink it, but it will do you good,' he said.

'Have one yourself,' she said, 'and I think all the others need something as well, to help them sleep. I'm sure I'll have nightmares.'

'I'll sit up with Mr Brooke,' Staines said, 'in

case he comes to during the night.'

'What would I do without you!'

A moment later, as Catarina was sipping the brandy, almost choking at the unfamiliar burning sensation in her throat, Dr Holt came into the room. He accepted a glass of brandy and sat opposite Catarina.

'He's in a bad way. I don't like that head wound,' he said, without any prevarication. 'He can't be moved. Can your servants manage to care for him? Staines is a reliable chap, and your maids seem sensible lasses. At least they didn't go off into hysterics.'

'Of course we will care for him.'

'Send for his valet; he can help look after his needs. And I think you ought to let his brother know. We'll do our best, but I'm making no predictions. I've seen men with less serious wounds develop a fever and be gone within the week.'

★　★　★

Nicholas was in the estate office early the next morning talking with his agent when his butler came in carrying a letter.

'My lord, I apologize for interrupting, but this has just been delivered; it's from Marshington Grange. The man who brought it said it was urgent. He's waiting for a reply.'

With a brief smile at his agent Nicholas broke the seal. He was finding it tedious back in England, doing all the humdrum tasks involved in running a large estate, though his agent and other senior servants were so well trained they were fully capable of managing without him, but he could not yet leave to go to Marshington.

The address was the Dower House and for a moment his heart leapt. Had Catarina repented of her refusal? But she would never have written to him to say so. And the man must have ridden through the night. He was suddenly apprehensive and scanned the brief few lines rapidly. Then he dropped the paper on to his desk and felt numb.

'My lord, what is it? Bad news?' the agent asked.

The butler went to the decanter and brought across a glass of brandy.

'Drink this, my lord, you've gone as pale as a ghost.'

Nicholas swallowed and tried to pull himself together.

'My brother has been badly hurt. Tell the man I will follow him as soon as I can pack some clothes. I'm sorry, but I will have to leave you to do the best you can, as I don't know how long I'll be away. Can you ask Lady Mortimer to come here, but please don't alarm Miss Olivia? Get Chettle to pack what I'll need for a week or two; he can come with me. I'll drive the curricle. Send to the stables.'

The butler was almost out of the room before this string of commands finished, already talking to a footman to pass on some of them.

'I'll go, my lord, but please give Mr Jeremy my good wishes,' the agent said, gathering up his papers and backing out of the room.

Nicholas nodded. When he was alone he sank his head in his hands for a moment. Catarina's note had said Jeremy had suffered a serious head wound the previous evening and was still unconscious when she wrote.

We are keeping him at the Dower House as the doctor advises he must not be moved.

It must be serious, especially if he was still unconscious several hours after the accident. Catarina had not said what had caused it, and Nicholas wondered if he had suffered a bad fall from a horse. He was an excellent rider, but there were always accidents.

His reflections were cut short as Lady Mortimer entered the room, looking anxious.

'Nicholas, what on earth is it? The servants

are all in a pother and you look dreadful.'

He explained. 'I must go to him; it sounds serious, but please don't worry Olivia. I'll send the groom back to you with a report when I discover just how badly hurt he is.'

'Of course you must go, and don't worry about Olivia. She is relishing being back at home. I can keep her mind occupied with plans for Christmas.'

There might not be any Christmas celebrations, Nicholas thought, as he set off, then he forced himself to pay attention to his driving. The roads were muddy and the horses found it heavy going, but it would be a disaster if he too had an accident. Maybe he would have been better advised to ride. But he would probably need Chettle and his tiger, and he needed a few changes of linen.

His thoughts raced ahead. He would make his headquarters at Marshington Grange, Catarina would be having enough extra to do if Jeremy had to remain at the Dower House. Could she hire a nurse? Was there a suitable woman in the village? He could perhaps relieve her of some tasks and Chettle would be useful; he'd had some experience of nursing with his former master before the old man had died.

Cursing the difficult conditions of the roads, he made what speed he could. It was

269

dusk before he pulled up his tired horses outside the Dower House.

★　★　★

It had been a terrible day. Jeremy remained unconscious. The doctor had been twice, and on the second occasion he suggested that the village midwife ought to be here to look after him.

Catarina had known the woman ever since she'd married Walter, and shuddered at the thought of having such a one in her house. She was fat, with greasy hair and dirty hands. She was for ever laughing raucously, or airing her opinions in her loud, unpleasant voice. Catarina had been thankful she would never have to depend on her assistance, since she would not ever have a child.

Catarina was about to say they would be able to manage when Jeremy's valet, who was in the room, said fiercely he was quite capable of doing all that was necessary for his master. Mr Brooke abominated being fussed by females.

He cast an apologetic glance at Catarina when he realized what he had said, but she smiled at him and gently shook her head.

'We can manage, I'm sure,' she told the doctor.

As the day wore on she began to wonder if they really could manage. Though Jeremy lay comatose, his plight influenced everyone in the house. Staines, having sat up all night, spent the morning sleeping and, somehow, without his calming influence, the household seemed unable to function properly. Cook complained that the bread refused to rise, the kitchen maid burnt all the toast and let one of the saucepans boil dry so that the kitchen filled with reeking black smoke. They forgot to replenish the fire in the nursery and Maria was unusually fractious. Clarice became tearful and said she wanted to go home to Portugal as soon as the baby was weaned.

So when Nicholas appeared Catarina welcomed him warmly.

'Thank heavens you are here! Maybe now everyone will be able to behave normally!'

'Catarina. How is Jeremy? Is he badly hurt? I have to thank you for taking him in.'

'You'll wish to see him immediately, my lord,' Catarina replied, suddenly recalling their last meeting and its unfortunate ending. 'He is still unconscious, but he is moving a little, restless, and we think that is a good sign.'

She led Nicholas up to Jeremy's room and left him there to talk to the valet. Half an hour later he came downstairs and found her in the drawing room. Staines had a glass of Madeira ready and Nicholas downed it in one swallow. Staines took the glass and refilled it, then quietly left the room.

'What happened?'

'He was attacked by several men, just inside the gates. We heard them shouting, but could not tell what they were saying. We don't know who they were. Mr Lewis and one of his men arrived with a shotgun and frightened them away. That is all I know.'

'He seems to have been beaten savagely, around the head especially. Those wounds are always the most dangerous. I need to talk to the doctor.'

'He is coming back this evening. My lord, will you have dinner here? I can have a small bedroom prepared for you if you prefer to stay here rather than sleep at the Grange.'

'Thank you. I have eaten nothing all day and suddenly feel ravenous. As for the bedroom . . . ' He hesitated and gave her a quizzical look. 'I would prefer to be near him, but it could harm your reputation.'

Catarina cared nothing for that.

'What reputation do I have to lose?'

Fortunately, she thought, Staines announced dinner at that moment and she led the way into the dining room. While he was present serving them they talked of Nicholas's stay in

Paris; he gave her Delphine's messages and good wishes, and she told him something of what was happening in the village, the general hardship and the discontent many of the villagers felt towards Jeremy.

'You think it was some of the villagers who feel hard done by who attacked him?'

'Who else could it have been? I've had plenty of time to consider it. It's highly unlikely some roving band would set upon him so viciously.'

'There are such bands. Many of the soldiers now have no occupation. One can see many in the towns and on the roads, begging, especially those who lost limbs. The stronger ones who cannot find jobs have resorted to more violent means of feeding themselves.'

Staines coughed. 'My lady.'

'Yes, Staines?'

'The man with Mr Lewis told me today he thought he recognized one of the men. He said it looked like Dan.'

'So he is still around,' Catarina said. 'Yes, he feels he has many grievances. He was suspected of setting fire to Mr Lewis's barn, so he has the potential for violence. And he could have persuaded the friends he still has in the village to join him. Now they are facing such a hard winter, without much food, they could have been willing to attack Jeremy.

They blame him, even though it's unreason-able, for all that's befallen them.'

'The young fool has partly brought it on himself. My lady, if you are agreeable, I will sit here with Jeremy tonight.'

'You must be exhausted, driving all the way from Brooke Court. Couldn't Staines sit up again?'

'I would not sleep. Not until he shows some sign of improvement.'

'There is a comfortable armchair I could have brought into the room, my lord,' Staines said. 'You will be able to doze. Or I could have a truckle bed brought in from my lady's room.'

Nicholas opted for the armchair. Just at that moment the doctor was announced and he accompanied him up to Jeremy's room.

Later, as Dr Holt left, he told Catarina Jeremy was showing signs of waking up, so he was hopeful he would make a recovery.

'Though we cannot yet tell whether his faculties have been impaired. We know so little about the brain and what can happen to it from such injuries as Mr Brooke has received. Send for me at any time if there are changes that worry you, but I hope that by morning he will have recovered his senses.'

★　★　★

When Catarina peeped into Jeremy's room before she went to bed, Nicholas was sprawled in the armchair, fast asleep. She told herself she ought not to, but she could not resist standing and looking down at him.

His hair was ruffled, not in its usual carefully dishevelled state, but as though he had raked his fingers through it repeatedly. He had torn off his cravat, and without it he looked surprisingly vulnerable. She saw how uncommonly long his dark lashes, spread over his cheeks, were. Unfair, a small voice inside her said. Girls would give a great deal for such natural assets. His cheekbones stood out, slanted, with hollows below them. He looked thinner than when she had last seen him, but perhaps she could not recall his features quite accurately.

A shadow darkened his chin and she could see the individual hairs of his beard. His lips were slightly open, relaxed, and Catarina wondered what it would be like to kiss them, to have them pressed against her own. She shivered. Nicholas opened his eyes and looked up at her, smiling.

Then he recalled why he was there and sat up, frowning, looking across at Jeremy.

'I didn't mean to fall asleep,' he said softly. 'This chair was a mistake. Is Jeremy the same? Were you guarding him for me?'

Catarina shook her head. 'He looks the same. Would you like me to wake someone to stay here with you?'

'No, I was used to having a quick doze whenever I could while I was in the army. I won't fall asleep again.'

To make sure of it he rose from the chair and placed a hard stool beside the bed.

'Then I'll say goodnight,' Catarina whispered, and went slowly back to her own bedroom. Why had circumstances conspired to make it impossible for her to accept his offer?

She was soon asleep, but in the middle of the night was awoken by shouts. After a moment she realized it came from Jeremy's room, across the corridor from her own. Stopping only to fling on a brocade dressing-gown she hurried across and flung open the door. Jeremy was struggling with Nicholas, who was trying to hold him down, raving and shouting curses, interspersed with cries which sounded like cries of pain.

Staines arrived on Catarina's heels and went to help Nicholas.

'The doctor left a sedative in case he became restless,' Nicholas gasped. 'It's on the table, but I can't reach it.'

Catarina went and found the small glass and, while Staines held Jeremy's arms, which had been flailing about, Nicholas managed to get him to swallow most of the medicine. It soon took effect, and Jeremy quietened, and looked as though he was sleeping naturally.

Nicholas stood up, sighing, and dragging a hand across his face.

'It happened so suddenly. One moment he was lying there, the next he was awake and trying to get out of bed. I'm so sorry we woke you.'

'You have a cut on your forehead,' Catarina said, stretching out her hand as if to touch it, then suddenly drawing back.

'He must have hit me with the splint on his arm. It's nothing.'

She took refuge in practicalities.

'It's bleeding. Stay here while I fetch something to cover it. Staines, could you ask Cook or one of the maids to make a pot of tea? I think we might all benefit from one.'

'I'll make it, my lady. Have you all you need?'

She nodded and fetched some of the bandages the doctor had not used, and some soothing balm made with comfrey leaves. Forcing herself to control her trembling as she touched him, she applied the salve while Nicholas sat in the armchair. The cut was not, as he had said, serious, but it had bled copiously. She wound a strip of bandage round his head and suddenly giggled.

'You look like an Indian in a turban. Joanna and I had some pictures in a book we were given when we were small.'

He grasped her hand and pulled her gently towards him. She shivered and tried not to snatch her hand away.

'Thank you, Catarina,' he said, and lifted her hand to his mouth, planting a firm kiss into the palm.

14

By morning Jeremy was in a high fever, and Nicholas refused to leave him. Catarina took in some lukewarm water and Nicholas and Jeremy's valet took it in turns to sponge him down.

He was never still, alternately raging and shouting, or muttering words no one could understand, so slurred was his voice. By evening, though, he seemed to have exhausted himself and sank into an uneasy sleep. Catarina persuaded Nicholas to come downstairs and eat dinner.

'You must have some sleep,' she told him. 'You will not be fit to care for him if you collapse from exhaustion.'

'Don't fuss! Oh, I apologize, that was unpardonable of me when you are being so kind.'

'You are too tired to know what you are saying, my lord. There is a bed waiting for you. Staines insists he will stay up tonight with Chettle who has been demanding to help.'

Nicholas resisted, but was eventually persuaded to go to bed after Chettle had promised to wake him should Jeremy show any signs of getting worse.

Catarina, who had slept badly herself, soon went to bed, but was woken in the middle of the night by piercing wails coming from Maria's nursery. She struggled into her dressing-gown and went to see what was the matter. Clarice, looking harassed, was sitting rocking the child in her arms.

'What is it?'

'She is cutting some big teeth, my lady, and has a fever. I have put a little clove oil on her gums, but it does not seem to help. And she throws away the teething ring whenever I try to give it to her.'

'I'll take her downstairs. She will waken his lordship, and he needs his rest. You try and sleep for the rest of the night.'

She carried Maria down into the library, which was a small room, and where she had been sitting the previous day. She had been sitting in front of a good fire and the room was still warm. Raking out the ashes she threw on some kindling from the wood basket and soon the fire was blazing, the perfume of apple logs filling the room.

Catarina curled up in one of the deep chairs, Maria on her lap, and began to sing quietly to the child. Normally Maria loved these songs, but she was so miserable with the pain of her new tooth cutting through the gums that it took a long while to calm her and for her to fall asleep.

She seemed so deeply asleep Catarina considered the advisability of carrying Maria back to her own bed, but decided it might wake the child. If she began to cry again she would wake Nicholas. Easing her arm, which was aching from the weight of the baby, she wriggled into a more comfortable position and was soon sleeping.

It was there Nicholas found her when he came downstairs in search of breakfast. The opening of the door woke her. Catarina blinked, wondering for a moment where she was. Then she tried to move and Maria began to wail again at being disturbed.

Her limbs were numb, and she winced as she tried to stand up. Nicholas came across the room swiftly and lifted Maria out of her arms.

Catarina smiled her thanks, then realized her hair was in a tangle. Some time during the night she had lost her sleeping cap and, worst of all, her dressing-gown skirts had ridden up while she slept and she was revealing her ankles and bare feet. She blushed with mortification, but luckily Nicholas seemed to be concentrating on the baby and hadn't appeared to notice.

Maria, startled, had stopped crying and was considering him closely.

'So this is your adopted daughter,' he said. 'How old is she? I've never had anything to do with babies, so I have no idea.'

'It's her first birthday in November, on the fifteenth of the month,' Catarina said, pulling her dressing-gown round her and searching for her cap.

'She's a very pretty child.'

Catarina had by now managed to struggle out of the chair.

'I hope she did not disturb you during the night. She was in pain from her new teeth.'

Maria, seeming to understand, opened her mouth wide and smiled beguilingly at Nicholas, who laughed.

'She did not disturb me; I slept well. And Jeremy seems a little calmer, the fever is less, they told me when I looked in on him. She is already a flirt.'

Like her mother, Catarina thought. Joanna was missing so much by rejecting her child.

'I had best take her upstairs, or she will soon be crying for her breakfast. What is the time? If Cook has not already prepared breakfast please ask for whatever you want.'

★ ★ ★

Nicholas watched Catarina leave the room, smiling at the look of confusion there had been on her face when she realized her ankles were visible. Very attractive ankles they were, too.

He'd almost commented the child looked very like her, had her eyes and hair, but had recollected just in time that she could not be Catarina's baby if Delphine's information was to be trusted. Why should it not be?

She had not reappeared by the time he had eaten, but while Staines had waited on him he said Jeremy had passed a reasonably peaceful night, though his fever had not diminished. Chettle and Jeremy's own valet, Bates, were continuing to sponge him down.

'We could understand some of the things he said, my lord,' Staines reported, 'and he seemed to be worried about some business to do with Mr Trubshaw. My lady wondered whether you might go up to the Grange and see him? Even though Mr Jeremy does not appear to know what he is saying, if you could report all is well it might reassure him.'

'I'll decide after I've seen him. Is the doctor coming this morning?'

'He'll be here.'

'Good. Now, Staines, don't you think you ought to be in bed? You look exhausted yourself, man, and I had a good sleep. You ought not to be bothering to wait on me.'

'I will sleep soon, my lord. But if I might be so bold, my lady has not stepped out of doors since the accident, and she is looking pale. Could you persuade her to drive with you for an hour?'

Would she agree, Nicholas wondered. Fate had thrown them together again and he was even more certain he still wanted her. Paris had not cured him of that longing, despite the uncertainty the Brazilian's words had at first produced. He thought he had divined the truth. But while Jeremy was so ill he could not think of making another attempt to win her. She would undoubtedly consider it inappropriate, even if she had changed her mind and was willing to accept him. But Staines's suggestion was sensible. She needed to keep up her strength.

There was no change in Jeremy's condition, but at least he was no worse. The doctor, when he appeared, seemed satisfied.

'The lump on his head is getting smaller and there is no sign of the open wound becoming infected,' he said, after examining Jeremy closely. 'Continue the sponging. If he wakes try to get him to take some chicken broth. I will come back tomorrow.'

Nicholas went to look for Catarina, eventually finding her in her small still room, pounding some dried herbs for use in the kitchen.

'I intend to drive up to the Grange to talk to Trubshaw. Staines believes Jeremy is worried about something. Will you come with me?'

Catarina opened her mouth to speak and Nicholas, convinced she was about to refuse, went on hurriedly, 'You know the estate, better even than Trubshaw, and we might be able to settle whatever it is and tell Jeremy. It might help quiet him. Besides, you look pale, and a drive in the fresh air would do you good. You cannot afford to become ill. Too many people depend on you.'

Catarina hesitated, then nodded.

'Very well, my lord. I confess it would be pleasant to get out of doors and though it is cold, for once it is a sunny day. I will be finished here in ten minutes, and then I will change.'

'I will have my horses put to. I've been using your stables, in case I had a sudden need for my curricle. We are all so grateful for your hospitality.'

They spoke very little on the way to the Grange, commonplace remarks about the weather, the state of the farms, work which needed to be done, but Nicholas was satisfied. Catarina seemed more at ease.

When Jeremy recovered she might be prepared to listen to him.

They found Mr Trubshaw in the estate office. He immediately asked how Jeremy was.

'Mr Brooke's valet gives me a bulletin. I have not been to enquire myself because I did not wish to add more pressure on you, my lady.'

'We understand,' Catarina said.

'My brother seems to be fretting about something. We wondered whether there is some unfinished business, something he was discussing with you just before he was attacked? If we could tell him all is well, it might aid his recovery.'

'There were the usual estate matters,' Trubshaw said, 'but Mr Brooke would be content to leave those to me, as he has done while he was away. The only new thing which might be causing him to worry is a deputation which came to see him the day before he was attacked.'

'A deputation? From the village?' Catarina asked. 'That sounds as though it is an important matter. What did they want?'

'They came to say it had been such a bad harvest this year they had barely enough grain to feed themselves this coming winter. They also needed to slaughter more animals than usual, including some of the oxen used for ploughing. In the spring they would have to purchase more, so they asked whether Mr Brooke would help, by not asking for rents.'

'What did he say?' Nicholas asked.

'He said he wanted to talk more with them, and he would come to the village on the following day to see them. He told me afterwards that he meant to see their grain stores for himself and count their animals, before he decided. But he was quite willing to consider the idea. And I know what they said was correct.'

'Do you think he may have been on that errand when he was attacked?'

'These men were sensible ones? Not hotheads?' Catarina asked.

He reeled off a list of names.

'They were mainly the ones who had agreed to amalgamate their holdings, with a couple of others.'

'Then tell them, please, on my authority, that they need pay no rent this quarter. We will consider it again come next Lady Day.'

They left Mr Trubshaw looking happier than when they arrived and promising to go and inform the villagers at once.

Nicholas was thoughtful as they began to drive back towards the Dower House.

'I do not believe these fellows were the

ones who attacked Jeremy. He would have agreed with them and told them so.'

'They are not the troublemakers,' Catarina said slowly. 'I know them all and they are honest and hardworking, all of them.'

'Then can you hazard a guess who was responsible?'

'There is Dan, he's grown wilder and more strange this year, but no one can find him. He has friends in the village, young men who do not have regular work, but depend on finding it at times like the harvest, and who must be suffering, even worse than the others.'

'Can you name a few?'

'I can suspect some, but I might be wrong. It would be impossible to prove anything if they all deny it.'

'I'll make it my business to see them in a day or so, when Jeremy is better. If he recovers.'

'Of course he will. My lord, you must not despair. He is already improving. When you tell him what you have done for the villagers, surely that will ease him.'

★   ★   ★

For a few hours it did seem as though the news soothed Jeremy, but that night he became more feverish, and tossed and turned so that it was all Nicholas and Chettle could do to calm him. Catarina, hearing his groans, went to see if she could help and, when she saw the state he was in, sent straight away for the doctor.

For two more days Jeremy suffered a high fever, and Nicholas barely slept. They all feared for his life, and Nicholas vowed that if he died all those who had attacked his brother would hang, if it took him the rest of his own life to track them down.

On Sunday the Reverend Eade preached a sermon against the wickedness of violence. Many of the villagers came up to Catarina afterwards to ask how Mr Brooke was, and to send him their best wishes for a full recovery.

'Them what did it ain't no more'n vicious animals,' one old man said. 'They should be druv out of village.'

'Who do you suppose did it?' Catarina asked, and the names he gave her matched the list she had made for herself.

As suddenly as it had started Jeremy's fever abated, and within a day he was rational and demanding more substantial food than the chicken broth and beef tea which was all the doctor would allow.

On the following day Nicholas came down to breakfast dressed in riding breeches.

'I'm going after them,' he announced.

Catarina had no need to ask who he meant.

'You'll take your groom? Please! We don't want you to be brought home with a broken head.'

'Don't be concerned, I won't be. I'm prepared for them; Jeremy was not. He thinks they stretched a rope across the path, pulling it tight as he reached it, so that it made his horse stumble. He said he was only trotting. That's all he remembers, his horse making a sudden stop, and then falling. That matches the cuts on his horse's legs.'

Catarina tried to comfort herself after he had gone with the thought that the attackers would not dare to assault Nicholas as well. Then her optimism faded and she worried because they had nothing to lose by attacking a second man. They could only be hanged or transported once, and if in a second attack they killed, they might try to escape justice by fleeing.

She was restless all day, and in the afternoon her mood was not eased by Mrs Eade calling.

'My dear Lady Brooke, we have missed you at our little sewing circle, but we do understand that you have been acting the good Samaritan, taking in poor Mr Brooke and having him nursed here at the Dower House. I understand he is much better now.'

'He seems to have turned the corner. We are optimistic.'

'Then he will soon be going back to the Grange?'

'Yes, when the doctor says it is safe to move him.'

'That will no doubt be a comfort to you. You must have had a full house with his brother and their servants.'

'We could not have managed without them.'

'Of course not, and no doubt the earl will be going back there now to make sure everything is in order for Mr Brooke's return.'

Catarina began to have an inkling of what was coming.

'The servants at the Grange are mostly the ones I and my husband employed, and I can assure you they are to be trusted to do whatever is necessary there, Mrs Eade.'

Mrs Eade gave her an impatient look.

'That is understood, my lady. But surely there is no necessity for his lordship to remain here now. He could visit his brother at any time.'

'He is welcome to remain just so long as he believes it necessary, or wishes to be close to Jeremy. That is for him to decide.'

'My lady! Of course you were married at a

very young age and have lived here quietly ever since. You cannot be fully aware of how it looks to the rest of the world for you to be entertaining two bachelors in your home, with no older woman to give you countenance.'

'You mean someone to chaperon me, I collect?'

'Well, if you wish to call it that.'

'I have no need of a chaperon,' Catarina said, her voice quiet, but anger simmering under the surface of her calm. How dared the old busybody come and try to tell her how to behave!

She stood up and began to pace round the room, striving to keep her temper under control. Mrs Eade sniffed.

'There is no need to take me up in such a fashion, my lady. I am considerably older than you, my dear, and, even though I say it myself, much more aware of the world and its censoriousness. Naturally no one believes anything wrong is taking place — '

'I think anyone with common sense would understand that Jeremy has been far too ill to try and seduce me, and the earl has been fully occupied looking after him, which has meant he has had little sleep, and is presumably too worried, if not too tired, for amorousness! If the world's gossips choose to disregard facts like those then I don't think their nasty suspicious suggestions are worth a single farthing!'

Mrs Eade was stuttering with indignation. 'If you refuse to listen to my advice I shall have to ask the Reverend Eade himself to call on you and try to bring you to a sense of what behaviour is proper! Now I will bid you good day!'

'I ask you not to trouble your husband, for I will tell him exactly what I have told you, ma'am. Good day to you.'

Mrs Eade heaved herself out of the chair, her face red. Catarina, after ringing for Staines to show her out, went to stand by the window and looked out of it, breathing deeply, desperately trying to keep back the angry tears which threatened to overwhelm her.

* * *

Nicholas found two of the lads who were suspected of attacking Jeremy working on a narrow strip of land at the edge of one great field. They were brothers, he guessed around sixteen and eighteen years of age. As he rode towards them he saw how skinny they were, dressed in thin rags even on a cold day like today, and the younger was marked with the pits left by smallpox. He felt a moment of unexpected compassion. If he were in such a sorry state, might he not think as they did?

They looked up as he neared them, fright clear in their eyes. They glanced round as if to judge their chances of running, but he was mounted, two grooms rode behind him, and Nicholas held a pistol in one hand. Their shoulders sagging, they waited.

'I believe you assaulted my brother some days past,' he said quietly. 'He nearly died. If he had you would have been hanged for murder. What had he done to you to make you think you had the right to try and kill him?'

'We dain't wanna kill 'im, 'onest,' the older one whined. 'We just wanned ter ask 'im fer money. We've no food in 'ouse, an all 'e wants ter do is tek the land from us.'

'What would you do with the money if you had it?' he asked, again quietly and with a suspicious calm.

'What d'yer think we'd do?' the younger one snarled. 'We'm starvin'; we wanted food.'

'Or ale, perhaps. I ought to send you to the assizes, but I'll make a bargain with you. If you tell me the names of your companions, I'll give you each a guinea, provided you promise to get out of Somerset by tomorrow night. You can waste it on ale and then starve if you choose, but I recommend you use it to get to Bristol, or Southampton, or some other sea port where they are in need of seamen. Perhaps, if you can get to America, or even New South Wales as free men, not convicts, you can begin to make something of your lives. Well?'

They looked at him suspiciously, and he was not at all certain they had understood what he wanted, or his conditions.

'Yer'll gi' us money? A guinea each?'

'If you give me the names of the others who attacked my brother. And promise to be away from Somerset by dusk tomorrow.'

They looked at each other briefly, then the older one nodded and held out his hand.

Nicholas smiled. 'Not yet. I want all the names. I also want you to fetch Dan from wherever he is hiding. Then I want you to bring them here so that I can speak to you all. One of my grooms will accompany each of you, so don't think you can escape them. They both have pistols and orders to shoot anyone who tries to escape.'

It took an hour to round up the other four, none of them apart from Dan over the age of twenty. They were sullen, and clearly did not believe Nicholas's offer of a guinea each to get out of the county.

'If you can decide amongst you where you

prefer to go, I will organize a wagon to take you.'

'Wi' us in chains?' one sneered. 'Yer must think we'm daft! Tek us straight ter gaol, rather.'

'I don't expect you to understand me when I offer my word as a gentleman. But if you do not believe me enough to accept my offer you will certainly be in gaol within days, accused of attempted murder. If any of you have families, you have tonight to make your farewells. If any of your relatives wish to go with you, I can send them on the wagon too. Now, what do you say?'

'We've no choice,' Dan said at last. 'I'm fed up wi' livin' rough. I've been wet an' cold an' 'ungry all summer, an' now winter's 'ere it'll be worse. And I'd rather work me passage ter that there New South Wales an' my Annie than be sent there in chains by a judge. I votes fer Bristol.'

He seemed to be something of a leader. After some argument the others reluctantly agreed with him.

'Be by the Bear at eight in the morning then. You'll receive your guineas after you've been driven to Bristol.'

As he and his grooms rode home he could sense they did not agree with his actions. One, the older, a man of forty, asked if he thought they would all turn up after they'd had a night to think it over.

'They might go into 'iding, like Dan.'

'You heard what he said, it's cold and winter's coming. Somehow I think they were scared of what damage they'd caused and will be thankful to get away, especially as I now know who they are.'

'Who's to go with them?'

'I shall go myself. I'll ride guard and take as many men as can be spared. I have no intention of allowing this scheme to fail.'

15

Mrs Eade was just passing through the gates of the rectory when Nicholas rode through the village. He bowed to her, calling out a greeting, and was rather surprised when she lifted her chin, glared at him and turned away without speaking.

What had offended her, he wondered? Normally she would have been full of irrelevant chatter, asking how Jeremy was, mentioning her own plans, as well as making endless suggestions for things she had decided were the responsibility of the squire.

As he walked up to the Dower House from the stables he found Catarina pacing along the garden paths. She did not hear him and was muttering to herself, her hands clenched into fists. Something had clearly upset her.

He paused at the junction of two paths and, as she swung round the corner, not looking where she was going, she collided with him. He instinctively clutched her to him. She gasped and began to struggle, then realizing who it was she uttered a sharp laugh and tried to push away.

'It's all right, Catarina. What has happened to upset you?'

She was breathing rapidly, but she ceased struggling and he found he did not wish to let her go. She felt so right in his arms, but she was holding herself rigidly, and he did not know if that was out of fury or because of being within his embrace. Suddenly she began to laugh.

'If only that odious, wretched woman could see me now she would believe me past redemption.'

'What woman?'

'The Reverend Mrs Eade, guardian of everyone's reputation, and mine in particular. She has had the impertinence to tell me it is causing scandal for you and Jeremy to be living here without an older woman to chaperon me. How dare she impute such things!'

Nicholas tried not to laugh.

'It has been said that women who go around imagining every other woman is behaving scandalously would, deep in their hearts, like to be doing the same themselves.'

Catarina chuckled and Nicholas felt the tenseness in her body relax.

'Can you imagine Mrs Eade conducting a liaison?'

'Can you think of any man who would be

willing to, with her?'

'Oh dear, we ought not to be abusing the poor woman in this fashion. My lord, please release me.'

He tightened his grip and, as she looked up at him, he dropped a kiss on her forehead. She opened her mouth to protest, but he silenced her by covering her mouth with his own. He felt her stiffen, but suddenly, with a strangled sob, she relaxed against him. For a moment she returned his kisses, then she began to tremble and he released her.

'We have to provide some positive grounds for the gossips, do we not, my love?' he asked lightly, tucking her hand through his arm and turning towards the house.

She nodded, but seemed incapable of speech. He wondered whether his impulsive actions had frightened her.

'Would you like me to move to the Grange?' he asked. 'Jeremy will be fit to move in a few days, but I could relieve you of my presence at once.'

'I am not prepared to let that woman believe her censure has had any effect on me. She has no right to dictate to me, to judge my actions. If you feel compromised, of course, you must leave, but I am tempted to ask you and Jeremy to remain here until he is fit to walk all the way to his own home.'

He chuckled. 'Then, given such a gracious invitation, my lady, we will do just that.'

★ ★ ★

Catarina was sitting in the drawing room after dinner that evening. Nicholas was with Jeremy and this was the first quiet moment she had had since that devastating kiss in the garden. It had felt so right, so natural.

She knew now without any doubt she loved Nicholas, but she would have to avoid any further such occasions. They were too disturbing. Soon Jeremy would be able to go back to his own house and Nicholas would go home. There must be matters which needed his attention. He had been in London, then Brighton and Paris, and could not have spent more than a few weeks at Brooke Court since the spring. Then, perhaps, she might be able to forget him.

She did not know how she would be able to look Mrs Eade in the face when next they met. This time she would not be able to deny any accusations of scandalous behaviour, unless once more she resorted to telling lies. But now they would not help her. Recalling that kiss she knew she would blush and the woman's suspicions would be confirmed.

When Nicholas walked into the room she

wanted to escape, but her legs refused to obey her and she remained sitting in her chair. At dinner the conversation had been mainly about the scheme of taking the lads who had attacked Jeremy away from the village. With Staines there they could not discuss personal matters.

Catarina had approved the scheme.

'I would not want them to be charged and turned into convicts. This way, if they can find their way to New South Wales it will be as free men. I understand there are many land grants, and it is possible to live well, now the initial difficulties have been overcome.'

'At first Jeremy was not in favour, but I persuaded him there would be less resentment in the village if we simply sent them away rather than taking them to court.'

Now, however, they were alone, and she felt embarrassed. She ought not to have responded to his kisses, but they had been so sweet, she had not been able to help herself.

He sat down facing her, close enough to reach out and touch her. She shrank back into her chair.

'Catarina, my dear, you cannot fail to know now how I feel about you. I made a dreadful mistake when I first tried to ask you to marry me and hurt you badly.'

She tried to interrupt, to tell him she

understood, but he did not allow her to speak. Leaning forward he managed to capture her hands. His were warm and so comforting Catarina longed above all else to forget her scruples and follow her heart. But she dared not. She had told too many lies. When he discovered it, as he must, he would despise her. Besides, she suspected he had spoken to protect her. Mrs Eade had suggested she was ruining her reputation, and he may have felt the justice of this and was endeavouring to preserve it by offering her marriage. She could never permit him to sacrifice himself like this.

He went on, 'I cannot apologize enough, but I want to spend the rest of my life making it up to you. I understood your refusal in London, you must have been hurt still. But after today, you cannot, I think, deny your feelings for me. Will you not reconsider and accept me? I know now I love you and I believe you love me. Catarina, my dear, I want you as my wife, more than I have ever before wanted anything.'

She had to be firm, she had to withstand the appeal, but it was the hardest thing she had ever done.

'My lord, I am honoured, but I cannot! There are reasons, insuperable reasons why I cannot marry you. My reputation does not need protecting. Mrs Eade is a foolish woman.'

'Catarina, that has nothing to do with it. I love you. I want you to be my wife. What are these insuperable reasons? Can you not tell me and we will see whether we can overcome them? I can think of nothing to stop us unless you are already married!'

'Please, my lord, I cannot tell you. There are secrets which are not mine to reveal. Now forgive me, I cannot remain.'

She dragged her hands away from his grasp and almost ran from the room. Upstairs she struggled not to succumb to weeping. That would serve no purpose. But oh, how she had longed to give way and throw herself into his arms.

★　★　★

Jeremy by now was able to move about a little and complained he was bored at having to remain in his bedroom all day. Nicholas and his valet carried him downstairs the following morning and installed him on a daybed in the back half of the drawing room, where he could see out of the window.

'Promise you will go back to bed when you feel tired,' Nicholas said. 'I'm leaving Chettle, so he can help your man get you back upstairs. I have to go and see that those miscreants are taken to Bristol. The wagon will be slow, so I will stay there tonight.'

Catarina and Jeremy chatted, played cards and ate a light nuncheon. Because of his broken arm she cut up the meat for him and peeled an apple.

'Thank goodness I am allowed proper food again,' Jeremy said, as he ate the slices of cold chicken and ham.

Afterwards he seemed sleepy, but he refused to go back upstairs.

'I'm perfectly comfortable on that daybed. I'd rather stay there, if I'm not in your way.'

'Of course not. I have letters to write, so I will draw the dividing doors to so as not to disturb you.'

Catarina sat at her escritoire and began a letter to Joanna. After ten minutes or so she heard horses, and glanced out of the window. Had Mrs Eade, as she had threatened, sent her husband to chastise Catarina? If so, the man would regret criticizing her behaviour. A carriage had drawn up just outside the gate. She could see the top of it over the hedge, but not who was in it.

It was not the Reverend Eade Staines showed into the drawing room. To Catarina's astonishment it was her uncle, Sir Ivor, and her cousin, Matthew. She rose to her feet to greet them. Staines offered wine.

'Uncle Ivor. Cousin Matthew. I was not aware you were back in England.'

Matthew grinned at her.

'Or you would no doubt not have been receiving visitors. I've come to claim my child.'

Catarina stared at him in amazement.

'What on earth do you mean?'

He sighed. 'Catarina, do not be stupid. You know that Joanna and I were married and she had a child. That child is mine. Now I am back from Canada and have sold out, I want to live with my family. With Joanna's fortune I can provide a good home for them both. Of course, Joanna's so-called marriage to that Brazilian is bigamous and she will have to return to England. And I understand he is wealthy, and will no doubt be happy to recompense me for having deprived me of my wife, and to keep the scandal quiet.'

'I see,' Catarina said. 'When it suited your purpose you told my poor sister the marriage had been a sham. You repudiated her, leaving her alone and desperate. You had other prospects, it seemed. What happened to the heiress you were planning to marry? Did she discover in time what a despicable rogue you are?'

Matthew laughed and moved towards the door.

'You will sing a different tune when we have the child. We know she is in the house; we have been talking to the people in the village. I am taking her back to Bristol with me now. You will write to Joanna and inform her, and say she can either come home and live with me, or stay with her lover. Of course, if she chooses to do that, she won't see a penny of the fortune her father left her. Legally it belongs to me, her husband.'

'If that marriage was legal. I need to have that proved before you can take your daughter away. Joanna left her with me when she went to Brazil and I intend to keep her.'

'How do you propose to stop us? I don't think your ancient butler will be much opposition.'

On the words he opened the door.

'I suppose the child is upstairs? Do you mean to be sensible and pack what she needs, or do we have to remove her by force?'

'You mean you would kidnap her?'

Matthew, with an oath, swung round at this new voice and saw Jeremy in the hall.

'Who the devil are you?'

'I own Marshington Grange; therefore this Dower House is also mine. I do not choose to have scoundrels such as you in it, so you will leave at once.'

Matthew sneered and moved forward.

'And I suppose you think you can stop us, even though your arm is in a splint. You'll get out of our way unless you want to be hurt again.'

Jeremy stepped aside. Matthew, with a smile of triumph, started towards the stairs only to see Staines and the two valets, both of them young and sturdy, blocking the way.

'What's this? Cousin, do you keep a male harem here in your snug little house? Are you missing Walter's attentions?'

'Get out before you are thrown out,' Catarina said. 'And don't try to come back. We are well protected, as you can see.'

'I'll go for now, but you'll regret defying me, Cousin Catarina! We will be back.'

Jeremy laughed as, trying to maintain their dignity, Matthew and his silent father backed out of the front door. He followed them and watched as they scrambled into their carriage and drove away. Then, growing suddenly pale, he fell into rather than sat in a chair beside the front door.

'I rather think I ought to go back to bed now. Staines, I suggest you secure all the doors and windows, be prepared to repel boarders.'

★ ★ ★

308

Jeremy slept for the remainder of the day. Catarina surmised he had heard at least some of what Matthew had said while he was in the back part of the drawing room, and had made a great effort to summon the help of his own and Nicholas's valet. She relished recalling the look on Matthew's face when, instead of being faced just with the elderly Staines he had found two young, able-bodied men ready to oppose him. He'd known Sir Ivor, who was in his sixties and had said almost nothing during their confrontation, would not have assisted him in forcing his way upstairs. She was impatient to ask Jeremy exactly how much he had heard. Joanna's secret was now probably no longer a secret, at least from Jeremy. Would he tell Nicholas? Who else would discover it? Did Staines know? Or the valets?

There was nothing she could do. She had briefly considered asking Jeremy not to tell Nicholas, but that would involve him in her own deception and she could not do that.

It would be at least afternoon on the following day before Nicholas returned and, if the wagon had not been able to reach Bristol in one day, it could be even later. Catarina wondered what Matthew would do. Did he intend to make another attempt to take Maria? Why did he want her? If he claimed the marriage between himself and Joanna was legal, he could control her fortune. He did not need the child; surely she would only be a nuisance?

The reason came to her in the middle of the night. Afraid Matthew might attempt to snatch the little girl during the hours of darkness, she had a truckle bed made up for herself in the nursery. Staines said the three men would take it in turns to patrol inside the house, so they had taken what precautions they could. Catarina still could not sleep. She was worried for Maria, the truckle bed was uncomfortable and Clarice snored.

Matthew, she suddenly realized, sitting up in bed as she woke from an uneasy doze, no doubt wanted the child as a hostage. He would promise not to harm her if she and Joanna did not attempt to claim Joanna's fortune. She had no illusions about her cousin. He would harm the child if it suited him, in revenge if nothing else.

Jeremy, Staines told her the following day when, heavy-eyed, she was trying to force some breakfast down her constricted throat, meant to stay in bed for at least the morning.

'He found yesterday a strain.'

'But without him we might have lost Maria.'

'Don't fret, my lady. His lordship will be

back tonight and we're all on our guard.'

She could not help worrying, not just about the danger to Maria, but also that soon Nicholas would know all about the lies she had told. She was in no state to deal with the Reverend Eade when he called in the middle of the morning.

He wore his most solemn expression when Staines showed him into the drawing room, the one he put on when he delivered some ranting sermon complaining about the real or imagined sins of his congregation.

'My lady,' he said formally, and refused her invitation to sit down. Instead he paced slowly around the room, coming to lean over her when he thought he had some telling point to make.

'I am here to perform a most unwelcome task,' he said. 'My wife is very hurt at the unseemly manner in which you treated her and her advice the day before yesterday. She is much older than you and, although I hesitate to describe us as worldly, she has been about in the world much more than you have. She is concerned for your reputation.'

'I think I can be trusted to look to my reputation,' Catarina said, furious at being treated to such a scolding as though she were a child. 'Neither she nor you have any authority over me, or any responsibility for me, so I will thank both of you to keep your — to refrain from interfering in my affairs.'

'You are impertinent, speaking to a man of the cloth in such an intemperate manner. But I understand what a strain you have been under since your dear husband died. It is my duty to forgive you.'

Catarina gritted her teeth and stood, the better to face him.

'I neither need nor want your forgiveness.'

He strode towards her and, despite herself, she backed away a couple of paces. Tall and broad, his hands held out in front of him, he was a formidable figure. She was afraid for one dreadful moment that he was about to seize her and, at the very least, shake her.

'That is not the only problem I have come here to resolve. I was visited yesterday by your uncle, Sir Ivor Norton, and his son. They tell me the child you have here is the son's daughter and you are trying to deprive her father of his rights. His wife, your sister, has apparently deserted him and run away with a rich Portuguese merchant.'

'The marriage they claim between my sister and my cousin was a fake! He deceived her; a friend played the part of a parson to make her think she was truly married. Then he deserted her. When she informed him she was expecting his child he repudiated her, and

312

said he was about to marry a girl he had met in Brussels, just before the battle. I have no notion what happened to her, but I suspect she discovered what a scoundrel he was.'

'That, my dear lady, is only what your sister has told you. If she wanted to desert her child and become this other man's concubine, she must have thought it a likely story. I am ashamed to think you believed it.'

'You seem determined to disbelieve me, sir. I will not listen to your bigoted, uncharitable, unchristian remarks any longer, or your slandering of my sister. Please leave my house, immediately.'

'Oh no, you cannot dismiss me so easily. I have come to take the child away to her true parent.'

'What? You can't do that! What right do you have to kidnap a baby?'

'Kidnap! How dare you accuse me of that!'

She really thought he was about to strike her.

'Yes, kidnap! You have no proof of what Matthew says, yet you believe him and not me. Have you seen the marriage certificate of this supposed legal marriage? Have you questioned the witnesses, asked who the clergyman was who conducted the ceremony, seen proof of his power to do so? How can you prove the child I have here is my sister's baby?'

'Sir Ivor is a respected gentleman, and his son has served his country in the army. I tend to believe such people.'

'My uncle is a harsh disciplinarian and as bigoted as you are proving to be, Mr Eade. Now, please do as I ask and leave my house before I have to ask the servants to throw you out.'

'Very well. I will not give you the heathen satisfaction of seeing a man of the cloth mishandled, but I will return with the magistrate and the constable. You will not presume to defy the law, I hope.'

Catarina stared in dismay. The only local Justice now was Sir Humphrey Unwin, and he would have no sympathy for her since she rejected his offer so decisively.

He swept out of the room. Catarina flew up the stairs to check that Maria was safe. She had a horrid feeling he might have been keeping her occupied while Matthew sneaked in and stole the baby.

When she saw Maria playing contentedly with a rag doll Clarice had sewn for her, she collapsed into a chair. Nicholas, she thought, come home, quickly. I need you!

16

Catarina almost wept with relief when Nicholas arrived as she and Jeremy were sitting down to nuncheon. Saying he was exceptionally hungry, since he had started back from Bristol early and it was a very cold day, he joined them. Jeremy declared that after a long sleep he was feeling better than ever, and began to tell Nicholas of the visitors they had endured.

'This man Matthew claimed little Maria was his, and that he was married to Joanna,' he reported, and then glanced at Catarina in remorse. 'Oh, I'm sorry, I shouldn't have said that, should I?'

'I think I had guessed the truth,' Nicholas said gently. 'Maria is so like you, my dear, but you and your sister are also very alike. She's Joanna's child, isn't she? Do you fear they will return?'

She nodded, accepting his statement, and explained how she believed Matthew intended to use Maria.

'Then the first thing to do is move everyone to the Grange. There are more people there, young, strong footmen and grooms, and we can repel invaders. I will send for carriages if you, Catarina, will tell your servants to pack what you will all need for a few days.'

'All of them?' Jeremy asked. 'Even the cook and the gardeners?'

'We don't want to leave anyone at the mercy of the Reverend Eade's tirades, do we? And you have plenty of room.'

'Yes, of course, but then the Dower House will be empty.'

'And no one can be bullied.'

Within the hour it had been accomplished, and Catarina, bemused but thankful, was settling Clarice and Maria in the nursery suite of rooms on the top floor of her former home.

When she sought out Nicholas to thank him she found him in the estate office writing letters and sending grooms riding off with them. He looked up and smiled at her. Her heart turned over with love for him.

'I've just one more letter to write. I'll come to the library when it's done.'

She went and sat before a roaring fire, all her anxieties set at rest, and feeling more at peace than she had done since Walter's death. The time for lies was over and she could relax. When Nicholas came in he pulled up a footstool and sat beside her, taking her hands in his and kissing them.

'We'll beat them,' he said. 'The tale Jeremy spun was a little confused. Tell me all about it.'

Hesitantly she began, telling him how Joanna, in deep distress, had come to her for help when Matthew deserted her, how they had spent the time in Lisbon until she was delivered, and how Joanna had met and fallen in love with Eduardo.

'She said all along she did not wish to keep the baby, and once Maria was born she rejected her. I could not bear to give her away, so I decided to keep her. Joanna didn't care,' she added bitterly.

'This so-called marriage,' he said slowly. 'Did Joanna tell you where it took place?'

'Matthew took her to a small church a few miles south of Bristol. They didn't have time to go far. She was foolish to believe it was a legal ceremony when they had to use the church at night, and secretly, but my sister has always been a romantic little fool!'

He suddenly stood up.

'My love, we must settle this as soon as possible. I will invite Sir Humphrey and your cousin here, the Reverend Eade as well, and we will examine the facts. Now forgive me, I have some more letters to write.'

* * *

Catarina did not at all relish the thought of facing her cousin and the rector again, and Sir Humphrey was no longer an indulgent elderly man who wished to marry her. He would be resentful and she feared he might take this opportunity to try to humiliate her. She breathed deeply and told herself she had to endure whatever they said. Words could not damage her, but she was confident Nicholas would not permit them to take Maria away, and that was all that mattered.

The Reverend Eade called later that day, but Catarina did not see him. She had been in the nursery, helping Clarice unpack all the ancient toys that were stored there, which had been the playthings of earlier generations of Walter's family.

Maria did not know which toy to look at first, so they ended up with the floor of the day nursery littered with all manner of things, dolls, chapbooks, balls and even the furniture of a doll's house.

Blodwen had packed some of Catarina's new dresses, so when she changed for dinner she chose the most flattering, one in a soft green with short puffed sleeves and an overdress of silver gauze. It was, perhaps, too elaborate for a simple dinner at home, but it suited her to perfection, and she could wear with it a string of emeralds set in a filigree gold necklace. From the admiring looks both Nicholas and Jeremy gave her she was satisfied she looked better than they had ever seen her.

At dinner Nicholas announced he had arranged for the meeting to be held in two days' time.

'How will you convince them?' Jeremy asked.

'Don't worry, they will be convinced,' he said, but refused to say more. 'Jeremy, what do you propose to do about the villagers?'

Jeremy frowned. 'I will have to permit them to go on as they always have, until the stubborn ones see the benefits of what I am doing and decide they will agree to changes. But they will all have a hard time this winter. I don't know how much I will be able to help.'

'I will supply whatever money you need, and help in finding food. But there is another matter which needs urgent attention. Do you wish to have the Eades remain as your neighbours? Would you not prefer to choose a man more congenial for your rector?'

'Yes, but how can I? I suppose Walter gave him the living?' he added, turning to Catarina.

'Yes, he did; on the recommendation of some old university friend, a tutor at Oxford.'

'Where does he come from, do you know?' Nicholas asked.

'I believe his childhood home was near Norwich.'

'Excellent. I have contacts there. I will make enquiries about possible livings, or even a position in the cathedral hierarchy. I am sure he will prefer to go back there, especially when he understands he will not be invited to dine at Marshington Grange in future. You don't wish for his company, do you?' he asked Jeremy.

Jeremy laughed. 'Nick, you are indeed a devil after your namesake! I certainly do not wish to have to be polite to him, and I certainly don't wish to listen to his tedious sermons.'

'Then I suggest you begin to think whether any of your old cronies took orders. Or there is the curate at home — perhaps he is ready for a parish. But don't make your choice too quickly. You'll have to live with the man for years.'

After dinner, Nicholas retired to the estate office with Jeremy, saying there were matters to be decided, as he must soon be going home to Brooke Court.

Catarina, feeling somewhat flat after the excitement of the past few days, and a little hurt Nicholas did not seem to wish to spend any time with her, soon went to bed. What did he intend for her? Did he still want to marry her, now he knew about all the lies she had told him? What would happen when Matthew and he came face to face? Could Nicholas really convince them of the truth about the sham marriage? Was Maria safe?

★ ★ ★

Catarina saw the Reverend and Mrs Eade arriving and retreated to the drawing room, while Jeremy's butler showed them into the dining room, where Nicholas had decreed the meeting was to take place. As far as she knew Mrs Eade had not been invited, but it was typical of the woman to insist on coming.

Soon afterwards Sir Ivor and Matthew arrived, Matthew driving a new, yellow-painted curricle drawn by two fractious Welsh cobs. They were so fresh she knew her uncle must have stayed the night at some nearby inn. Then Sir Humphrey appeared, driving a very staid gig. With him was the village constable, looking, Catarina thought, decidedly uneasy. She felt sorry for the poor man, being asked to take action against her if Sir Ivor and Matthew could convince him they had a right to remove Maria from her care.

Nicholas, for reasons he did not explain,

had sent the carriage to the village. When it returned it drove straight round to the stables.

Jeremy then appeared, limping slightly and with his broken arm still in a splint.

'What's old Nick up to?' he demanded. 'I know my brother when he takes it into his head to play a lone hand, but I'd like to know what he expects of us. I don't want to say anything out of turn.'

'I don't expect he'll permit that. We'll soon know what is going to happen, no doubt,' Catarina said, trying to calm him, but feeling anything but calm herself. 'Just don't talk unless it's to answer your brother's questions.'

Her stomach was churning with anxiety. Would Nicholas be able to convince Matthew he had no right to take Maria away? If he failed, she would be utterly devastated. She had come to love the child as if she were her own, and could not face the prospect of losing her. Nor did she dare contemplate the sort of life Maria would have if she were left at the mercy of Matthew and his father.

Nicholas appeared before her thoughts could get out of control. He was dressed with great formality, in buff pantaloons, a dark blue, perfectly fitting coat, a white waistcoat with white embroidery, and a cravat tied in what Catarina thought was the Osbaldson.

'Are you ready?' he asked, and Catarina, unable to speak, nodded and rose to her feet.

He smiled comfortingly, put his arm about her shoulders and hugged her then led her through the hall into the dining room opposite. He ushered her to a chair next to the one he took at the head of the table and gestured to Jeremy to sit the other side of her. Was he surrounding her, protecting her, Catarina wondered a little hysterically? She looked round at the others, clustered at the other end of the table. Staines was standing just inside the doorway, so immobile she soon forgot he was there.

Matthew gave her a triumphant smile.

'I think we'll soon convince his lordship and the authorities, in the persons of Sir Humphrey and the constable, that I have a just case,' he said.

Nicholas rapped on the table.

'My lady,' he said, turning to Catarina, 'it is the child you brought home from Lisbon we are concerned about. Can you tell us about Maria's birth, when, where and to whom?'

Catarina took a deep breath. When she spoke she was thankful her voice did not tremble.

'My sister Joanna gave birth on the fifteenth of November last year, in Lisbon. She had previously told me Matthew, our cousin, was the father.'

'Thank you. And you adopted the child, brought her to England?'

Thank goodness he was not dwelling on Joanna's rejection of the baby.

'Yes. Joanna had met and was marrying a Brazilian who was about to return to Brazil.'

'A very long journey for a young baby,' he commented, and Catarina admired how he managed to suggest an acceptable reason for Maria's being left behind.

'So the child's birth and parentage are established. Were her parents lawfully married?'

'Of course we were,' Matthew interrupted.

Nicholas looked at him, his eyebrows raised. Catarina shivered. She had never seen him with so arrogant an expression on his face.

'That is the important point, is it not? Where did the ceremony take place and when?'

'In March last year. Just after Catarina's husband died. At the church of St John outside Bristol.'

'At night, Joanna told Catarina.'

'Joanna preferred it that way. She wanted to keep it a secret.'

No she didn't, you did, you despicable toad, Catarina thought.

'And it did not take place, I assume, by banns, since she was not married from the home where she was living. What sort of licence did you obtain?'

Matthew sighed impatiently. 'What does all this rigmarole matter? I had a licence.'

Nicholas ignored the question.

'From whom did you obtain it?'

'The bishop, of course.'

'And did you reside in the parish of St John before the marriage?'

'Why should I have?'

'Joanna did not, either. A common licence can be used only if one party has resided in the parish for four weeks. Also, people under age need proof of the consent of parents or guardians. Joanna was only eighteen, a minor.'

'She had my consent,' Sir Ivor interrupted.

Catarina thought he was beginning to look worried. She glanced at the Eades and saw a look of puzzlement on the rector's face. Mrs Eade was tugging at his sleeve, but he paid her no attention.

'Mr Norton, you claim your licence was a common one. But marriages celebrated with such must take place where one party has lived for four weeks, and can only be celebrated between the hours of eight in the morning and noon. Yours did not.'

'Well, it must have been the other sort, then. I forget. Is this important? We were married.'

'You both signed the parish register at the time I assume, together with your witnesses.'

'Of course.'

Nicholas looked across at Staines, who slipped from the room. Then he turned to Catarina.

'You have the letter your cousin sent Joanna, repudiating the marriage?'

Catarina took it from her reticule and handed it to him. He read it out slowly.

'That was a joke,' Matthew blustered.

'Isn't it time this farce came to an end?' Sir Ivor demanded. 'We are wasting time. My son and my niece were married.'

'And he therefore is trying to control her fortune, now she is so far away and unable to dispute it.' Nicholas turned round as the door opened. 'Ah, gentlemen, please come in. Can I introduce the curate of St John's parish, and the bishop's secretary? Do sit down, gentlemen.'

They took the seats facing Catarina and Jeremy. The curate placed a large book on the table in front of him. Nicholas smiled and opened it at a page where there was a marker.

'Here we have the marriage register of St John's parish. There is no entry of this supposed marriage between Mr Norton and Joanna. Perhaps you wish to verify that fact?'

'They must have torn the page out!' Matthew snarled.

'The pages are numbered, sir, and none are missing,' the curate told him.

'Then I have the name of the church incorrectly.'

Nicholas turned to the other newcomer.

'Sir? What have you discovered?'

'There is no mention of either Mr Matthew Norton or Miss Joanna Norton in the bishop's transcripts for that time.'

'What the devil do you mean? What are these things?'

The Reverend Eade, who had been silent until now, spoke.

'Each parish is obliged, every year, to send to the bishop a record of all entries in the parish registers. It seems clear to me that if there is neither a record in the register itself, nor in the transcripts, no marriage took place. I have been grievously misled, Mr Norton, Sir Ivor. My lady, pray accept our apologies for associating ourselves with these — I can only call them knaves. I will be preaching a sermon on the wickedness of trying to deceive for monetary gain. Come, my dear, I am leaving, since there is nothing for us to do here.'

They departed, much to Catarina's relief. She did not think she could have endured speaking to them.

Matthew was looking sick, and his father furious.

'Why did you have to drag me into this imposture?' Sir Ivor demanded. 'I believed you, but you're no son of mine to behave like this!'

He stormed out of the room and Matthew, throwing a glance of fury at Nicholas, who ignored him, followed.

Nicholas was thanking the curate and the bishop's secretary, and asking them to stay for a nuncheon, but they both said they were happy to have been of assistance in preventing such a miscarriage of justice, but ought to be setting off back to Bristol as soon as possible. Staines showed them out.

Sir Humphrey, who had remained silent throughout, coughed.

'Well, Catarina, I am pleased it has all been satisfactorily settled. I hope to call on you in a day or so.'

Nicholas glanced at him.

'I fear that will not be possible, Sir Humphrey. I am taking Catarina with me to Brooke Court tomorrow. We will be married from there, since I doubt she wishes the Reverend Eade to conduct the ceremony after the way he has behaved to her.'

'I can't marry you!'

'Why not? Apart from the fact that I love you and you appear to be fond of me — if your reaction to my kisses means anything — now I've told everyone you can't possibly jilt me. There's the scandal, too, of my staying in the Dower House when you were unchaperoned. And I made sure to obtain a special licence,' he added, with a wicked grin.

They were in the drawing room of Marshington Grange after a celebration dinner. Jeremy, saying he was tired and his arm was aching, had taken himself off to bed, but Catarina had caught him winking at Nicholas as he left the room.

'That's not important. People will soon know about Joanna, and that Maria is her child, born out of wedlock. That's an even worse scandal!'

'If the Regent and his brothers can have children out of wedlock, and acknowledge them, I don't think your sister's doing so will be considered so very important.'

'Her husband might hear. Besides — '

'Besides what?'

Catarina wished he would not look at her like that. It made her incapable of thinking logically.

'I told so many lies! You once said you abominated lies more than anything else.'

'You only told them to protect your sister. I find that completely reasonable and would probably have done the same.'

Catarina felt like being utterly childish and stamping her foot in anger. Why did he have to counter all her arguments and sound so odiously reasonable while he did so?

'I can't marry you,' she repeated.

She was totally unprepared when Nicholas rose from the sopha where he'd been lounging, drinking tea, and came across to her.

'Then there is nothing else for it,' he said, and swung her into his arms.

'What are you doing? Put me down! Nicholas!'

He grinned, carried her out of the room and up the stairs. At the top he turned towards his own room, not the one she had been given.

'I'll have to ruin you,' he said.

'Nicholas!'

'I'm not intending to force you, my love. You can tell me to stop at any time. And I promise I will. But you are staying in my bed until morning. Ruined, you'll be. What will Mrs Eade say?'

She was betrayed into a giggle, then

decided he was completely mad, too puffed up with his own success in vanquishing Matthew to care about convention. But being held in his arms, pressed closely against his heart, was such a safe, delicious feeling, it would be unbearable to be forced to leave him. Perhaps after all she could accept his offer.

He dropped her on to the bed in his room and stood, laughing down at her.

'Catarina, you are such a darling and you've had such pain since Walter died. I want above all else to make it up to you. I do love you, unreservedly, and I think I have done since I first saw you in this house. You looked so young and lost in your widow's weeds. Which reminds me, we can dispense with this gown, I think. Let me be your maid.'

Before she knew what was happening he had removed her gown and shrugged off his own coat. He sat down on the bed and took her face in his hands, looking deep into her eyes.

'My dear, say you love me.'

Catarina swallowed, and gave in to the inevitable. He knew about all the scandal, and if he didn't care, why should she? She'd been attracted to him from the first, but having just lost Walter so suddenly, had not recognized the feeling, the desire which had swept through her very soul. She had never been in love with Walter, and had been too young when they married to have suffered any sort of calf love before that time.

'I love you,' she managed.

Within seconds, it seemed, he had discarded the rest of his clothing and was removing her shift. He sat beside her and began to roll down her stockings. She shivered at his touch, especially when he trailed his lips down her legs, feathering kisses. He left the candles burning, and the glow from the fire-light lit the room, but it didn't matter, she wanted to look at him. She had never before been naked in front of a man, but the feelings he was causing to flood her whole body made her forget that. When he lay down beside her and began to stroke her body, then to cup her breasts in gentle hands and tease her nipples with kisses, she arched against him, not knowing what she wanted.

He roused her slowly, carefully, murmuring endearments, until she was clasping him and begging for release. When he moved to lie on top of her she gasped, but was ready for him, until, as he began to enter her, he found an obstruction. She felt him pause, but by now was so desperate for fulfilment she urged him on, knowing by instinct what to do. They clung together until the paroxysms which had shaken them slowed and finally stopped.

He was holding her close against his heart.

'Why didn't you tell me? I'd have been more gentle.'

'Tell you?'

'That you were a virgin. That you have never made love before. That Walter was never a true husband to you.'

She sighed. It was her final secret.

'He could not, because of an accident. But he was always kind, and very good to me.'

'I intend to be a proper husband, my sweetest Catarina. I love you, adore you, and want you by my side for the rest of my days.'

We do hope that you have enjoyed reading this large print book.

Did you know that all of our titles are available for purchase?

We publish a wide range of high quality large print books including:
Romances, Mysteries, Classics
General Fiction
Non Fiction and Westerns

Special interest titles available in large print are:
The Little Oxford Dictionary
Music Book
Song Book
Hymn Book
Service Book

Also available from us courtesy of Oxford University Press:
Young Readers' Dictionary
(large print edition)
Young Readers' Thesaurus
(large print edition)

For further information or a free brochure, please contact us at:
Ulverscroft Large Print Books Ltd.,
The Green, Bradgate Road, Anstey,
Leicester, LE7 7FU, England.
Tel: (00 44) **0116 236 4325**
Fax: (00 44) **0116 234 0205**

SUPERVISING SALLY

Marina Oliver

Phoebe is delighted to go to Brussels as companion to Sally, rather than be an unpaid governess to her sister Jane's children. Her hopes are dashed when Zachary, Earl of Wrekin, claims Phoebe is too young for the task, and refuses to escort her. She finds herself unable to control the rebellious Sally, who gets into many scrapes even before they leave London. However, when Phoebe rescues Sally from a calamitous action, Zachary relents. But Jane's husband and his unpleasant sisters cause irritation on the journey. Then Napoleon escapes from Elba and everything is in turmoil for Phoebe.

A DISGRACEFUL AFFAIR

Marina Oliver

Sylvie Delamare's great-uncle Sir George sends her a mere £20 — claiming it to be a whole half of her inheritance — and she's infuriated. Her parents had been wealthy, so she wants to go and confront him in Norfolk. Meanwhile, she is invited to visit Lady Carstairs, her friend's aunt in London, to be presented. However, Sir Randal is suspicious of Sylvie, after seeing her with Monsieur Dupont, who he suspects is one of Napoleon's spies. Then when Sir Randal follows Dupont, he meets Sylvie in Norwich on her way to see Sir George. And when he offers her a lift — he becomes embroiled in her affairs . . .

A   ®